This book is dedicated to all grandmothers — those who are avengers and those who wish they were.

Contents

About The Granny Avengers

THE GRANNY AVENGERS *is a new series written by* Carolina Danford Wright. *Marfa Lights Out* is the second book in the series. Each of the protagonists in this series is old enough to be a grandmother. Each is brave and on the side of truth and justice. Some of these heroes act on the spur of the moment because it is the right thing to do. Some, because of circumstances, seem to stumble into being avengers. Other Granny Avengers take over when the criminal justice system has failed to do its job. You will enjoy getting to know these feisty women as they struggle to right the wrongs of the world.

Map of Texas

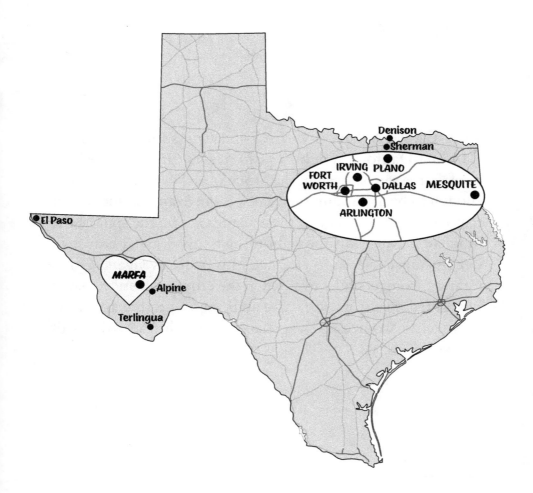

The Present...
Marfa

Chapter 1

I *decided to move to Marfa because I was tired, and* the small, high desert town in the middle of nowhere West Texas seemed like a place where I could rest. Marfa was calling me. It's the county seat of Presidio County and the epicenter of the Chinati Foundation, home of artist Donald Judd's famous collection of one-hundred aluminum rectangular boxes.

Marfa may be even more famous for its mysterious lights. Also known as ghost lights, these glowing orbs have been observed just outside the town of Marfa for generations. Those who have seen them have attributed these hovering, flickering, twinkling, colorful mystery balls to paranormal phenomena such as ghosts, UFOs, or will-o'-the-wisp. Really? I have never seen the Marfa Lights, but the Donald Judd aluminum boxes are very real and very wonderful. In spite of these claims to fame, Marfa has been able to maintain its small-town appeal, and after looking at real estate for about five minutes, I bought a house there.

Housing prices are going up in Marfa, but I was moving from Washington, D.C., well-known for having some of the nation's, and maybe the world's, most inflated real estate. I was selling an outrageously over-priced home in our nation's capital, so I could afford the somewhat over-priced home I had to have on North Austin Street in Marfa. My new place was going to require a lot of work, but I could afford the house and the expense of fixing it up so it would be the way I wanted it to be. Some of my friends thought I was crazy to move to Marfa and undertake a major renovation project at my age, but I'd fallen in love with the town and with the house. It's hard to argue with love.

I'd lived in the District of Columbia for many years and had suffered through the crime, the taxes, the traffic, as well as the baloney of various political administrations. I'd thought I would be able to endure the eight years of the current crowd, but my patience ran out midway through the second term. I had to get away. My husband had died a decade earlier of congestive heart failure, partially a victim, I will always believe, of the stress that resulted from his many years spent driving on the Washington Beltway. The year after my husband died, my son was killed in Iraq by an IED, another casualty of the insanity that has long reigned in this country's seat of politics and power.

My daughter Anna is a lawyer and recently moved to San Diego. She and a college friend started their own law firm in Southern California. Not only is she enjoying better weather and less traffic, she's making a great deal more money. I've never been a big fan of California, but Anna is happy. So I'm happy. She has almost married twice, but escaped disaster both times—her words.

There was no longer any reason for me to stay in D.C. I would always grieve for the loved ones I'd lost to the place. Now that my daughter had moved on, and with no grandchildren anywhere in sight, it was time for me to move on, too. I had many friends and many favorite restaurants in the District. I wished I could take the Lebanese Taverna with me. I would miss them all, but I was tired of city life, and especially tired of life in this city. I sold my house for an obscene amount of money and got rid of most of my furniture. I wanted a new life in a new place. This old lady was going to get a new dog and a new car to go with her new house in her new town.

I'd decided I was going to become a recluse when I moved to Marfa. I wasn't going to join any clubs or volunteer to do anything. I was still debating with myself whether or not I was even going to register to vote. My osteoarthritis and my age would give me permission to disengage. I always use a blue and white cane and sometimes use a wheelchair. I wondered if Marfa's powers-that-be would allow me to drive around town in a golf cart. I was not going to ask permission; I was just going to do it.

I was making my house as handicap accessible as I wanted it to be, and I was putting a heated swimming pool in the back yard. The pool would be big enough for me to really swim in it, and I'd been able to convince myself that the pool and the accompanying exorbitant utility bills that would be required to heat it were a medical necessity.

Having retired from several careers along the way, I was ridiculously happy in my current occupation as a writer of mystery novels. Early on, I'd been an eighth grade teacher in the New Orleans public schools, and after graduate school and a PhD, I'd been a professor of economics at two universities. Then I'd designed for and managed my own women's clothing business, and most recently I had spent twenty years as an architectural designer.

Always a voracious reader, I'd discovered during the past eight years, that I have a rich imagination and began writing my own books. Being a writer, I used to think, was the perfect job for a recluse. Having written and published several novels, I now realize that much is expected of an author in terms of promotion and marketing. I love to write, but I aspire to the J.D. Salinger school of authorship. I want to write and publish my books and never be seen again. Thank goodness, I had published my first book under a pen name. If my pseudonym ever becomes famous, I personally will be spared the fuss and exhaustion of having to deal with celebrity or notoriety.

Marfa, here I come, ready or not!

Chapter 2

*B*ecause *I was buying my house from an estate, the* transaction was complicated, and the settlement was delayed. The delay had allowed me extra time to study the blueprints over and over again and plan my house renovations and landscaping in detail. I'd hired a highly-recommended contractor, and he promised he would be ready to go on the project as of September 1st. While my house was being fixed up, I'd decided to indulge myself and live at the Hotel Saint George, a wonderful and recently repurposed hotel in downtown Marfa. It was going to cost me a fortune to stay at the Saint George for three months, but I loved the place. It was fairly close to my house on North Austin Street and had great food. There was a roll-in shower in the bathroom of my hotel suite. I would be able to closely supervise the renovation of my new home in the mornings and return to the Saint George's restaurant for a delicious lunch and a Mexican coke. Mexican cokes are made with cane sugar rather than with high fructose corn syrup.

I closed on my D.C. house and sent ahead the furniture, clothes, books, and household goods I wanted to take with me to Marfa. It would all be stored until my house was ready. I bought myself a big gas-guzzling Ford Expedition. It was white, and it came with all the bells and whistles the salesman could talk me into. I packed my laptop and other things I couldn't live without into my new truck and visited friends in Virginia Beach, Virginia; Asheville, North Carolina; Madison, Mississippi; and Mansfield, Arlington, and Fort Worth, Texas along the way. Marfa was hot when I arrived during the last week of August. At an altitude of almost 5,000 feet, it isn't as hot as it could have been, and it's a dry heat. I was patting myself on the back, however, that I had budgeted to upgrade the HVAC system in my Austin Street house.

The Hotel Saint George was delighted to welcome me. How many people, after all, reserve a suite for three months? I was their new best customer. I quickly made friends with the waiters and waitresses and everybody who worked in the bookstore gift shop. It hadn't been difficult to convince the bookstore to carry the series of adventure books I'd written for young people. While the work was being done on my house renovation, I was going to have fun staying at the Saint George.

In a shocking display of showing up on time, the contractor met me at my new home at nine in the morning on the first of September, just as he'd promised. We'd exchanged hundreds of emails but were meeting each other in person for the first time today. I liked George Hernandez immediately. We were on the same page, and I was relieved that he respected my opinions. He'd known from the beginning that I was a senior citizen, but sometimes when an old lady with white hair hobbles up to a meeting leaning on a cane, she's dismissed as irrelevant.

George won me over immediately as he greeted me with a big smile and helped me climb out of my enormous car. While we discussed the plans, his crew was already demolishing the derelict structure at the rear of the property that had to go to make room for my swimming pool. We made a few minor changes in the plans, but for the most part, it looked as if my renovation was going to proceed on schedule. I hung around and met George's men, answered a few questions, asked a few questions, held up paint samples, and took some measurements. I like to fix things up.

The house on North Austin Street had most recently been owned by an older couple who had run a restaurant out of their home. They'd lived in the back of the house, and the restaurant had been open for breakfast and lunch only, Thursday through Sunday. The husband was a retired anesthesiologist, and he waited tables. The wife loved to cook, and having a restaurant had always been her dream. I'd never eaten there, but word was that the food had been terrific. The couple had grown older and had to close the restaurant. They'd moved to an assisted living facility and subsequently passed away. The house had been vacant for more than three years. The real estate agent had done a bit of clean up in the yard, but the landscaping and the gardens needed professional attention. I planned my herb garden and my cutting garden, wondering what could actually survive in this arid climate.

From my large and shady front porch, I had a view of the picturesque and historic pink Presidio County courthouse built in 1886. I wondered if I'd ever actually sit on my front porch. If I intended to be a recluse, wouldn't I have to stay indoors? I'd selected a low-maintenance, beautiful, and expensive fence to enclose my backyard, swimming pool, and garden. I told myself it was an essential safety feature to be sure no children or critters accidentally fell into the pool. My contractor was building a garage addition with a ramp to make it easy for me to go from my car to my mudroom. After the renovation, the garage would be big enough to hold the Expedition and a golf cart. I'd decided to buy the golf cart now and wait until later to ask permission to drive it around town. The Hotel Saint George had already promised me a convenient reserved parking spot for the cart, right by the front door. I had a handicap tag to display on my rear-view mirror. The golf cart was ideal for running back and forth to Austin Street to keep an eye on the progress of my house.

There hadn't been much time to rest yet, and resting had been my reason for choosing Marfa. I settled into a routine, and most afternoons, I even found some time to work on a new novel. Life in this small town was looking good. I'd promised myself I wasn't going to get involved in the community and I wasn't going to get to know anybody. Before I knew it, of course, I knew way too many people. The folks in West Texas were friendly and happy. How could I not get to know them and like them?

Years earlier, I'd visited Donald Judd's exhibit of aluminum rectangular boxes, housed in two brick buildings on the outskirts of Marfa. I had been awestruck by his genius. Not usually a fan of the latest thing in art or architecture, I loved Judd's work. I could see why his artistic presence in the town had attracted worldwide attention and higher housing prices. If aluminum boxes sound boring, believe me, Judd's exhibit is not boring. Every one of the rectangular boxes is different.

The display is beautifully done, and it is fascinating. I hated it that Donald Judd was dead. He'd died in 1994. Part of me wished I'd moved to Marfa while he'd still been alive. But having so much of his work in the area did compensate. Judd was still alive here in Marfa because his work lives here. I'd promised myself that in my new life, I wasn't going to get involved in anything other than my writing, but the Chinati Foundation and the Judd Foundation were awfully tempting. I'd made a good decision to move to Marfa.

I've never been an extremely neighborly person. My Myers-Briggs personality profile has consistently let me know that I'm an introvert, but at the same time, I really love people. How can both of these things be true? My Austin Street property was on a sizeable lot, but it was in town and had fairly close neighbors. Because contractors, pool people, and landscapers need access, my fence can't be built until after the renovation work is completed. I was doing my best, during my daily visits to the house, to avoid all contact with nosy neighbors. They were probably curious about who had bought the property and what I was doing to it. I was going to allow that random and speculative curiosity to expand and take itself wherever it wanted to go. I was hiding out, and I wasn't talking.

I'm not a good liar, and my true feelings tend to spread all over my face and are more than obvious in my body language. Even though it never seems to work out for me, I continue to indulge my fantasy that I want to be mysterious and eccentric. I am actually fairly conventional and absurdly nice, but my wishful thinking about becoming a recluse lives on. I'd considered wearing a wig whenever I went to Austin Street to consult with George and his men, but decided that was silly and too much trouble. Wigs itch like crazy.

I'm certain the neighbors have already found out from Sotheby's exactly who has bought the house, how much I paid for it, and everything about everything else. Do I even need to mention that driving a golf cart around town, perhaps an illegal golf cart, is not exactly the way to maintain a low profile?

One day as I was about to leave the construction site, a woman who looked like she was even older than I am, staggered up my front walk. She had long grey hair that floated around her head and shoulders like a curly cape, and she was very unsteady on her feet as she approached the door. I thought about ignoring her presence but didn't want to appear rude in front of George's friendly and cheerful workers. I felt some empathy for her because I am also unsteady on my feet. I hobbled on my cane to meet my neighbor.

The moment she began to speak, I realized she'd been drinking. The aura and aroma of alcohol surrounded her, and she was slurring her words. "I'm Melody, and I live next door. Welcome to Marvelous Marfa. I'm an artist. Everybody in Marfa thinks they're an artist, but I really am one. Are you an artist?"

I shook her hand. "It's nice to meet you. I'm Margaret Lennox. Everybody calls me Margaret." I motioned for her to sit on the bench beside me. I can't stand up for long periods of time and always need a chair or a bench nearby. George's crew knows this about me, and they tirelessly move my chair from place to place as we troubleshoot and make construction decisions about various rooms in the house. The bench on my front porch is made out of raw, cheap pine, thrown together by the men so I can have a place to sit down after walking to the house from my golf cart in the driveway. A classic English cottage-style bench is on order but has not yet arrived. The homemade bench is a bench made for one, but Melody snuggled up next to me as she sat down. I wondered where this encounter was heading and wished I were back at the Saint George eating lunch and drinking a Mexican coke.

"What are you doing in Marfa? Everybody wants to know where you've come from and how you could afford to buy this house. You must be spending a fortune fixing it up." Melody was nothing if not blunt. Had old age destroyed her social filters, or was it the booze talking? Maybe Melody the Artist was always like this, even when she'd been younger and even when she was sober.

"I moved to Marfa to get away from my hectic city life on the East Coast. I fell in love with this house, and I'm hoping to be able to move in soon. There's still a lot of work to be done." I was trying to give out as little information as possible, but Melody's interrogation was relentless.

"Are you building a swimming pool? Everybody thinks you're building a swimming pool. The neighbors are all glad you tore down that awful looking corrugated metal shed thing in your back yard."

"Yes, that had to go. I couldn't figure out exactly what its purpose was anyway." I hoped to keep the conversation focused on the ugly shed I'd had demolished.

"You have a hard time getting around, don't you? You're even more crippled than I am, and I'm betting I'm older than you are. What's your ailment?"

"I have osteoarthritis, and I do have a difficult time getting around." I was anxious to get away on my golf cart, but I couldn't find a polite way to stem the flood of questions from my tipsy neighbor.

"When you move in, you can come over for a drink. I make my own wine, you know. Everybody says it's delicious.

I'm an artist, did I tell you? Are you an artist? Everybody in Marfa thinks they're an artist."

It was time to leave. "You'll have to excuse me, Melody. I have a meeting, and it starts in twenty minutes. It's been nice meeting you. Good luck with your art." I didn't tell my neighbor that in fact my upcoming meeting was with a bowl of the soup of the day and a fructose-free coke at the Hotel Saint George.

"Who's your meeting with, Margaret? I do sculpture out of found objects. I'm an artist, a sculptor. Are you an artist?"

"I look forward to seeing your work sometime. I have to go now, or I'm going to be late." I didn't want to tell her I was a writer, and I didn't want to be late for my lunch. I briefly chided myself and considered that maybe Melody had dementia. I told myself I should try to be nice to her because I might have dementia someday. I grabbed my blue and white cane and started for the golf cart.

Melody followed after me toward the driveway. "Can you give me a ride downtown on that thing? Everybody knows you're living at the Saint George. Everybody wonders how you can afford it."

"I'm not going downtown right now." I lied. "I have a meeting, and I have to leave now."

Melody was put out that I wouldn't give her a ride downtown, and I felt guilty for rejecting her. My neighbor was determined to have the last word. "Well, I'll see you tomorrow. I know you come here every morning. I've been watching you."

I'll bet you've been watching, I think to myself. I climbed into my golf cart and headed for downtown. I would need a nap today after the conversation with Melody. Maybe I'd made a mistake to try to get away from it all. Melody lived next door to me. Was she going to be a constant thorn in my side? The realist in me reminded me that it was not possible to get away from it all anymore, if it had ever been possible. I would have to try to set limits on my neighbor who made her own wine and drank too much of it in the morning. I would have to get good locks installed on my doors and on the gate that provided access to my fenced-in back yard. I could pretend I wasn't home and refuse to answer the door. I could hide under the bed.

Chapter 3

I *stayed away from my house for the next three* days. It was a weekend, and George's crew didn't come on Saturday and Sunday. Maybe Melody would forget about me. There was a fundraising event on Saturday evening at the Chinati Foundation, which had its headquarters at a former U.S. Army post, Fort D.A. Russell. Donald Judd had purchased the Army post in the 1970s and turned it into a place to display his art. I had paid $250 to attend the cocktail party. What had happened to my promise that I wouldn't join anything or make any friends? And I hated cocktail parties. I'd made an exception and decided to attend this party because I loved Donald Judd's work.

Finding a convenient parking place is often difficult when one is handicapped. Handicap parking spaces fill up quickly. Because I wasn't familiar with the location of the cocktail party and can't walk long distances, I'd hired a driver to deliver me to the Chinati reception and take me home when it was over. One of the busboys who worked at the Saint George would drive my car, let me out close to the door, and wait for me while I attended the party. If I needed any assistance, he would help me walk up any unexpected stairs. It would be money well spent.

I was overdressed for the fund raiser. I had on black jersey palazzo pants and a matching black jersey scoop-neck top. I was wearing my favorite pearls. It was October, so I wore a colorful shawl and my long leather coat. Most of the other partygoers were wearing blue jeans, and they all knew each other. I was an old woman leaning on a cane, and although my blue eyes and white hair are attractive, I didn't belong.

It was my own fault that I wasn't mingling. I really just can't mingle anymore. I can't stand for long periods of time or walk around and chat with a drink in my hand. And that's what you do at a cocktail party. I found a chair on the periphery of the room and sat down. A couple of people came up to talk to me, but the crowd was energetic and constantly moving. I felt out of things and again vowed I wouldn't attend any more cocktail parties. What was I thinking? I would just send a check next time. I was about to text my driver to tell him I wanted to go home. He could pull up to the entrance where he'd let me off. Just as I began to tap on my cell phone, a young man with a neatly trimmed blond ponytail came up to me and introduced himself.

"I'm Ellery, and I think you live down the street from me in town."

Ellery looked like a very nice young person, and I was thrilled that he'd made the effort to speak to me. I put out my hand. "Hello, Ellery, I'm Margaret Lennox. Delighted to meet you. Yes, I'm renovating a house on Austin Street. Do you live on Austin Street?"

"I live in the tiny blue house around the corner, on West Jackson Street. I've seen the workers at your house, and I'm excited that someone is fixing it up. It's been vacant too long. I've always loved your place. It's a real Texas classic. I have a feeling you're keeping all the original charm." Ellery's blue eyes crinkled when he smiled, and he seemed to mean it when he said he was happy to meet me.

I really liked this young man who lived in my neighborhood. "I love your house, too. Every time I drive by, I wonder who lives there. Even in October I can see you have a magnificent garden and a wonderful greenhouse. Lucky you! And yes, you've got my number. I'm trying to keep as much of the original Austin Street house and charm as possible. The work takes longer to finish than one thinks it will, but isn't that always the story with renovations? I hope to be in by Thanksgiving, but it will be close."

"You hired the best contractor in the area, and I'll bet he's finished with your house ahead of time. He did my house a few years ago. He does beautiful work. Your pool and landscaping might not be done by the end of November, but I'm thinking you will be able to move into your house before Thanksgiving." Did everyone in Marfa know I planned to put in a pool?

"I'd love for you to come over and see what's been done so far." What was wrong with me? What had happened to the secret recluse inside myself, that eccentric soul who wanted to retreat from the world? It seemed I couldn't wait to show off my house to this nice young man. "I'll be there on Monday morning if you want to come by. Are you an artist? Melody says everybody in Marfa thinks they're an artist."

Ellery laughed out loud. He had a genuine and contagious laugh. "So you've already met Melody, and no doubt she's been grilling you about how you can afford to buy your house and fix it up. Don't worry. She does that with all the new people. She'll eventually get tired of you. As soon as somebody else buys a house in the neighborhood, she'll move on with her nosy neighbor routine and start hassling them. She's harmless. Drinks too much."

"That's hard to miss. I've wondered if she has dementia or if she's just socially inept. I guess it's the homemade wine."

"She does make wine, but I suspect it's vodka that keeps her going. She's actually pretty sharp, if you can catch her when she's sober. And, surprisingly, her sculptures are in demand, and they sell for high prices."

"Now, you are telling me something I wasn't expecting to hear. I'm glad she's able to support herself with her work. I had my doubts when she showed up at my house a few days ago. She said she works with found objects."

"She refuses to cut her hair, and she makes her own personal fashion statement by *wearing* found items, too. She goes through garbage cans and dumpsters and landfills to find materials for her sculpture—and to find her wardrobe. She's a true eccentric and definitely marches to a unique drummer. She'll leave you alone after a while. Don't despair or think about moving away."

"I appreciate the information. I'll admit I was worried that she would become a major PITA. You've reassured me."

"I write music, to answer your question about my being an artist. I write songs and music scores for movies and play piano, guitar, the flute, and the clarinet. I love what I do. I'm a member of a jazz ensemble that mostly gets together for fun. Occasionally, we play a gig someplace, but our primary mission is to entertain ourselves. Marfa does have an inordinately high percentage of artists per capita. I hate to ask you, but are you an artist?" Ellery laughed out loud again when he said that.

"I'm a writer. Fiction. I'm curious about your name, Ellery."

"Yep, you've got me. My mother loved mystery novels, especially the old-fashioned ones. Ellery Queen was a particular favorite. And my last name is King. Can you believe it?" He laughed again.

I laughed with him. "I love Ellery Queen, too. Those two brothers made one terrific mystery writer."

"I've got to go. The Chinati Foundation hired our jazz group to play for a while tonight. It's been a real pleasure meeting you, Margaret. I look forward to the tour on Monday morning." He took my hand and made a small bow. Then he was gone. I was so happy to know Ellery King. He was a sweetheart. I was tired and wanted to leave, but I decided to stay a while longer and listen to the music. The group's performance was exceptional, and Ellery's love of jazz was contagious. It was fun to watch him play. Music was obviously his passion. Ellery was an artist.

I was sorry when they'd finished their concert, but it was past time for me to go back to the hotel. The cocktail party had been a big outing for me. I texted Guillermo, my driver, and he picked me up at the door and drove me back to town. Marfa may not be as away from it all as I'd thought it would be, but it was going to be an incredibly interesting place to live.

Chapter 4

*S*ure enough, Ellery had been right about George Hernandez. He and his men finished the painting and everything else by November 18th. The landscaper was still working on the exterior, but I could finally move into my Texas classic. I scheduled a cleaning crew and made arrangements for my furniture and household goods to be delivered from storage. I loved being in my new house.

I'd hired You Are Home!, a company out of Dallas to put things away for me. It was an expensive service, but I wasn't able to lift and unpack boxes, hang up clothes, and climb on ladders anymore. Hiring You Are Home! had been a stroke of genius. All I had to do was sit in a chair and tell the two efficient young women exactly where I wanted them to put everything. They folded each sweater and towel in a beautifully professional way and followed my directions precisely. I knew exactly where everything was, but I hated to use anything or take anything out of a drawer for fear

I would mess it up. It all looked so perfect now, and I'd never be able to fold things the way those two experts had. I'd watched closely, but my arthritic fingers no longer went where I wanted them to go.

With help like this, I would for sure be settled in my house before Thanksgiving, so I called Ellery and asked him what he was doing for Thanksgiving dinner. I said goodbye to my friends at the Hotel Saint George but told them I wouldn't be a stranger. I'd made arrangements to pick up takeout from the hotel restaurant three nights a week.

My cooking and entertaining days are pretty much behind me, but Ellery was almost family by now. I was going to brine and roast a turkey breast and make celery and onion dressing and my fabulous cranberry relish for myself. I love turkey, especially leftover turkey sandwiches. Since I was already half-way there, why not buy some already-made mashed potatoes, steam some frozen vegetables, and invite a friend? I could still make great gravy and would order a pumpkin pie from the Saint George. Ellery knew how difficult it was for me to get around. He knew I didn't cook much anymore, so he wouldn't have high expectations. I arranged for the groceries to be delivered. The dressing and relish had to be made at least a day or more in advance. I would set a table for two. After dinner, Ellery would put the dishes in the dishwasher for me. It would be fun.

While living at the Saint George, I'd interviewed several women as possible candidates to be my housekeeper. I was more than willing to have a man as a housekeeper, but none applied. I wanted someone to come in for a few hours five days a week to clean, do laundry, run errands, cook, and generally wait on me. I'm not lazy; I'm old and crippled. I can't do everything I used to do for myself. After speaking with a number of applicants, I hired Consuela Rodriguez, a middle-aged Hispanic woman who has promised to help me learn Spanish as well as take care of me and my house. Consuela couldn't start until after the Thanksgiving holidays, but I liked her very much. She was worth waiting for.

The day before Thanksgiving, Melody made another appearance. I was just putting the turkey into its brine when she banged on the back door. She'd pretty much stayed away while I was moving in. Maybe she was afraid I would put her to work. She seemed relatively sober today, so I motioned for her to come in. I'd designed my kitchen so I could sit down to do prep work like peeling and chopping vegetables. It was just a step to the stove and another step to the sink. I was making it work. Melody, nosy as always, wanted to know what I was cooking.

"Do you have family coming for Thanksgiving?" I had told her I didn't cook anymore. If she remembered my telling her that, she would wonder what in the world I was doing with a skillet full of sautéed onions and celery in butter on my fancy gas range. "It looks like you're going to a lot of trouble for just one person."

I knew that before she left, I would invite her to join Ellery and me the next day, but I put off issuing the invitation as long as I could. "I like turkey sandwiches, and I can make a turkey breast last for weeks." I was determined that she was going to have to work for the rest of what she wanted to know and for her dinner invitation.

"It looks like you're making more than a turkey breast. It looks like you're making turkey stuffing, too. Of course, you know, everybody here in Texas makes their stuffing with cornbread. I see bags of Pepperidge Farm bread cubes here on the counter, but I don't see any cornbread. Of course, you're a Yankee, so you would use plain bread, rather than cornbread."

"I know Texans prefer cornbread stuffing, but this is my special recipe." Melody was being a bit of a snob about the dressing, and I ignored her tone of voice. I liked Pepperidge Farm bread cubes and my own Scarborough Fair dressing recipe with parsley, sage, rosemary, and thyme. I always used fresh parsley, but I usually substituted poultry seasoning for the other three herbs. It was delicious, and it was what I loved and what I wanted.

"You're making so much. Are you having guests?"

"I like to make a large batch and freeze it. I make stuffed pork chops with the dressing." I knew she was angling to be invited for dinner, but I was being naughty and wanted to make her ask straight out.

"Stuffed pork chops? I thought you said you didn't cook. Stuffed pork chops are a lot of trouble."

"Do you cook, Melody? Are you making a turkey?"

"I used to be a gourmet chef, but my sculpture takes up too much of my time these days. Now I prefer to be creative with my work rather than in the kitchen." Melody was thin as a rail, and I suspected she drank rather than ate most of her meals...these days.

I finally took pity on her. "I've invited Ellery King to have dinner with me tomorrow, and I'd love to have you come, too. It will just be the three of us, and I'm serving dinner at 4:00 p.m."

Melody smiled a rare smile. "I'd like that. Ellery is such a sweet man. I've wondered why he doesn't have a girlfriend or a boyfriend. His music seems to be his one and only love. I'll bring a bottle of my homemade wine."

Before I could tell her I had the wine situation under control, she was out the door. I hoped she wouldn't be too smashed by four o'clock the next afternoon, and I hoped Ellery wouldn't mind my inviting Melody. He was easygoing and knew how pushy Melody could be. He probably already expected her to be joining us for dinner.

My cell phone rang, and it was Ellery. I panicked and hoped against hope he wasn't cancelling. I needed him tomorrow as a buffer. Dinner with just Melody and me was not going to happen.

"Ellery, please don't tell me you're cancelling. Melody was here, and I had no choice but to invite her to have dinner with us tomorrow."

Ellery laughed his wonderful hearty laugh. "Not to worry. In fact, I was calling to see if I could bring a friend with me. He's somebody I work with, and he's unexpectedly flying in from L.A. tonight. If it's too much for you, I told him he'd have to go to a restaurant for dinner, but I thought it wouldn't hurt to ask."

I was so relived Ellery wasn't pulling out of the dinner, I would have told him it was okay to bring his entire jazz band. "Of course, please bring your friend. I'd love to have him. The more people Melody has to grill, the easier it will be for me. Who's your friend?"

"He's a work colleague as well as a good friend, and his name is Augustus Gemini. Thanks for being flexible, Margaret. You'll enjoy Augustus. He's outrageous and funny. He's very L.A., but he loves Marfa and never misses a chance to visit. He flies his own plane, so he comes here often. He will be eager to see what you've done with your house. He talks about getting a place in Marfa, but I doubt he'll ever follow through with that. He's a huge fan of Donald Judd, and I think he gives oodles of money to Chinati and to the Judd Foundation. Dinner will be fun. Augustus can easily handle Melody, and the two of us will clean up afterwards while you and Melody have an after dinner drink together. Ha Ha! Sorry, I had to say that. Really, though, we'll clean up, I promise."

"I'll hold you to it. See you both at 4:00." Things were getting a little out of hand, but I thought I could set the table for four as easily as I could set it for two.

Chapter 5

I set the table in my dining room for four, and it was elegant with white linens, sterling silver flatware, and blue and white china. I was able to pull the food together before my guests arrived. The turkey breast was resting on its large oval serving platter. I had to admit, I'd bitten off more than I could chew, making a fancy Thanksgiving dinner. It was exhausting, and by the time Ellery and Augustus arrived, I was ready for somebody else to do the carving and the serving and everything else that still needed doing.

The two men arrived bearing gifts. Ellery handed me a gorgeous end-of-the-summer bouquet from his garden, the perfect addition to my Thanksgiving table. We'd not had a freeze yet, and Ellery had a greenhouse. The flowers were lovely. Augustus brought three dozen long-stemmed multi-colored roses and a huge box of candy. He was, as promised, very L.A., dressed in a tight suit complete with cropped pants.

His bleached white hair was spiked with purple highlights, and he had on high-heeled leather boots. Definitely over the top, he could have been anywhere between twenty and fifty. He was charming and smart and funny. I loved him and was laughing at his banter before he'd been in my house for thirty seconds. He warned me not to call him Gus.

Augustus made himself at home and found my best cut crystal double old- fashioned glasses and the kitchen shears. He ruthlessly cut off the long stems of the roses and filled the sparkling crystal with water and tight bunches of the colorful blooms. He placed the glasses full of roses here and there, in between the votive candles on the dining table. With Ellery's fall flowers as the centerpiece, the table was transformed into a work of art. Augustus presented me with the box of candy, and it was five pounds of handmade caramels dipped in bittersweet chocolate. The candy was from a private Hollywood chocolatier to the stars who only made candy to order. Five pounds of dark chocolates! I was beyond thrilled.

I made my delicious gravy, and the food was ready. Ellery put the serving dishes on the table. Augustus lit the candles and stood over the turkey platter where he deftly and expertly carved the turkey breast into perfect slices. Ellery opened the Pinot Noir and filled the wine glasses. Just as we were sitting down, Melody blew through the back door and into the kitchen. It was almost 4:30, but she didn't seem to be wobbling. She had a bottle of wine in her hand and set it down on the counter with a bang. Taking her place at the dining room table, she mumbled something about cats and devil's food cake. Augustus looked questioningly at Ellery who shrugged his shoulders and made the introductions. Melody immediately began to grill Augustus about who he was, what he did, and where he'd come from. She asked repeatedly if Gemini was really his last name. She asked repeatedly if he were an artist. Augustus was more than able to hold his own with my next-door-neighbor, and pretty soon, Melody was laughing. That was a first for me; I'd never heard her laugh before.

We had an outlandishly good time, and I finally gave the Thanksgiving blessing just after we'd eaten dessert. We finished the fabulous Saint George's pumpkin pie with whipped cream, and Augustus asked if there was just a touch of bourbon in it. I'd thought there was something extra in the pie that gave it a special kick, and Augustus had put his finger on it. We went around the table to say what we were thankful for. Augustus was thankful for lots of absurdly funny things, many of which I'd never heard of. Ellery was thankful for musical things and friends and his garden. Melody was pretty sloshed by now, and I think she said she was thankful for cats and devil's food cake and girdles. I asked her if she had a cat, and she said she kind of had a cat. No one asked about the girdles. I was thankful for my new town, my new house, and my new neighbors. Most of all, I was thankful I didn't live in Washington D.C. anymore.

I gave Augustus a tour of the house and told him about the renovations. He loved my huge bathroom with its stone floor and the white and silver tiles I'd chosen. Although I suspected he had ultra-modern furnishings in his own Los Angeles home, he said the antiques in the master bedroom suite worked perfectly in my house. He helped Melody get home safely, while Ellery finished cleaning up the kitchen. Hugs all around. It was one of the best Thanksgivings I'd ever celebrated. There was plenty of perfectly sliced turkey for a week's worth of sandwiches, and the rest of the leftovers were either frozen or otherwise neatly stored in my refrigerator. Who needed a housekeeper?

I spent a long time sitting under the hot water on the stone bench in my grand open shower. It had been a big day, and I was worn out. I climbed into my four poster bed and tried to read a book. I was truly thankful for many things, and the crisp sheets, the clean Texas air, and the Pinot Noir didn't let me stay awake for very long. Life was good in Marfa.

The main railroad tracks through town run behind my house. The real estate agent had apologized for this when I first looked at the property. The proximity of the tracks didn't bother me, and there was a wide dirt road and a small field of scrubby bushes between my future backyard fence and the railroad bed. The clackety clack took me back to simpler days, childhood times when there were a lot of trains around. There was comfort in the sound of a train going by, a sound that meant people were coming and going and adventures were afoot. That night, the train whistle woke me up. I wasn't used to my new surroundings yet but knew I would soon learn to sleep through all the aberrant sounds. There was no railroad crossing near my house, but whoever was driving the train and sounding the whistle tonight was insistent. I heard a shrill screeching noise. It could have been the train or the scream of a human being. I was mostly asleep and decided I would figure it out in the morning.

Chapter 6

The next morning I was up early. I'd wanted to sleep late after all the Thanksgiving Day hoopla, but something woke me up. As I hobbled to the kitchen to start the coffee, I caught a glimpse of the blinking red and blue lights gathered near the railroad tracks behind my house. It was the police. Did Marfa even have that many police cars? There must be Texas Rangers there, too. I had to find out what was going on. Whoever was in charge probably wouldn't let me get close to anything. I hobbled to the window of my walk-in closet and dressing room which had the best view of my back yard and beyond. It was just getting light enough to be able to see what was happening on the other side of the dirt road. It addition to all the police cars, there was an ambulance, a hearse, and a coroner's car. Somebody was dead.

I hurried to get dressed and filled my travel coffee cup. I would take the golf cart. If they wouldn't let me get close to the action, I could always sit in my back yard and watch them over or through my fence. The fence was still under construction, and I was determined to see what they were doing. Somebody might want to question me.

When I approached the assembled multitude in my golf cart, I was turned away from what had to be a crime scene. I had already anticipated that no one would be glad to see me. People in uniforms were stringing yellow plastic tape around some bushes beside the tracks.

"You can't go beyond the tape, lady. This is a crime scene. We'd prefer you go on home." The man in charge didn't quite say, "where you belong," but he almost did. I knew that's what he was thinking.

"I live right here, you know. That's my house." I pointed to my property. "You might expect that I'm curious about what's happened literally in my own back yard. Well, almost in my own back yard."

"This is an ongoing investigation, and I'm not at liberty to share anything with you at this time."

"I understand that, but I can see the coroner's car and the hearse. At least one person is dead. You can't deny that." The young Texas Ranger set his jaw and glared at me. I could see that he was by the book and wasn't going to share anything, so I turned my golf cart around and went home. I ate breakfast on my unfinished back patio and watched the comings and goings. I used my binoculars so I could better see what was happening. A photographer was taking a lot of pictures. I couldn't see a body until the coroner stood up and walked to his car. Then I thought I saw one dead person being zipped into a body bag and loaded into the hearse. Marfa was the county seat of Presidio County, so the coroner's office must be here, unless they were sending the body to Austin. I figured Austin was where the state's medical examiner would be. It was two more hours before all the red and blue blinking lights left the area.

I'd been looking forward to having a turkey sandwich for lunch, but if there was ever a day that demanded my presence at the Hotel Saint George for lunch, today was that day. I wanted to be there when the dining room opened at eleven. My friends who waited tables at the Saint George would have all the gossip. They always did, and no matter how much the authorities tried to put a muzzle on what was happening, these folks knew the scoop. I couldn't wait to get to town, and I forgot how tired I'd thought I was. I would rest up from Thanksgiving and sleep late tomorrow.

There was hearty beef barley soup with mushrooms on the Saint George's menu today, and I ordered a bowl. I questioned the waiter about what was going on behind my house, and he didn't disappoint.

"They found a dead woman beside the railroad tracks this morning. A jogger discovered her body in the bushes about six. At first they thought she'd wandered onto the railroad tracks and been hit by a train. Then they decided she might have fallen from a passing train. However, the latest word is that she was already dead when she landed in the bushes. They think she was dead before somebody threw her off the train. And her death wasn't from natural causes."

"Who is she and where was the train coming from?"

"The train was coming from L.A., and nobody knows who she is. She's a Jane Doe, unknown. The coroner will know more after he's done the autopsy and has the results of the toxicology report. They'll know then if she was drunk or on drugs. She's not a local, and I guess she didn't have any ID or a purse or anything on her. That's all I know."

Ruben, the man who ran the bookstore and gift shop in the hotel, was usually another dependable source of information. I had some Christmas shopping to do, and the gift shop sold wonderful things. Artists and artisans gravitate to Marfa; just ask Melody. One of my favorite textile artists makes fabulous silk scarves that are sold in the gift shop. Her scarves are colorful and soft and totally original. This year, I was giving all the women on my Christmas list one of these unique creations. The scarves were expensive but undeniably beautiful. The colors are vibrant and intense. The scarf artist grew plants in her garden that she used to make the dyes for her scarves. She used botanicals and other interesting objects in a reverse printing process to create her remarkable designs.

I would pump the bookstore manager for the latest news and get some Christmas shopping done at the same time. Unfortunately, Ruben didn't know much more than my waiter had already told me. He confirmed that the woman who was dead was not a local person and that law enforcement believed she'd either fallen or been thrown from the train coming from LA. The odd thing was that the train had been a freight train loaded with huge box-shipping containers, not a passenger train. People weren't supposed to be riding on freight trains. I bought six gorgeous scarves in various colors and drove home in my golf cart.

I wondered if the police would want to ask me some questions. Had I seen or heard anything? The woman had been found, after all, right behind my house. It had happened in the middle of the night, but the authorities could at least ask me if I'd heard anything suspicious. I hadn't, but it would have been nice of them to ask. Actually, I'd heard what I thought was a loud train whistle screaming in the night, but

I had no idea what time I'd heard it. I imagined that trains come and go all night long behind my house, but if that were true, how could the authorities know the dead woman had been thrown specifically from the L.A. train?

I knew the sensible thing would be to stay away from the crime scene. The yellow tape was still there, and I wasn't bold enough to mess with anything inside the perimeter that had been set up by law enforcement. As I drove my golf cart back to Austin Street, my curiosity began to get the better of me. I promised myself I wouldn't touch anything inside the crime scene tape, but there was nothing to stop me from looking around outside the cordoned-off area. I drove around and around the bushes where the body had been found. I could see where the body had landed on the brush and broken it down. I shivered as I looked at the outline a human being's body had left in the vegetation. Some poor soul, a woman, had landed there, thrown from a train, nameless and alone.

I grabbed my cane and poked through the grass and the dirt on the periphery of the area of the crime scene. Because I was trying to do my investigating from the seat of my golf cart, I wasn't very efficient. If I could walk around, get down on my hands and knees, and really look through the bushes, I told myself I might be able to find something. Who was I kidding? The CSI people had no doubt gone over the area with a fine-tooth comb. They would have already found everything there was to find. I'd always wanted to be Nancy Drew, but I was way past the age when I might have been able to discover something the professionals had missed. I was ready to admit defeat. I told myself I would make one more circle around the site and then go home and take a nap.

There was one clump of grass I couldn't quite reach with my cane when I was sitting on the golf cart. On this last trip through the bushes, I decided to get off and poke around on foot. It was always painful to get off the cart after I'd been sitting for a while. My joints stiffened up, and it took several steps to get my legs working properly and to get my momentum going.

I staggered a bit as I made my way into the unexamined brush. I hoped I wouldn't provoke a snake as I prodded with my cane. Not expecting to find anything of interest, I was shocked when I pushed aside a dirty, crumpled plastic bag and saw what looked like a woman's shoe lying on the ground. I leaned over to pick it up, but I didn't want to touch the shoe with my hands. I stuck the tip of my cane into the shoe, and after a few tries, I was able to lift the shoe out of the weeds and put it in the golf cart. I dropped it on the front seat on the passenger side, climbed back into the driver's seat, and drove home. How ridiculous was I? The shoe probably had nothing at all to do with the woman who'd been found dead, but the shoe was this Nancy Drew's only clue.

As I drove back to my garage, I couldn't keep my eyes off the shoe. It had a flat heel and looked cheap. The polka dots were black against what had once probably been a white or cream-colored background. The shoe was now faded and stained. It didn't look like any shoe I'd ever seen for sale in the United States. In other words, it looked foreign to me. It was a very small size and could belong to a child. The sole was almost worn through, and the shoe was soiled, inside and outside. The stiff, black and white polka-dotted fabric was thin and discolored. It looked as if it had been wet many times. The shoe was only a little bit sturdier than a shower shoe, and it was old. It looked very uncomfortable.

I headed home. I still didn't want to touch it with my hands, and when I parked the golf cart, I found a box of plastic gloves and a clean cloth in my garage. With difficulty, I pulled a pair of the tight gloves onto my arthritic fingers and picked up the shoe. Holding the dusty clue in the cloth, I carried it into my kitchen and put it on a clean white dish towel spread out on the kitchen table. I took a picture of it with my phone. I knew in my heart of hearts that, if the shoe turned out to be a real clue that might be related to the woman's death, I would turn it over to the police. But first I would document and take pictures of everything. Only then would I call law enforcement and give them my shoe clue.

I still had on the plastic gloves and cautiously examined the shoe. My feet aren't very big. I wear a size 7 shoe, but this shoe was much smaller than my own. It had to belong to a child or to a very tiny woman. I turned it over and took pictures of the well-worn sole. With trepidation, I gingerly reached my gloved hand inside the shoe and found the lining in the bottom was loose. There was something underneath the piece of cheap plastic insole that lined the inside bottom of the shoe. I could feel a thickness under the lining and what felt like coins under the area near the toes. To walk in shoes that had coins inside had to have been very uncomfortable. I grasped the lining with my fingertips. The glue that held the plastic in place was old, and the lining easily peeled away. Sure enough, there were two gold coins inside the lining of the shoe. The gold coins looked like antiques and had some kinds of unusual writing on them. The writing could be Asian or Greek or Russian. The letters on the coins were in an alphabet that was unfamiliar to me. I didn't know anything about coins or exotic alphabets, so I would have to do some research or hire an expert to identify their origin.

Just as surprising as the coins was the folded paper money that was also tucked inside the lining of the shoe. Both bills were Euros, and they each had the number 200 printed on them. Ancient foreign gold coins and high-denomination Euros inside a cheap shoe? The shoe had to be related to the murdered woman. What other explanation could there be for the shoe I'd found beside the railroad tracks? Still wearing my plastic gloves, I carefully photographed both sides of each of the bills of paper money and both sides of the two gold coins. I photographed the shoe from several angles. I put the Euros, the coins, and the shoe into a gallon-size Ziploc plastic bag.

I was new in town, and nobody in law enforcement knew me. This morning I'd managed to get myself on the wrong side of the Texas Ranger who'd been guarding the crime scene behind my home. Investigators wouldn't be happy to learn they'd missed something, if in fact the shoe I'd found was related to their case. As I thought about what might have happened, it didn't seem too far-fetched that when she was thrown from the train, one of the woman's shoes had flown off her foot and landed some distance away from her body. In the violence of falling or being thrown off a train, anything could happen. Maybe the woman's other shoe had still been on her foot when her body was found, or maybe the police had found the other shoe closer to her body. I had to call the police and wondered if it would be better to call the local sheriff or the Texas Rangers. I decided to call the Texas Rangers. They'd probably end up with the case anyway, until they turned it over to the FBI.

Chapter 7

iguring out how to communicate with the Texas Rangers wasn't easy. I didn't want a tour of their head-quarters. I didn't want to take my group to the Texas Rangers' museum, and I didn't want to hire a speaker. There just wasn't any option to choose to report having found evidence in a possible murder case. I wish I had asked the name of the ranger who'd shooed me away this morning. He probably would not have been willing to reveal his name, even if I'd asked.

I ended up calling the local 911 and making the operator mad at me. I wasn't reporting a crime in progress, a life or death health emergency, a burglary, or a fire. She didn't want to talk to me about anything else. "I live right behind the railroad tracks where a woman was found dead this morning. This afternoon, I found what I think is one of her shoes and some money near the crime scene. You need to send somebody to my house to talk to me." I hoped the mention of money might get the woman's attention.

After many phone transfers and two disconnections, I managed to talk to somebody who was interested in what I had to say. The Texas Rangers would send somebody to the house — later that afternoon. I waited, and finally there was a knock at the door. When I opened it, there was the Texas Ranger from this morning. He wasn't any happier to see me than I was to see him.

"Ms. Lennox, I'm Detective Jeremiah Drayton. He took off his hat and put out his hand."

I shook his hand. "Come in Detective Drayton, I believe we talked briefly this morning at your crime scene." I was trying hard to be agreeable and not tick off the detective. I took him to my living room and asked if he wanted any coffee, tea, or ice water. He didn't, thank goodness. Carrying a tray with anything on it is pretty far outside my skill set these days. We sat down. He was in my home now, so he was being more mannerly than he'd been this morning.

"My understanding is that you've found something you think might be connected to a crime scene." Drayton got right to the point.

I was amused that he wasn't even willing to refer to the area behind my house as "our" crime scene or "the" crime scene. It was "a" crime scene. The way he referred to it, it could be a crime scene anywhere in the universe. "I was riding my golf cart behind my house this afternoon, and I found a shoe. There are yards and yards of yellow tape that are printed with the words 'crime scene' on it back there, so can we agree to refer to it as 'the' crime scene? It's right behind my house. It isn't on Mars." I was trying hard not to slip into my snarky, if not sarcastic mode, but this guy was making it very difficult to talk to him.

Drayton smiled a tight and not very friendly smile. "You say you found a shoe? What were you doing, driving your golf cart around...," he paused, "the crime scene? I told you this morning to stay away from there."

"I didn't touch your crime scene. I stayed strictly outside the crime scene tape. I know better than to go inside that tape. I found the shoe in a clump of bushes about two yards from your perimeter. I don't know whether or not the shoe has anything to do with the dead woman you found out there this morning. It's a small woman's shoe, and it had money hidden inside of it. There were Euros and two antique gold coins inside the lining of the shoe." I wondered if mentioning money would get this guy's attention, and it did.

"Money? Inside the shoe? I guess you'd better show me this shoe and the money you found."

I picked up the Ziploc bag from the end table next to me and handed it to Officer Drayton. He frowned and started in on me again. "How do you know a woman was found dead behind your house this morning? And why were you driving your golf cart around there?" He was scolding me.

"Everybody in town knows you found a dead woman behind my house this morning. They know she was dead before she was thrown or fell off the train, and they know she didn't have any identification on her when she was found. It's a small town. Being secretive about everything is just ridiculous." He bristled when I said the word ridiculous.

"I'm not allowed to talk about an ongoing investigation." He turned his attention to the shoe and the coins and the Euros. He examined it all through the plastic bag and didn't open the bag or take anything out of it. He seemed especially interested in the two coins.

"Did you touch any of this when you picked it up?" He was ready to scold me again, but I'd outfoxed him this time.

"I picked the shoe up with the tip of my cane and put it on the seat beside me. As soon as I got home, I put on plastic gloves before I examined the shoe. I never touched the shoe or the money with my hands, so you won't find my fingerprints on any of it." Drayton clenched his jaw, looking a bit disappointed, I thought, that he couldn't jump all over me for contaminating the evidence.

"Well, at least you didn't contaminate the evidence. You're going to have to show me exactly where you found this shoe. Why don't we do that now?"

He put the plastic bag with the evidence I'd found into his car and brought me back a receipt for the bag's contents. We rode to the crime scene in my golf cart, and I showed him the exact clump of brush where I'd found the shoe. He got out and walked around a little bit. He looked at the ground and stepped off some distances. Then he put a marker of some kind in the ground. He took some photos with his cell phone. We rode back to my house. He wasn't going to come in the house this time, but he was going to caution me. I could see it coming.

"You are not to discuss what you've found with anyone. Someone from my office will call you next week to take a statement about exactly where and how you found the shoe.

"I will look forward to the call. I promise I won't talk about the shoe or the money. But I'd like for you to let me know what's happening. I'd like to know if the evidence *I found for you* leads to anything." Jeremiah Drayton was a grumpy Texas Ranger, and he didn't want to tell me squat about what was going on.

"As I've said to you, I can't discuss anything about an ongoing investigation."

I turned away and hobbled back into my house without saying another word. He knew he'd pissed me off. I was glad he'd received that message. I was tired after yesterday, and with all the excitement of today, I should have stayed in for the night. And I'd had lunch and already questioned the wait staff at the Saint George. If there were more news about the murdered woman, I certainly wasn't going to hear it from Jeremiah Drayton. If I was going to learn anything at all, it would be from my friends at the hotel.

The turkey sandwiches could wait another day. I got on my golf cart and rode into town. Since I'd lived at the Saint George for such a long time, the staff was always glad to see me and always found me a table in the dining room, no matter how crowded it was. I was looking at the menu when someone tapped me on the shoulder. It was Ellery King. I invited him to sit down and join me, for a drink or for dinner. He seemed genuinely glad to see me and said he would have a drink with me. He wanted to thank me for Thanksgiving.

"Augustus and I had a great time celebrating Thanksgiving with you yesterday." Was it just yesterday? "Every bite of your food was fabulous, and Augustus loved you and loved your house. He can't wait to come back. He says he wants us to come to L.A. so he can take us to his favorite restaurant there. I told him that probably wasn't going to happen, but he did have a wonderful time. He was very curious about our neighbor, Melody Granger. Apparently, he knows her work, but he didn't know she was a drunk."

"I've never seen her work. She's never invited me to come over, but one day, she probably will, whether she wants to or not." Ellery knew what I meant.

I ordered a Mexican coke. I had to drive my golf cart home. Ellery ordered a beer. I talked him into having dinner with me. I ordered the curried lamb on rice pilaf, and he ordered the lobster fettuccine. We split a chocolate dessert. Ellery told me he was going away the following weekend. He seemed excited about the trip. His jazz band was traveling to a town on the border, Terlingua, Texas, for a four day get-together, a convocation of sorts, of jazz combos. He planned to leave next Wednesday.

Terlingua had a vivid and dubious reputation, for many reasons. It was said to be a ghost town, and everyone agreed it was located at the end of the world. Hippies of all ages, shapes, and sizes had been gathering there for years, and drinking and drugs were not unheard of in this remote West Texas refuge for the unconventional and those who wanted to be left alone. It has been called a magnet for dropouts, drifters, seekers, free-spirits, and lost souls looking for a new start. From what I'd heard, the folks who gathered there were looking for an excuse not to have to start doing much of anything.

Supposedly, law enforcement goes there only under duress. One story that floated around was about a female government official of some kind, maybe a census worker, who went to Terlingua and was attacked and badly bitten by a javelina. She never returned, and you can scarcely blame her for that. A few years ago, there'd been a tragic murder in Terlingua. The well-known and much-loved owner of Terlingua's La Kiva bar was brutally bludgeoned to death in the parking lot of his own bar. One of the bar owner's good friends had been charged with the murder. Even with a change of venue, the accused was found not guilty. Mystery and scandal still surrounded the case. One could probably conclude that the bar owner wasn't much-loved by everybody.

Ellery said that six jazz groups from around the Southwest were planning to gather the following weekend to play for each other and whatever audience turned up to listen to them improvise. One group was coming from as far away as Tucson. It sounded fun. I don't very often wish I were younger, but I did wish I had the energy, the physical stamina, and the maneuverability to make the trip to see Ellery's jazz jam in Terlingua.

"It sounds wonderful, Ellery. If I were younger, I'd be there to hear you."

"Even if you were younger, Margaret, I wouldn't recommend that you come to see my group perform. You are much too law-abiding and refined for Terlingua. Trust me, you would hate the place. Most towns want people to move there, and their Chamber of Commerce and the local boosters tell people and businesses why their town is a great place to live and work. Terlingua, on the other hand, actively discourages people from moving there. They send out public service announcements, of a sort, to try to talk people out of coming. They openly say, 'You probably won't like it here.' I wouldn't be going if it weren't such a great musical opportunity. I'm shocked anybody there wants us to come. We'll be playing at the famous and infamous La Kiva Bar. Terlingua has a chili cook-off in November, and that's much more Terlingua's style than a jazz band symposium. I'll let you know how it goes."

"It sounds exotic and dangerous. You're right. I am a good bit past the exotic and dangerous part of my life. But if it's so unfriendly, why is your band going there?"

"The drummer in my band and the sax player in one of the other bands are cousins. They've wanted to go to Terlingua and play music for years. So this is the weekend that's going to happen. I'll drink a Mind Eraser for you. Ha! That's a joke. I probably won't even have the nerve to drink one for myself."

"What's a Mind Eraser? It sounds to me like most of the people who live in Terlingua have already taken care of that...the mind erasing thing."

"The Mind Eraser is a combination of vodka, Kahlúa, and club soda — kind of like an alcoholic version of a coffee-flavored ice cream soda without the ice cream. The bar's website used to say it was to be 'inhaled through a straw from the bottom up as fast as possible.' Sounds deadly to me. I'm more of a beer and wine kind of guy."

"I guess you're right. I'd better stay in Marfa. But why would they want to leave out the ice cream?" Ellery offered to split the bill with me, but I paid for our drinks and dinner and drove Ellery home. He was such a nice young man. I told him to be careful in Terlingua. It sounded pretty rough down there.

I was so captivated by what was going on in Ellery's life that I'd completely forgotten to ask the waiter about the latest on the dead woman from the train. I'd have to go back to the Saint George again for lunch or dinner tomorrow.

Chapter 8

*T*he next day I drove my golf cart to the grocery store and bought my groceries for the week. It was Saturday, so the Stone Village Market was busy. I waited in line to place my order at the deli counter. I shop at all the grocery stores in Marfa, but this store makes really great sandwiches. I intended to order a roast beef and provolone on rye with Thousand Island dressing, along with the rest of my deli order. In any small town, the grocery store is a good place to pick up information about the latest scandals...and the latest murders. I struck up a conversation with one of the other customers who was waiting at the deli with her number in hand. So much for the reclusive image I was trying to cultivate.

"I used to think small towns were safer than big cities, but with the events here in Marfa lately, I've begun to wonder if that's true." People were usually polite to old ladies like me and answered me when I spoke to them.

"I know, isn't it terrible? I can't imagine why or how anyone could be thrown off a train in the middle of the night. They still don't know who she is or where she came from, and I'm betting they'll never find out. She's foreign, you know, but not Hispanic. I heard the police think she's Chinese, something to do with her shoes. I told Albert, my boyfriend, that everybody's shoes are made in China these days. If they try to figure out your identity or your nationality from your shoes, they're going to think everybody's Chinese. Albert said it wasn't just her shoes. You can do DNA tests now to figure out a person's background. Apparently she looks Asian, even looks Chinese, so they might not have to do a DNA test. Somebody said she had Chinese money with her, and some valuable coins. They say she was dead before they threw her off the train, of course, so who knows what's really going on? If the train came from L.A. or El Paso, she could have been killed in one of those places, and really Marfa might not have anything to do with any of it."

"Nobody thinks she was killed here or is from here?"

"Oh, no, she's definitely from someplace other than Marfa. She just ended up here. I think the last time somebody was killed in Marfa was a few years ago when a couple of cowboys got drunk and got into a fight. It wasn't really a murder; it was manslaughter. The trial was a big deal, and the guy who went to prison is out now. If they figure out where this woman was killed, they will have their investigation and their trial wherever that is. It won't be here in Marfa. She definitely wasn't killed here. It's just our bad luck—and hers—that she ended up here. I think I heard that the train started out in L.A. The authorities believe, or so the grapevine has it, that she was probably dead when the train left from there. You know what crime is like in a place like L.A."

"So really, small towns are safer than cities. The woman wasn't even killed here, just found here."

"That's what the coroner thinks. Albert works in the post office, so he knows everybody and hears about everything that's going on."

The only new information I'd learned from Albert's girl-friend was that the word regarding the coins was already out. I hadn't taken the time yet to research the coins on the internet, but I promised myself I'd do that tonight. The coins had been heavy and irregular and looked antique and handmade. I had good photographs of both of them, front and back, on my cell phone. I collected my sandwich, a pound of sliced provolone, the pound of Boar's Head thinly sliced honey ham, a loaf of the store's homemade rye bread, and some Campari tomatoes. The Stone Market gourmet sandwich was for my dinner even though I had turkey at home. I try to make my sandwiches taste like the ones the Stone Village Market makes, but they never do. So every time I shop here, I take home a sandwich.

It was time to head to the Saint George for lunch. I carry a small cooler in the back of my golf cart to keep perishable grocery store food cold so I don't have to make a trip to my house to put it away. I put my sandwich and the other food in the cooler and went directly to lunch. Nobody had said anything yet about my golf cart not being wanted on the streets of Marfa. I loved driving it around and hoped I would be allowed to keep it. Lunch at the Saint Georges would be my main meal of the day, and I wanted to buy three more scarves for Christmas gifts.

Chapter 9

*M*y new housekeeper arrived on the Monday morning after Thanksgiving. Consuela Rodriguez was forty-three but looked ten years younger. She had a lot of energy. When I'd hired her, I had explained in detail everything I expected of her, including cleaning, cooking, washing clothes, and taking care of me. She was also going to help me learn Spanish. Consuela had three children, so working part-time for me while her kids were in school suited her schedule.

She arrived at my house after seeing her kids off on the school bus and left work in time to get home before they did. I was accommodating about holidays, and I told her if she had to take time off when the kids were sick, that was fine with me. She appreciated my flexibility. Her husband worked for a pool servicing business. Lucky me! He didn't clean pools, but he repaired the pool pumps and heaters that were always breaking down. My pool wasn't completed yet, but when it was I would be signing up with his company's pool maintenance service.

Consuela dove right into the work. I'd only lived in my house for a little over two weeks, so it didn't really need much cleaning. Some laundry had accumulated, and she immediately knew which things needed to be hand washed and which could go into the washing machine and dryer. We discussed how often I wanted my sheets changed and the towels in my bathroom washed.

Consuela said she would bring me coffee and breakfast when she first arrived in the morning, if that worked with my schedule. It did. Consuela was smart as a whip and figured everything out on the first day. She asked me what I wanted for lunch and for dinner. She would make my dinner, if I wanted her to make it, and leave it for me to warm up. I told her I frequently went to the Saint Georges Hotel for lunch or dinner or both. She would also do my grocery shopping.

My new housekeeper understood that I was a writer and that I would be writing in my office most mornings. I told her I wrote under a pen name, and I didn't want her to talk about my writing or my pen name with anybody. She was fine with keeping my identity as a writer confidential. She didn't seem to want to stand around or chat with me too much. She said she liked to work, and she was a hard worker. She was agreeable to all my requests.

We made some lists, and she began telling me what the Spanish words were for the various items on the grocery list and on our other lists. It was a good start to my learning a new language. Our arrangement was going to work out fine, and I could tell we would settle into a comfortable routine in no time.

Consuela knew a great deal about cooking and about gardening. I told her I wanted to plant an herb garden, a perennial garden, and a cutting garden the next spring. Her eyes lit up when I told her I would need her help figuring out what would grow in the desert climate. Consuela had an extended family who lived in the area, and they all celebrated together during the Christmas holidays. She looked sad when I told her I would be spending Christmas alone.

I'd briefly considered traveling to San Diego to visit my daughter for Christmas, but I'd have to drive to El Paso to get the plane. That was three hours in the car and then a one-hour flight. My daughter's new firm was just getting started, and her business was surprisingly brisk. She wanted to take advantage of being the new kid on the block and take as many cases as she could. I decided I could fend for myself through the Christmas Holidays. I wondered if Ellery had any family or if he would be in town for Christmas. I wondered if the hilariously funny and outrageous Augustus Gemini would be spending the holidays in Marfa or in L.A.

I did most of my Christmas shopping over the internet. It was so convenient. I'd already purchased fabulous scarves from the gift shop at the Hotel Saint George. Gifts were on their way to friends and family before I could say scotch tape or tissue paper. I wasn't going to cook, and the Saint George was making a fancy Christmas Dinner. I'd made a reservation for two. I would invite Ellery to join me if he was going to be in town.

I'd ordered an already-decorated Christmas tree from a catalogue. It was a small tabletop tree, and it was incredibly beautiful and incredibly expensive. The arthritis in my fingers kept me from being able to put ornaments on the tree anymore. I ordered some wreaths for the doors and windows of my house. Consuela could hang those up for me. I was ready for Christmas! That was easy. I knew I would end up making cookies or something else, but with the gifts, the decorations, and the dinner taken care of, the pressure was off.

With my Christmas preparations behind me, I enjoyed a ham and turkey sandwich with mustard and mayonnaise for lunch. I was remembering the days when preparing for Christmas began months in advance. I was glad to have the memories from those days but also glad I didn't have to put up and decorate a twenty-five foot Christmas tree anymore or throw a Christmas wassail party for five hundred. When I'd driven the Christmas train, I'd driven it hard and fast. What a relief to be old and not have to prove anything to anybody anymore. I had wanted to do it all at the time, and I had done it all. Mostly I'd loved doing it. But this year, I was going to allow somebody else to do the work.

A few days later, I called Ellery to invite him to be my guest at the Saint George for Christmas dinner. He doesn't have a landline, so I was surprised when he didn't pick up. He usually answers when I call, if he's not busy with something. I figured he was busy and left a voicemail message for him to call me. I asked him about the jazz symposium in Terlingua. He should have been back in Marfa by now, home from the La Kiva gig. When Ellery hadn't called me back after three days, I began to get worried. He should have been home by last Sunday night or Monday, and it was now Friday. I decided to drive my golf cart to his house and knock on the door.

I admit I was being a nosy neighbor, but I was concerned. I drove my golf cart as close to Ellery's mailbox as I could to get a look inside. It was stuffed full, and I realized he hadn't picked up his mail in a week or more. I got off the golf cart and hobbled to his front door. I knocked and leaned against his porch railing while I waited, but nobody answered. He wasn't home. I hobbled around to the side of his house where there was a shed. He used the shed as a garage for his car and for all his garden equipment. His ancient, dusty Range Rover with its questionable four-wheel drive wasn't in the shed. I began to wonder if Ellery had ever come back from his trip to Terlingua. I called his cell phone again, expressing my concern.

I hobbled back to my golf cart and drove home. I wanted to go to the Saint George for lunch, but there were things I had to take care of at home. I couldn't get Ellery out of my mind. He had gone off to spend a long weekend at a remote and dangerous place, a place where he'd told me I shouldn't go. I thought he had intended to come home on Sunday night, and it was already the following Friday. Where was he? He wasn't responsible for checking in with me, and it was none of my business where he went or how long he stayed there. But I'd grown fond of the young man and wanted to be sure he was all right.

Augustus Gemini had written me a beautiful and enter-tainingly funny snail mail thank-you note to tell me what a good time he'd had at Thanksgiving dinner. He went on con-siderably about not remembering the last time he'd needed a stamp for anything, telling me he only wrote on paper when he was dealing with people who were over sixty years of age. He'd included his business card which I'd put in the center drawer of my desk. It was a heavy vellum, oversized business card, engraved in purple ink. It said Augustus Gemini was a "GEMINI OF ALL TRADES AND MASTER OF ALL." There was a phone number, three email addresses, a twitter address, and some other things I couldn't figure out on the card, all ways to communicate with Augustus Gemini. I would either call or send Augustus a text and ask him if he'd heard from Ellery. I hoped Ellery had decided to go to L.A. to work on a movie.

I went home and Consuela made me a ham and cheese sandwich. I had some delicious leftover potato salad I'd brought home from the Saint George. Consuela had a pitcher of fresh iced tea with lots of lemon, and I wished Ellery were there to have a sandwich with me. I started on my bills and paperwork, and when I'd cleared my desk, I decided to take a nap. I paid Consuela who was finished for the day and for the week. She told me to have a nice weekend. My house was clean. My clothes were all washed and ironed and neatly folded or hung up and put away. I had food for the next two days. I drifted off to sleep.

I don't know how long I'd been sleeping when I heard someone pounding on my front door. Nobody was expected, and I was a recluse, after all. I decided I wasn't home and rolled over and tried to go back to sleep. Whoever was at my door was persistent, and the knocking wouldn't stop.

I hobbled to the door. It was Melody. I should have known. She was completely schnockered. She looked very upset as well as very drunk.

"Melody, what's wrong?" I had to invite her into my house. She stumbled through the doorway and collapsed on my living room couch.

"My cat's been poisoned. She's dead. I'm devastated."

"Dead? Your cat is dead? Poisoned? I'm so sorry. What happened?"

"I've been dumpster diving in Dallas. I get all of my art materials for my sculptures out of dumpsters and landfills and people's garbage cans. I've pretty much cleaned out everything in Marfa, and people throw away the best stuff in Dallas. Lots of very rich people there. I go up to Dallas Ft. Worth a couple of times a month, if I can, and fill up the back of my truck with stuff. It's a long drive, and the trip takes me at least three days. It's a whole day to drive there, and a whole day to drive back to Marfa. They have great material in the dumps and landfills in Dallas, so I make the effort. I make all my sculptures out of found objects, you know." Melody started to cry. "I just got back. When I got home, Girdle was dead."

"Can I get you anything to drink? Some water or some tea?"

"No, but can you come over and bury my cat? I just can't do it."

I couldn't do it either. Not because it would make me too sad but because I physically couldn't dig a grave. I would immediately have called on Ellery for this job, and he would have been happy to do it. He's a gardener and great with a shovel, but he wasn't anywhere to be found.

"I can't do it either, Melody. I'm sorry. I'm not physically able to dig a grave for your cat. Is there anyone you can call who could take care of this for you? I understand why you can't do it yourself, and you shouldn't have to." I felt sorry for her but there was little I could do. I didn't know anybody I could call to dig the grave. Consuela might be able to do it, but grave digging wasn't really in her job description. Maybe I could pay her husband to do it. "Why do you think somebody poisoned your cat? Are you sure about that? If you think your cat was deliberately killed, you need to call the authorities."

"I know somebody killed Girdle because she's foaming at the mouth and there's blood everywhere. Somebody did this on purpose."

"Do you want me to call the sheriff? I can do that for you. He may want to take the remains away to have them analyzed, to see if Girdle really was poisoned."

"Oh, no. I could never let them take her away...or do an autopsy on my darling."

"I don't think they would actually do an autopsy. I think they might do some blood tests. I don't really know, but I can ask the sheriff what's involved." When she didn't say anything, I looked over at Melody. She was sound asleep on my couch.

I decided to go over to her house and have a look at the cat. Maybe I was being pushy, but Melody had come to me for help. I had never been to Melody's house, but I assumed she had left her door unlocked. It wasn't easy for me to get to her house. It was not really far enough away to take the golf cart, but it was too far for me to walk. I took the golf cart. I pulled into Melody's driveway and hobbled to her front door. It was unlocked, and I let myself in.

Her whole house was her studio. That was my kindest interpretation of the mess I found inside Melody's living room and dining room. I had no reason to believe any of the other rooms were different. Every square inch was filled with "found objects." There had been some attempt to sort things into categories, but not much. It was almost at the level of the hoarding homes you see on television shows. It wasn't quite that bad, but it soon would be.

I tried to give my neighbor the benefit of the doubt. She was an artist, as she had pointed out to me on numerous occasions. She would tell me this was how really creative people live, that the artistic personality found order in their art, not in keeping their houses neat and tidy. I shuddered. I was too organized to be designated as having an artistic personality, and so I could not possibly understand what felt comfortable to Melody. If this level of chaos was what made her feel comfortable, no wonder she drank.

I wondered how in the world she had ever found her cat. I couldn't find her in these massive piles. I looked and looked and finally found the poor thing on Melody's back patio. The covered porch was where Melody actually did her work. The rest of the house was just a place to store her materials, her found objects, her junk. There were three massive sculptures underway in the open air space behind Melody's house. I was fascinated, but I would have to come back later to take a closer look. I needed to make Girdle my first priority.

I found the cat lying dead under a bench on the patio. Melody had not exaggerated. It did appear as if her cat had been poisoned. She had been frothing at the mouth before she died, and there was blood everywhere. The black and white cat had been small and skinny when she was alive. The poor thing was even more shrunken in death. I didn't know anything about rigor mortis in cats, but I was guessing Girdle had been dead since yesterday or the day before. She had died sometime during the three days Melody had driven to Dallas to go dumpster diving. Did Melody the artist really need to acquire more "found objects" with every room of her house already packed to the gills? I decided it was not for me to say. After visiting Melody's home, I finally had the answer to her question. I was not an artist.

I took some photos with my phone of Girdle lying on the patio. The photos were to show the frothing at the mouth and the blood. Then I searched the house for something to wrap the cat in. I found a clean pillowcase in the linen closet. At least I thought it was clean. I picked up Girdle and wrapped her in the pillow case. With great difficulty, I carried her out to my golf cart. I put her on the front passenger seat and called the sheriff on my cell phone. It was after normal business hours, but I didn't think the sheriff paid attention to that.

I'd decided not to call 911, although Melody probably would have. After negotiating the phone tree and several live human beings, the Sheriff's office told me to call Animal Control. I did that. When I explained what had happened, Animal Control told me to call the sheriff's department...again. Finally I got through to somebody who promised to come to my house and pick up the cat's body. I told them I wanted tests done to find out what kind of poison had been used on the animal and that I was willing to pay for it. I'd only had to threaten to write two letters to the editor of the local newspaper and make one call to *Sixty Minutes*, before the sheriff's office promised to send somebody out.

By the time I was off the phone, I had developed a somewhat lengthy and very convincing spiel about local pets being at risk and a mad cat poisoner being on the loose in Marfa. I had given a very graphic description of Girdle's appearance after death. I think the real reason they were sending someone out was to squelch my hysteria. I wasn't really hysterical, but putting on the hysteria show had been the only way to get any action.

I drove the golf cart home and carried Girdle to the rear of my house. She would begin to smell soon enough, and Melody didn't need to see her. I was worried that Melody wouldn't be willing to go back home if she had to deal with her dead cat. Better to have Girdle at my house and tell Melody to go home. I would deal with the problem.

I Googled poisons that produce frothing around the mouth. Strychnine was my best guess because of the foaming, but it could also have been cyanide. It looked to me as if Girdle had also vomited blood as she'd been dying a very painful death. Artists sometimes use unusual and dangerous chemicals to give their work a certain finish or patina. I wondered if Melody ever used either strychnine or cyanide as part of her artistic processes. Where in the world had Girdle found the poison? I knew strychnine was sometimes used in rat poison. Had Girdle eaten a rodent that had eaten strychnine? I vaguely remembered seeing a bowl of milk on the patio at Melody's. The milk looked as if it had been there for several days, and I should have taken more notice of it when I was there. I would mention it when someone from the sheriff's office came out. It occurred to me that someone might be trying to poison Melody and had put strychnine or cyanide or both in the milk in her refrigerator. They got Melody's cat instead.

What was happening in my neighborhood? Ellery was MIA, and Melody's cat had been poisoned. A week ago, a woman had been found dead behind my house. Was this what usually happened in small towns? I didn't think it was.

Chapter 10

While I *waited for someone from the sheriff's* office to show up, I called Augustus Gemini. I told him who I was and left a message on his voice mail. I said Ellery King had been missing since Sunday and that I was concerned. I asked Augustus if he'd heard from Ellery. I also asked him if Ellery had any family who might know where he was. I'd never heard Ellery mention family, except for his mother who had named him. He'd spoken of her in the past tense, as if she were deceased.

Melody was still snoring away on my couch, so I sat in my kitchen and waited for the law. I was glad it wasn't going to be the smarty pants Jeremiah from the Texas Rangers who was coming to see about the cat. My phone beeped to let me know I had a text. It was from Augustus:

Haven't heard from Ellery. Tried to call him. No answer. I will investigate. Hope you are well. Love, Augustus Gemini.

So much for my wish that Ellery had gone to L.A. to work on a movie. I texted Augustus back:

    Any family I can contact?

I got an immediate answer:

    No family. Sad story. I will try to find him.
    Why was he in Terlingua?

I responded:

    Yes, Terlingua for a jazz symposium. La Kiva Bar.

It was dark outside when someone finally knocked on my door. It was a sheriff's deputy, and it was a woman. I hoped she would be sympathetic and take Melody's cat's death seriously. Deputy Marjorie Whitefeather was efficient and friendly. We walked through my house, and she briefly glanced at Melody sprawled out on the couch. We went out to my back patio and looked at the cat. She picked Girdle up in the pillow case and took her to her cruiser. When she came back inside, she washed her hands thoroughly at the kitchen sink. We sat at my kitchen table, and I showed the deputy the photos I'd taken of Girdle at Melody's house. Deputy Whitefeather asked me to forward the pictures of the dead cat to her phone.

"The cat belongs to your next door neighbor, Melody Granger, the woman who's asleep on your couch? You brought the cat over here and called the sheriff's office?"

"Melody was in no shape to do anything. She was very distraught. She said her cat had been poisoned, and when I saw the cat, I agreed with her. I Googled both strychnine and cyanide poisoning, and I think one or both of those was what the cat ingested. There's a bowl of milk on Melody's patio. I noticed it when I went over to get the cat. You might want to take that milk in for testing."

"Ms. Lennox, we are concerned when anyone loses a pet, but we don't have the resources to do extensive testing when an animal is poisoned. We will do what we can to find out what happened to the cat, but as for testing the cat's food, we don't get into that."

"What if the poison was intended for Melody? Why would anybody want to hurt her cat?"

"Law enforcement in the area is familiar with your neighbor. She has a problem with alcohol, and two years ago she had her driver's license suspended. We believe she drives her car out of town but doesn't drive it around in town, where we can see her driving. She's more than a bit of an eccentric, and she's a menace on the road."

"She's an artist." Why was I mimicking to Marjorie White-feather the things Melody had said to me? I didn't know why, but I was doing it. "She is very eccentric, but I know she didn't poison her own cat."

"I'm not saying she did. I'm just saying, she drinks and gets confused."

Why did I now want to defend Melody's behavior? I decided I would somehow get hold of the milk from the cat's dish and have it analyzed at my own expense. Getting that done in Marfa, Texas would probably be not be possible, but I was absolutely determined to do it.

The deputy got up to leave, but I was going to insist she give me more information. "I'm going to have to tell Melody when she can have her cat's remains returned to her. I know she will want to have a burial and a service for the cat."

Marjorie shrugged her shoulders, "Yes, I am sure she will. It will be a few days. Can I have your phone number?

I'll call you when you can pick up the cat. I'd rather talk to you than take a chance on Melody's sobriety. Can you come and pick up the cat?"

"You can call me, and I will come to get the cat. Somebody will have to carry the cat out to my car." I figured I would drive my car rather than the golf cart. There was no point in asking for trouble. I wasn't even going to mention the golf cart, although it was, at this very moment, sitting front and center in my driveway for all the world to see.

"I'll be in touch." Deputy Whitefeather left, and I stood at the door as she walked down my front walk. She looked pointedly at the golf cart in the driveway; then she turned around and looked pointedly at me. I wasn't fooling Marjorie. Everyone in town had to know I was driving around in a golf cart most of the time.

Melody had told me she'd driven to Dallas to search for art materials, so Marjorie Whitefeather was correct that my neighbor, who had lost her driver's license some time ago, was driving out of town. No wonder Melody had tried to bum rides off me when I was driving the golf cart back and forth between my house and downtown Marfa. I could feel guilty for refusing to give her a ride, but her drinking and the loss of her driver's license were her problem and her responsibility.

I decided it was time to wake up Melody and send her home. I would reassure her that Girdle wasn't on her patio any longer. I would tell her about my talk with the deputy sheriff, at least the part that pertained to her cat. I would tell her I was going to pick up the cat when the sheriff's office was finished with her. I would reassure her there would be no autopsy on her beloved Girdle. I hoped Melody would be able to pull herself together and make it home.

When I woke her up she said, "I'm going to need help burying Girdle, you know. I went to Ellery's house today, to ask him to dig her grave, but he wouldn't answer the door. He's very good with a shovel, and I know he'll dig her grave for me."

"Ellery isn't home. I'm sure he will dig Girdle's grave when he gets back." I was urging Melody out the door. "I'll take care of everything. Go home and get some rest. I know you are sad, but we will have a nice burial service for Girdle." Melody stumbled out the door and across my yard to her own front door.

I was worried about Ellery, and I was upset about Melody's cat. Then I remembered the milk on the patio. What if the milk in the refrigerator was also poisoned? I grabbed my cane and took out after Melody. I wanted to get to her before she found the cat's bowl and threw the milk away and before she helped herself to a glass of milk from her refrigerator. She was just about to toss the bowl of milk into the sink when I got to her kitchen.

"I think we need to save that milk as evidence, for the sheriff. I'm worried that somebody put poison in the milk. I want to take your milk from the refrigerator, too, just in case."

"Why would anybody want to poison Girdle? Why would anybody want to poison me? I'm an artist."

"I don't know, and maybe nobody is poisoning anybody. But just to be on the safe side, I want to take both Girdle's bowl and your carton of milk. I looked around for clean jars with lids or some kind of containers to hold the suspect milk. I had to wash out two glass jars. I boiled some hot water on Melody's stove. She watched me with curiosity and amusement. I boiled water to sterilize the jars and the lids.

I filled one with the milk from Girdle's bowl and the other with milk from the milk carton. I washed the cat's bowl and rinsed it out with boiling water, too. I rinsed out the milk carton and put it in a plastic bag. I would throw it away at my house. I was afraid to throw it in Melody's trash. In fact, she didn't have a trash can. All trash was treasure for my artist neighbor. I didn't want Melody to think the plastic milk container was a valuable found object and try to do something with it. Better to put it safely in my own garbage.

It was difficult to juggle my cane and all the containers I was transporting in the dark. Plastic bags helped. I hadn't brought the golf cart this time. I made it home with everything. I labeled each of the glass jars that held my evidence and put them in my own refrigerator. I made a big sign that said "POISON" for each jar and warned everyone not to touch the two glass jars. I carefully rinsed out Melody's empty milk container again and discarded it in my garbage can. I was physically worn out after all this unexpected running around. I loved animals and seeing sad little Girdle had upset me more than I wanted to admit.

I decided to treat myself to a late dinner at the Saint George. I could usually find all kinds of excuses to go to the Saint George, but today I really did need to be cheered up. I had to eat, after all. I was exhausted after everything that had happened today, and I had told Consuela not to fix me any dinner.

On my way to the Saint George, my cell phone rang. It was Augustus Gemini, and I wanted to answer before he hung up. Maybe he had news. I pulled over to the side of the street and answered my phone.

"Augustus, do you have news?"

"Margaret, I do have news, and it isn't good. I've found Ellery. He's in the hospital in El Paso. Somebody tried to poison him with cyanide and strychnine, if you can believe it. He's going to make it, although I guess it was touch and go there for a while. He was in the hospital for quite a few days before he was able to tell anybody his name."

"Strychnine and cyanide?" Augustus couldn't possibly know what I suspected about these poisons, and he couldn't possibly know why hearing those words had totally freaked me out.

"Yes, he almost died. If he'd had one more sip of that soy milk, he would have died. Thank goodness it was spoiled, and he spit it all out before he swallowed any to speak of. So he's going to be fine. The doctor says it will be a slow recovery, but supposedly he doesn't have any permanent damage to his liver or kidneys."

I was stunned when I'd heard the word "milk." "How in the world did you get all of this information? I thought with HIPAA and all of that, nobody would be willing to tell you anything."

"I lied to the doctor and said I was Ellery's brother. He was so glad to have someone call him and show an interest in Ellery, he told me everything."

"What can I do? Can I go and visit him?"

"It's a three-hour drive from Marfa. You're not going to drive there. Tomorrow I'm flying my plane to El Paso. I'll be there first thing in the morning. Nothing but the best for our music prodigy. I will take care of everything, and I will call you with an update three times a day. I know you love Ellery. So do I. I promise I will bring him back to you, as good as new and as soon as possible. Gotta go. Say a prayer."

I desperately wanted to have the chance to tell Augustus about Melody's cat. I would email him the whole story as soon as I got home from dinner. I had the feeling he preferred email and texting to speaking live on the phone. He'd made an exception today to call me about Ellery.

After I got home from my dinner at the Saint George, I composed my email about Melody's dead cat and sent it to Augustus. I told him everything I knew about Girdle's death. At least he would be up to date with what was going on in Marfa. Tomorrow I would find a lab where I could take the samples of milk from Melody's house to be tested. Finding out what had happened to my neighbor's cat was going to be an effort, but that mission had now taken on a new importance and urgency. And I wanted details about Ellery's encounter with the soy milk. I also threw out the milk in my own refrigerator. I didn't think it was poisoned, but why take chances?

I read some more about strychnine poisoning and about cyanide poisoning, and what I read was really scary. Ellery was lucky to have survived. Even a tiny amount of either poison can be deadly. Terlingua was not a good place to have anything bad happen to you, that is, anything that required medical care or going to a hospital. Terlingua was a very long way from the closest medical facility. I thought the medical center that served Terlingua was in Alpine, Texas, and that was a trip of more than eighty miles by car. I assumed Ellery had been taken to Big Bend Regional Medical Center by helicopter. So how had he ended up in El Paso?

Chapter 11

he next morning, I put the glass jars that held
the samples of milk from Girdle's bowl and from
Melody's refrigerator into a cooler packed with ice. I
loaded the cooler into my Expedition. The closest private
lab that would test the milk was in Alpine, Texas, and I was
going to drive the jars there. It was Saturday, but the lab in
Alpine had agreed to do the testing and to allow me to drop
off the two samples today. It was expensive, and they wanted
a certified check as payment before they would even look
at my jars of milk. I stopped at the bank on the way out of
town and got the check. Thank goodness banks in Marfa
were open on Saturday mornings. When Melody's cat had
died, I'd wondered if I was overreacting by wanting to have
the milk tested. But after hearing about Ellery, I'd decided
there was a poisoning epidemic in my neighborhood, and I
was going to pursue it. Even if it turned out to be nothing,
I had to satisfy myself.

I decided to have lunch at the Reata Restaurant while I was in Alpine. I'd often had dinner at the Reata and always liked to eat lunch there whenever I had the chance. I would eat a late lunch and take home leftovers. I wouldn't have to worry about making dinner. I almost always had the tortilla soup, although sometimes, the soup of the day called to me, especially if it was black bean. I was torn between the club sandwich with hand-cut fries and the grilled cheese with tomato and bacon. Both were outstanding choices. Today I decided on the grilled cheese. I think they grilled the sandwich with garlic butter. It was so good.

Driving back to Marfa after lunch at the Reata was always a challenge. Even though I'd fortified myself with multiple glasses of iced tea to keep myself awake, the food was so delicious and so filling, I struggled not to doze off at the wheel. The lab would call me in a few days with the results of the tests on the milk. Ellery was constantly on my mind, and I wondered why I hadn't heard from Augustus Gemini.

My new Ford Expedition allows me to talk on the phone hands-free, and I can also listen to texts that people send me while keeping my hands on the wheel. But I can't answer texts. I have always been very strict about not using my cell phone when I'm driving. I kept hoping I would hear something about Ellery's condition. Because I had the feeling Augustus Gemini didn't like to talk on the phone, I figured his communications would be in the form of a text message, so I was shocked when I received a phone call from Augustus for the second day in a row.

"Margaret, this is Augustus. I have just been in the ICU to see Ellery. I gave him your best and told him you were the one who had called to alert me that he was missing."

"I'm so glad to hear from you. I was beginning to get worried again, when I hadn't heard anything. How is he?"

"He's very weak, but he is out of the coma. He was very sick and was unconscious for several days. He isn't able to have long conversations, but he seemed glad to see me. He tried to smile. He's being moved out of ICU to a private room in a couple of days. The nurse I brought with me will be with him most of the time. She will sleep in the room. He isn't himself, but I think he will be glad to be out of the ICU. He seemed to react positively when I explained to him about the private duty nurse. There's a police guard on his room. Apparently, whenever there is an attempted murder, the hospital routinely keeps a law enforcement officer outside the door until the patient is discharged."

"So they really think it was attempted murder? Were you able to find out anything at all about that?"

"It definitely was attempted murder, and no, I wasn't able to find out anything at all about why anybody might have wanted to kill Ellery. I don't think anyone has told him yet that somebody tried to poison him. He mumbled something about cyanide and bitter almonds, but I don't think he's realized yet that somebody intentionally poisoned his soy milk."

"What's with the soy milk? I've served him regular milk, and he doesn't have a problem with it. Is he lactose intolerant or something?"

"I think he just sometimes likes to drink soy milk. I haven't been able to question him about it yet, but I think he took a cooler with some food and drinks on the trip to Terlingua. It's tough to buy food there. There isn't any very good grocery store, and except for bars that sell food there isn't really a good restaurant. The La Kiva Bar has food, but in Terlingua, you are kind of on your own for groceries, except for the chili cook-off in the fall, of course. I'm just so delighted that his soy milk was spoiled and he spit it out. I don't think he swallowed more than a couple of drops, if that. If the milk hadn't been spoiled, he'd be dead now."

"Did you get my email about Melody's cat? I saw the cat, and it's my opinion the cat was poisoned, probably with either strychnine or cyanide, possibly both. I don't know if Melody was the target or if her cat was. My suspicion is that the milk was poisoned, and the cat got it by mistake. I just dropped off samples of milk from the cat's bowl and from the carton of milk in Melody's refrigerator at a commercial lab in Alpine, Texas. The test results will be back in a few days. Why in the world would anyone want to poison Melody and Ellery? I've been wracking my brains over that one."

"Did you have any milk in your refrigerator? Did you get it tested?"

"I had some milk in my refrigerator, and I threw it away." Augustus was silent at the other end of the line. "I probably should have taken it in for testing, too, shouldn't I?"

"If your milk had been poisoned, too, it would have probably cleared you as a suspect. And it could have set up a serial poisoner scenario. Can you get the milk carton out of your garbage? It seems like someone in your neighborhood is trying to kill off the neighbors, doesn't it? Has anybody else been found dead, or sick?"

"Not that I've heard about. I don't know many of the other neighbors. I'm trying to stay to myself and write. I'm trying not to be neighborly. I adore Ellery, and Melody thrust herself into my life unannounced, of course. I don't know anybody else in the neighborhood, and that's on purpose."

"Are there any people who live alone, people who wouldn't be missed if they didn't show up for several days? Could there be someone who's died in their house and nobody has found them yet?"

"I just don't know the answer to that question, Augustus. Sorry."

Augustus sounded discouraged. "There aren't really any authorities to speak of in Telringua, which is where Ellery actually drank the soy milk. He brought the milk from Marfa, and now he's in the hospital in El Paso, under the watchful eye of the El Paso County Sheriff's Office. So you can see, jurisdiction is a nightmare. Nobody wants this case on their roster, and everybody is saying the actual crime took place elsewhere. In fact, nobody is doing any investigating. A dead cat is just not enough to convince anybody that there's a serial poisoner out there. When you get the lab results back from the cat's milk and if it's positive for cyanide or strychnine, prevailing opinions might change quickly. Until we understand what's going on, I think you should be careful. Melody should be, too, but that's easier said than done. You can take care of yourself, and I will take care of Ellery until he's able to function on his own. He's still very ill. I promise I will be sure he's safe. Once he's out of the hospital, the sheriff in El Paso won't be watching out for him any longer. He will be on his own. I will hire a body guard for him as soon as he's able to leave the hospital."

"Thanks, Augustus. I appreciate your keeping me in the loop. I look forward to your updates. I wish there were something I could do for Ellery."

"Do you know how extraordinarily talented Ellery is? He's very modest, so you probably don't know that he's very well-known in his field. People in the film industry would love for him to move to L.A. Because he's in such demand for writing musical scores for films, he could have ten times as much work as he wants. He's very particular about what projects he agrees to work on, but everybody in Hollywood would love for him to do their music. He wants to live in Marfa and won't even think about moving to Los Angeles. He will visit there occasionally to work on scores, so I guess we should all be thankful he's willing to do that. He's very gifted, and I will do everything I can do to see that he stays safe and recovers completely. He's young and will eventually get his strength back, but keeping him alive in the long run is going to mean finding out who has it in for him—and for the neighborhood cats. I don't think the poisoning is connected to his work in any way. I think it has to do with something that's going on in Marfa, and I can't begin to imagine what that might be."

"I can't imagine what that might be either. A dead woman was found behind my house the day after Thanksgiving. It wasn't on the news, but everyone in town knew about it. The Texas Rangers are handling the case and are being very closed-mouth about her. Everything I know about her I've found out from the staff at the Saint George Hotel. The woman was apparently thrown off the train that came from L.A., and she landed beside the train tracks that run behind my house. I went snooping after the crime scene people had left, and I found a shoe which I'm sure belonged to the dead woman. There was money in the shoe—two heavy gold coins that looked to me like they were antiques plus two paper bills. Those bills were each worth 200 Euros. The money was hidden underneath the inside lining of the shoe. It would have been uncomfortable to walk in the shoes with the coins in there. I photographed the shoe and the money and then turned it all over to the Texas Rangers. They've never contacted me again or brought back the shoe or the money. I don't think the dead woman who lost her shoe has anything to do with these poisonings. But I must say, when I decided to move to Marfa, I thought the most exciting thing that might happen here would be that somebody would stand outside the Donald Judd aluminum boxes exhibit to protest the use of metal to make art...or something stupid like that. That hasn't happened, of course, but a lot of other things have happened. This town was advertised to be a low key, relaxed, artsy-fartsy place with two hotels. Now it seems like murder central. I should have moved to Terlingua."

"I agree that the woman who was thrown off the train probably isn't connected to the cyanide and strychnine, but it is odd that these things happened within just a week or so of each other. Would you mind sending me the photos you took of the woman's shoe and of the money that was inside the shoe? Did you ever look up the coins on the internet to try to find out what they were worth?"

"I intended to do that and just never got around to it. Since I don't have the coins anymore and I don't expect they will ever be returned to me, I guess I kind of forgot about them. I'd be happy for you to research them for me, not that I will ever see them again, no matter how valuable they might turn out to be. 'Finder's keepers' and all of that. They are gone, probably locked up somewhere as evidence in a murder investigation. I'd like to know something about them, though. They were heavy gold and looked old and valuable."

"Send the photos to me. I'll find out all about them. I will let you know what they are and how much the Texas Rangers are stealing from you. I'll also try to find out where the shoe came from. There's a wardrobe expert in the film industry here who knows everything there is to know about every shoe that was ever made. It's amazing how much she knows about shoes—antique shoes and shoes from every modern era, every decade. She always knows to the penny how much everyone at a party paid for his or her shoes. She will love having a shoe mystery to work on."

"I met a woman at the grocery store who said everybody's shoes these days are made in China."

"My friend will be able to tell exactly when the shoe was made and exactly where in China it came from. I promise you. She is *the* expert."

"The train that woman who lost her shoe was thrown from was a freight train, one of those trains that carries miles of gigantic shipping containers on flatbed cars. You see freight trains like that everywhere. There is a passenger train that comes through Marfa three nights a week, the Sunset Limited from Los Angeles to New Orleans. That train, of course, also travels back to Los Angeles from New Orleans three times a week. It doesn't stop in Marfa; it stops in Alpine. The night the woman was thrown from the train wasn't one of the nights when the Sunset Limited came through town. So this woman wasn't thrown from a passenger train. She was definitely thrown from a freight train, which seems very odd. But what do I know? It all seems bizarre and mysterious to me."

"I will see what I can find out about your coins and the shoe. The Euros are pretty standard fare, but send the pictures of those, too. Maybe they are stolen, and I can find out something from the serial numbers."

"Thanks for your interest. I don't think the woman from the train has anything to do with Ellery's situation, but I am curious about the coins. And thanks for keeping me informed about Ellery. He's such a wonderful young man. I've become very fond of him, and I'm praying for his recovery."

"I'm praying, too. I will stay in touch. Don't worry. He's going to be fine."

Chapter 12

*O*n *Sunday, I got a call from the lab in Alpine, and* my worst fears were confirmed. Both the milk from the cat's bowl and the milk from Melody's refrigerator had tested positive for strychnine and for cyanide! The lab was sending me a written report but felt it was important enough to call me with the results. I asked about the concentration of poison in the milk, and the technician I was speaking with told me there was a very high concentration of both poisons in the milk. My heart was pounding as I thanked her and ended the phone call.

Ellery had nearly died from the soy milk. Poor little Girdle had died, but I was sure Melody had been the intended victim. There was a serial murderer in the neighborhood, but why in the world would anyone want to kill Ellery or Melody? If I were going to find any less harmful people in the world, I was going to have to dig up Mother Teresa. I was kicking myself for throwing away my own milk carton, but the garbage men had come and gone. It was time to talk to Melody. I hoped I would hear from the sheriff's office about her cat today or tomorrow.

I rode over in my golf cart, and Melody came to the door immediately. She looked around to see if I had Girdle's body with me. She looked deflated and disappointed when she didn't see the cat. I wondered if she was going to invite me into her house at all. "Melody, I need to come in and talk to you." It seemed as if she was not going to let me come in since I didn't have her cat with me.

"Where's Girdle. You told me you would help me give her a funeral and bury her. I still don't have anybody to dig a grave for her. Where in the world is Ellery? He should be home. If he were here, he would dig Girdle's grave for me." We were standing outside her front door. She had a rusted metal glider on her porch, and I finally had to sit down on that.

"Yes, I know he would be happy to dig her grave for you, but he's still out of town." I intended to tell Melody about Ellery, but I wanted to get a read on how sober she was this morning. I also wanted to get some information out of her first. "I need to ask you some questions about your milk."

"About my milk? What about my milk? I buy it at Porter's."

"Do you ever buy milk for anybody but yourself? Specifically, do you ever buy milk for Ellery?"

"I bought Ellery some soy milk before he went on his last trip. I was going to the store and asked him if he wanted me to get him anything. He said to buy him some soy milk." I knew Melody was telling me the truth.

That answered one of my biggest questions. "How much soy milk did you buy for him when you went to Porter's that time?"

"I think I bought him three bottles. He takes soy milk in a cooler when he goes on trips. Why? What's this all about?"

"Do you ever drink the milk you buy or did you just buy milk for Girdle? This is important."

"Yes, if I eat breakfast, I put milk on my cereal." She seemed to be telling the truth about the cereal, but the way Melody drank, I was guessing she skipped most of those bowls of cereal first thing in the morning and went straight to the homemade wine or the vodka.

"You didn't drink any of the last carton of milk you bought, did you? You just put some out for Girdle. Can you remember?"

"I don't really remember whether or not I used any of that last container of milk. That was regular milk. It wasn't soy milk, and you took the rest of that carton of milk. So now I don't have any milk at all. What did you do with my milk? Are you bringing it back?"

"Your milk was poisoned, Melody. Somebody put cyanide and strychnine in your carton of regular milk, and that's why Girdle died. The poison was intended for you, and you were extremely lucky that you didn't drink any of it. You would have died a very quick and painful death if you'd drunk any milk out of that carton. Please, we need to talk. Can I come in?" I decided I needed to go into the house, even if Melody didn't want me there. Melody reluctantly stepped aside and allowed me to enter. I didn't look at anything and tried not to feel claustrophobic with all the piles of found objects everywhere. Melody headed straight for the kitchen. I followed her.

For once, Melody was speechless. She was standing up, and I pulled out a chair from her kitchen table and made her sit down. She stared at me with wide eyes. I had the feeling she wanted to go straight for the vodka bottle at that very moment, and not even pretend to drink any of her homemade wine. She really was in shock. I sat down in another chair. Her voice sounded panicky. "Why would anybody want to poison me? I don't even know anybody, except for you and Ellery and some of the other neighbors. What's going on?"

"I don't know, Melody. I think you should be very careful about everything you eat and drink. I have no idea how this person was able to poison your milk, but somebody did. Thank goodness you didn't drink any of it."

"Why were you asking me about Ellery? He didn't have any milk from that carton. He only had the soy milk that was in smaller bottles. I gave him three of those. Is he all right?"

"He's going to be all right, but he was poisoned also. He drank a little bit out of one of the bottles of soy milk, but it had gone bad by the time he tried it. He spit it out because it didn't taste right, and thank goodness he did. He's in the hospital in El Paso. He almost died, but he's going to be fine. Augustus Gemini is with him. The soy milk was poisoned, too."

Melody's face turned white. She looked as if she were going to be sick. "I love Ellery. I would never do anything to hurt him."

"Of course you wouldn't. Nobody is suggesting you tried to poison him. You bought the milk. The poison was intended for you. Do you have any idea why anyone might want to hurt you?"

"I told you, I don't even know anybody, except for my neighbors."

"What about your family? Is there anybody who might want you to pass away sooner than you want to?"

"I don't have any family. My only brother died in Vietnam, and he was never married. It was just the two of us. My parents have been dead for a long time. I'm leaving my estate to the Chinati Foundation. I need a drink." She stood up, and I could see she was headed for the kitchen cupboard. She didn't seem to care that I could see she was diving directly into the vodka or that she was revealing where she kept her not-so-secret stash.

I called out to her before she put her hand on the cupboard door. "I think we need to go to the police with this information, and you need to be sober to answer questions." I could see she was completely ignoring me. It was as if I hadn't spoken. She was headed for oblivion. My only recourse would be to physically restrain her, and I didn't have the will or the physical strength to do that.

I wanted to look around the kitchen to see if I could find the receipt from Porter's. I wanted to have a record of exactly what day Melody had purchased both the carton of cow's milk and the three bottles of soy milk. Now intent on her mission to drink as big a glass of vodka as she could, she didn't seem to care that I was poking around in the kitchen drawers and in a small desk where she sometimes sat to do paperwork. "I'm looking for the receipt from the day you bought the milk from Porter's. That's why I'm going through your papers." She continued to ignore me and poured herself another glass of vodka. At this rate, she would be unconscious by the time I called the authorities.

Finally I found a bunch of grocery receipts stuffed down inside one of Melody's work boots. I went through all of them until I found the one I thought was the receipt from the day she'd bought the milk. The problem was, the receipt said she'd purchased a quart of fresh Vitamin D whole milk plus *six* bottles of soy milk. She'd told me Ellery had asked her to buy him three bottles. If she'd given Ellery three bottles, where were the other three?

By this time, Melody was almost beyond being able to communicate, but I had to ask her anyway. "Did you drink any of the soy milk?"

"Oh, no," she slurred her words. "I can't stand soy milk. It tastes like cat pee."

My next stop, after I left Melody, was going to be Ellery's house. I had to see if there were two more bottles of soy milk in his refrigerator or in his pantry. Or maybe I would be lucky and find five bottles, all unopened. I thought the plastic bottles of soy milk were the kind you could leave in the pantry until you opened them. After they were opened, they had to be refrigerated. I hoped I would find at least the two missing bottles of milk somewhere in his house. I hoped neither of them had made its way to Terlingua or anywhere else. I would take one as evidence to give to the sheriff, and I would take one to the lab in Alpine to have it tested. But where were the other three bottles of soy milk? Searching Melody's kitchen, let alone her house, was an impossible task. I would make a quick search before I left today, but I would have to wait until she was sober again to ask her about the three missing bottles. From what she'd said about her opinion of soy milk, I had to assume she didn't have any in her pantry or in her refrigerator.

After fifteen minutes of searching, I'd not found any more bottles of soy milk at Melody's. Melody was now sitting on her couch and would soon be passed out. I left and locked the door behind me. I drove my golf cart to Ellery's house. I knew where in the garden he kept his backdoor key hidden, and I let myself into his kitchen. His house was the antithesis of Melody's. Bless his heart. Ellery had left everything neat as a pin before he'd gone to the jazz symposium in Terlingua. I sighed with relief when I found two unopened bottles of soy milk in his pantry. I put them in a plastic bag to take home with me. Thank goodness he hadn't drunk any of it before he'd left on his trip. I was very grateful for any piece of good luck.

I went back home and decided I would return to Melody's the next day and try to ask her about the three missing bottles of soy milk. It was too late to do anything about it today, but maybe she would be sober in the morning. I would search again for the three bottles. I had my doubts that she would be able to find the missing soy milk or anything else I might be looking for in her house, but I was going to give it one more try.

I would drive to Alpine the day after tomorrow and have the two unopened bottles of soy milk tested. The lab there was going to wonder if I was some kind of criminal or crazy person if I kept turning up with containers of poisoned milk. But circumstances would intervene before I had a chance to make another trip to Alpine.

The next morning I slept late. I'd worn myself out over the weekend—dealing with poor dead Girdle, driving to Alpine, searching for the missing soy milk, and trying to question Melody. It was Monday, and Consuela had arrived at my house before I woke up. I had put a big sign on the plastic bag in my pantry so she wouldn't touch the two bottles of soy milk I'd rescued from Ellery's house. As soon as she arrived at my house this morning, I planned to tell her all about what was happening. She brought me breakfast in bed. She said she'd figured I was worn out from a busy weekend and decided I deserved to eat in my bedroom. She arrived with a tray of popovers, fresh orange juice, and coffee. I had her sit down and told her all about what was going on with my neighbors and Girdle and the poisonings. All of this had happened since she'd left on Friday, and I felt she needed to know. I sensed she had something to tell me too, but I wanted her to know about the potential danger in the neighborhood as soon as possible.

"There's something I need to tell you, too, Ms. Margaret. The sheriff and the coroner are at Jinx Carruthers' house. He lives on the other side of Melody. I think he must have died. He was very old, in his nineties, and he was a total recluse, a real recluse." She gave me a slight smile. I had told her how I was trying to be a recluse and wasn't doing a very good job of it. "He probably died of old age. The authorities made a point of checking on him regularly, you know, doing a kind of wellness check. But most of the time he wouldn't let them inside the house. He would come to the door and scream at them to go away. They were there just to see if he was okay, so when he came to the door, they had accomplished their mission. Apparently, he hadn't answered the door the last couple of times they went to the house, so they got a warrant to break down the door and search the premises. They found him dead at his kitchen table. My nephew told me."

"Oh, no. I never met Mr. Carruthers. Melody mentioned him a couple of times, but I never saw him in his yard. I'm ashamed to say, I didn't even know the name of the person who lived in that house. I'm not a very good neighbor."

"Don't feel bad about it. Jinx Carruthers wouldn't have let you into his house anyway, even if you had gone by with a big basket of brownies. He probably wouldn't have answered the door, and if he had, he would have yelled at you and told you to go away. Lots of people have tried to do things to help him out, and he wouldn't have any parts of any of it. He screamed at everybody who came to the door."

"Why is the coroner over there? Is there any reason to suspect his death wasn't from natural causes?" I had a creeping, sinking feeling in my stomach that maybe I now knew the whereabouts of the missing bottles of soy milk.

"It was an unattended death, and he didn't have a doctor. He'd been dead for a few days before he was found. I think they just called the coroner to be sure he really was dead and to pronounce him. I will go over there and talk to some people, if you want me to do that."

Consuela was obviously curious, and I know I was. I told her to go over to Carruthers' house and find out whatever she could. One of her nephews was an EMT, and he would eventually tell her everything she wanted to know. I was concerned that maybe Melody had bought soy milk for Jinx. I dragged myself out of bed, got dressed, and tried to prepare myself to search Melody's house and call the Presidio County Sheriff's office.

When Consuela came back to the house, she had a worried expression on her face. I was in my study, trying to write, when she knocked on the door and asked to come in. She didn't usually disturb me when I was working unless it was an emergency. I knew by the look on her face that she had something to tell me, and it was something I wasn't going to want to hear.

"Bad news, Ms. Margaret, bad news. Jinx Carruthers did not die of old age. The authorities think he was poisoned. They are speculating that it was cyanide or something similar, and they are going to do an autopsy and a drug screening—the whole nine yards. They are treating it as a homicide. It appears as if his house was vandalized. But he has so much stuff in there, it was hard for the authorities to tell if it had actually been ransacked or whether he was just a hoarder. One other curious thing is that somebody tore some of Jinx's plumbing fixtures out of the wall of his bathroom. Somebody definitely vandalized the bathroom, but nothing was taken. Whoever tore out the plumbing fixtures didn't steal them. The sheriff is very puzzled by the crime. The report I got was that Jinx was eating his morning cereal when his face fell into the bowl. He died instantly—sprawled across his kitchen table. They are taking the cereal bowl, the box of cereal, and the milk away for testing. After what you told me about Melody's cat and about Ellery, I have a feeling they are going to find Jinx died of cyanide and strychnine poisoning."

My worst fears had just been confirmed. There was a homicidal maniac somewhere in Marfa. And they were not just in Marfa; they were in my neighborhood. Their target had been Melody, but because she had given the fresh Vitamin D milk to her cat and the bottles of soy milk to her neighbors, others had died and almost died in her place. Melody was eccentric, and she had been in trouble with the law because of the DUI. But she was not a killer. I worried that whoever had tried to murder her and had failed would try again and be more successful the next time. If they had put the poison into the vodka instead of into the milk, Melody would be dead now.

"Keep your ears open for updates, Consuela. I eventually will have to talk to the sheriff's office, but I'd like to know everything they know before I go to them with my evidence."

"Please be careful, Ms. Margaret, you don't know for sure that whoever is doing this has only Melody in his sights.

He may be a serial killer, and who knows who he will go after next?"

I sent a detailed email to Augustus Gemini telling him everything I'd found out about what had happened with the lab results from Alpine, the two bottles of soy milk I had liberated from Ellery's pantry, and the latest news about Jinx Carruthers.

The Past...
New York to Texas

Chapter 13

*I*n April of 1917, Marcel Duchamp shocked the art world when he submitted a controversial piece of sculpture to the first annual exhibition of the Society of Independent Artists in New York City. The Frenchman had begun his very successful artistic career as a painter. Later in his career, along with Pablo Picasso and Henri Matisse, Duchamp helped to define the revolutionary developments in sculpture and ceramics in the early part of the 20th century. After 1912, Duchamp focused less and less on painting, and by 1915, his "Readymades" period was fully underway. Duchamp's "Readymades" were found objects he chose and presented as art. Some of his earliest "Readymades" were *"Bicycle Wheel"* (1913) and *"Bottle Rack"* (1914).

In an attempt to shift the focus of art away from the physical craft toward an intellectual interpretation of art, Duchamp chose to exhibit an article of everyday life as a work of art at the Society of Independent Artists first exhibition at the Grand Central Palace in 1917. Duchamp's exhibition entry was a porcelain urinal, an ordinary piece of plumbing, a standard Bedfordshire model purchased from the J.L. Mott Iron Works at 118 Fifth Avenue in New York City. Duchamp brought the plumbing fixture to his studio at 22 West 67th Street, tilted the urinal backwards ninety degrees, and named it "*Fountain*." He painted on, and, perhaps in a way, signed, the urinal: "R. Mutt 1917." He submitted *Fountain* as a work of art in the exhibit. His artistic goal was to erase the usual function and significance of the urinal and give the object a new aesthetic meaning. He was engaging in a revolutionary act. He was calling for a paradigm shift in the definition of what it was to create a work of art.

The artwork for the 1917 New York exhibit was not selected by a jury, as was the case for many art exhibitions of that time. Theoretically, all works that were submitted were to be displayed. However, the show committee insisted that *Fountain* was not art and banned it from the show. Various explanations were given for rejecting Duchamp's offering. One excuse given was that the committee said the $6.00 entry fee for the piece had not been paid. Accounts about how the urinal's rejection were handled ran the gamut. Some said that *Fountain* was physically and purposefully removed from the show. Others said it remained on the premises but was "hidden from view" during the show (in a coat closet?). Duchamp himself said the showing of his art was "suppressed." The committee's formal rejection stated: "*Fountain* may be a very useful object in its place, but its place is not in an art exhibit, and it is by no definition a work of art."

Duchamp was a member of the board of the Society of Independent Artists, the organization that rejected *Fountain*.

Duchamp had submitted the urinal, his own contentious artistic entry, under a pseudonym. The committee that rejected the urinal as not being a real piece of art, did not realize it was Duchamp's submission. Because *Fountain* was rejected from the show, Duchamp resigned from the board of the Society of Independent Artists and withdrew his other artwork from the exhibit.

As expected, the rejection of Duchamp's entry stirred tremendous controversy in the contemporary art world. After the exhibition closed, *Fountain* made its way to the studio of photographer Alfred Stieglitz, who a few months earlier had championed the work of artist Georgia O'Keeffe and introduced her to the world. Stieglitz photographed *Fountain* at his gallery and studio at 291 Fifth Avenue in New York City. Along with a letter from Stieglitz and an anonymous editorial, the photo of *Fountain* appeared in the second and final edition of *The Blind Man*, an art journal published briefly in 1917 by a group of New York's avant-garde artists and writers.

The editorial in *The Blind Man*, that addressed the rejection and controversy around Duchamp's attempts to break down the boundaries between art and ordinary objects of everyday use, was prophetic. The editorial claimed that *Fountain* was of significance for the future of art and creativity and would influence works of art that would come after it. In 2004 a group of 500 renowned artists and historians selected *Fountain* as "the most influential piece of artwork of the twentieth century." That's significance!

After being photographed by Alfred Stieglitz for *The Blind Man*, the original *Fountain* was never seen again. It is interesting to note that Stieglitz closed his gallery on Fifth

Avenue in June of 1917, two months after photographing Duchamp's *Fountain*. Where did *Fountain* go? Duchamp commissioned sixteen replicas of the piece during the 1950s and 1960s, but the original *Fountain* was lost to the ages.

Chapter 14

*R*egnaldo, *the rag-and-bone man, was exhausted* by the end of the day, every day of his life. He collected people's cast-off junk and tried to sell it to other people. It was a backbreaking and thankless job and scarcely provided the poor man with enough to eat. He slept in an abandoned warehouse with his collections of castoffs, hoping to find buyers for these potential treasures. That day, he thought he'd struck it rich. A famous artist and photographer was closing his gallery at 291 Fifth Avenue. Regnaldo had been keeping his eyes on the location for weeks. He watched as the workers crated and moved out countless paintings, pieces of sculpture, and other works of art. Would there be anything left for a scavenger like himself after all the good stuff had been taken away?

Finally they were gone, and Regnaldo was the first to get into the building to go through the detritus that had been abandoned. His cart was parked outside, and he began to sort through the junk. It was July 1917, and it was hot as he carried what he thought might have even the slightest value out to the street. He couldn't afford a horse to pull his cart, so he harnessed himself up to the cart and pulled it behind him through the streets. Consequently, he was very strong. This was an advantage in his business for many reasons, not the least of which was that the other rag-and-bone men who might want to impinge on Regnaldo's territory were reluctant to challenge him. He had his pick of the junk in this prestigious part of New York City. He could lift almost anything and carry it to his cart by himself.

Plenty of paper, pieces of wood, and other packing materials had been left behind. There were lots of dirty rags. These were things Regnaldo already had buyers for. He gathered up all he could get into his cart. Underneath the discarded crates and packing materials, he saw the corner of what he thought might be a large piece of porcelain plumbing. He could get good prices for plumbing fixtures, and he was puzzled about why there was something like this lying around any place other than a bathroom. Before he uncovered it, he hoped it might be a claw foot bathtub or a pedestal sink. Even a toilet, if it wasn't too stinky, would bring him some money. When he finally unearthed it, he found his treasure was a men's pisser. Fancy folks called it a "urnal" or something like that.

It looked new, like it had never been used. That would be wonderful, if no one had ever peed in it. It looked like an item that would bring him some money, and sure enough there were the blue stamps on the underside that said "Bedfordshire" and "J.L. Mott." Regnaldo knew from experience that this was a quality find. He pulled the "pisser" out into the middle of the room. As he turned the piece of porcelain over, his heart sank. Somebody had painted on the side of this brand new fixture "R. Mutt 1917." They had painted the name and date in bold letters with black paint. Regnaldo wondered what in the world he could use to get the black paint off the piece. He thought turpentine might do the job, but he was worried that turpentine might also destroy the beautiful white glazed finish. He would take it to his warehouse and work on cleaning it up.

A few weeks earlier, the United States had declared war on Germany. On April 6, 1917, Uncle Sam had finally decided to join the Europeans and send American boys abroad to fight in the "War to End All Wars." Regnaldo wasn't worried that he'd be sent to war, but what he didn't anticipate was that he would lose his previously abandoned warehouse to the war effort. He'd never known who the building belonged to. Years earlier, after watching it for several weeks, to see if anybody showed any interest in it, he'd decided the warehouse had been abandoned. He would use it to store his treasures. He had been living in and using the warehouse for almost four years when the United States entered World War I.

A few days after he'd cleared out the remains of the stuff left in the gallery on Fifth Avenue, he came back to his warehouse to find men dressed in military uniforms swarming the warehouse and clearing his treasures out of the building. He stayed out of sight and tried to listen to what they were saying. They were talking about fixing the roof and repairing the bricks on the exterior. They were talking about putting locks on the doors and installing shelves for weapons inside. He realized that all along, his warehouse had belonged to the United States government. They'd had no use for it until now. Since the country had decided to go to war, the military was commandeering every empty space the government owned and putting it to good use.

Regnaldo lost his warehouse, his junk, and his livelihood. He would have to move on to a new location. He didn't think Brooklyn would offer the same quality of junk that Manhattan had provided, but he was going to give it a chance. He had no choice but to leave everything in the warehouse behind, and he pulled his empty cart behind him to Brooklyn.

Renovations were planned and had to be done quickly. The Sergeant Major from the Army Corps of Engineers and the representative from the Quartermaster Department were giving orders about cleaning out the warehouse. An enlisted clerk was writing down these orders as fast as he could write, but it was two against one. The clerk was falling behind, and he was sure he had missed a few things. There was no working bathroom in the warehouse. The warehouse had been supplied with an outdoor privy when it had last been used decades earlier. That privy had disappeared long ago and would not have been suitable for the needs of the modern United States Army of 1917. Somebody had to figure out a way to get running water to the warehouse and install a modern bathroom. It didn't have to be fancy, but it did have to be inside. After all, this was New York City, and this was the second decade of the Twentieth Century.

A staff of munitions supply personnel would be working in the building that was already provided with electricity. The electricity had been turned off years ago, and no one knew if it still worked. Someone would have to call Consolidated

Edison and have the power turned back on. The wiring would have to be checked to see if it was up to date. Masons, painters, carpenters, electricians, and plumbers would all be busy making the building shipshape. The warehouse would become an important munitions supply depot.

The USA was already at war in July of 1917, and the military was trying to catch up. America's young men were streaming through the city to board ships in New York Harbor, heading for the killing fields of Europe. Every available government facility and resource was being commandeered to help support the international mission to destroy the Huns. Things were chaotic, and weapons and ammunition were being moved into the warehouse in Manhattan before it even had a working bathroom. The place had been cleaned out, and almost everything that had been found inside was taken to a landfill in Queens. Just a few things had been deemed worth saving. These were things the quartermaster thought might be able to be reused. Some piles of new lumber, three large wooden office desks left over from a long time ago, a hot plate that still worked, a couple of relatively clean plumbing fixtures, and three hundred boxes of new #2 pencils were allowed to remain.

The warehouse was a large, solid brick building that needed a new roof. As drawn on the blueprints, the proposed bathroom wasn't very big. But because somebody had seen what they thought was a new urinal already on site, the contractor decided to put two toilets and a urinal in the new bathroom. The plans were approved, and the Army's plumber and his crew were given orders to expedite the renovation project. Previously, there had not been any water or sewer lines into the warehouse because no people had ever worked there. The plumber struggled to get the water lines into the building and the sewer lines out of the building. The water lines had to be hooked up to New York City's water supply, and the sewer lines had to be hooked up to the New York City sewer system. All of this required permits, and that was just for one bathroom.

The project was dangerously behind when the staff moved into the building. Desks and chairs were in place, but there wasn't any running water. The plumber had ordered two toilets and two sinks. He'd been told a urinal was already available in the warehouse. The Army sometimes got a bee up its collective butt in an attempt to save money, and they tried to use surplus items when they could. The bathroom was finally ready for the fixtures to be installed, but no one could find the urinal that had supposedly been set aside and left to be used in the new bathroom. No one could remember where they'd seen it in the chaos of people and supplies coming and going. Nothing was where it was supposed to be.

The Army couldn't get a permit to turn on the water and hook up to the sewer until all the fixtures were installed. The plumber became so frustrated, he walked to the nearest plumbing supply store and bought a urinal with his own money. He arranged for it to be delivered to the warehouse that same day. The urinal was finally put in place. The city approved the bathroom; the water was turned on; the sewer was hooked up; and the staff of the munitions supply depot was at last provided with the modern conveniences. Nobody bothered to search any longer for the missing urinal that had found its way to a basement storage closet.

In 1966, the brick warehouse, abandoned after World War I, requisitioned for use again during World War II, and abandoned once again a few years after that war ended, was slated to be torn down. The United States Army was selling off properties, and this warehouse location on Manhattan Island had become a very valuable piece of real estate. A new, modern skyscraper was going to be built on the site the warehouse currently occupied.

Generations of homeless people had called the warehouse home for decades and were very inconvenienced by the news that their building was headed for demolition. Several of the more enterprising homeless men and women hurried to strip the building of anything and everything useful that remained. Donny O'Malley had been living in the basement for six years, and he'd found a urinal in a closet. It was an antiquated model, but it didn't look as if anyone had ever used it. When he wiped off the dust and grime of the years, it looked almost new. Somebody had painted their name and the year 1917 on the side, but other than that, the urinal was in great condition. It didn't have any cracks or chips in the porcelain. It should bring Donny a couple of dollars, maybe even three. He loaded it into his grocery cart and took it with him when he moved out of his basement home, the day before the wrecking ball arrived to take down the brick warehouse and make room for a concrete monstrosity in the style of 1960's modern architecture.

Donny was a creature of habit, and having his home taken from him turned his routine upside down. He'd not really found another place to live and was sleeping in Washington Square Park with his cart beside him. One night while he was asleep, somebody stole his cart, the cart that held all of his worldly possessions. Donny was devastated, but resigned to his fate, he stole another empty cart from a nearby grocery store and began again.

Gladys was also homeless. She lived under the new Verrazzano-Narrows Bridge. When she'd seen Donny asleep in Washington Square Park, she'd helped herself to his cart and everything in it. She pushed the cart back to her spot under the bridge and set up the urinal as a place to store her meager supply of food. Rodents and insects were always getting into her food stores, and the sturdy porcelain bowl-like fixture looked like the answer to her prayers. To protect her food, she stole some plastic wrap from a grocery store and draped the wrap around the urinal to make it airtight.

Gladys had "friends" who occasionally stopped by her camp to check on how she was. She thought of them as the "do gooders" who gave her money and pretended to care about her when it got really cold in the winter. One of her do gooder friends was a young man named Rodney. He would stop by with hot dogs from the nearby hotdog stand. Gladys was happy to have the hotdogs, but what she really wished Rodney would bring her was a big bottle of Thunderbird. Rodney occasionally bought things from Gladys. She didn't think he really wanted any of the things he bought from her, but it was his way of giving her money without giving her money outright. When Rodney saw the urinal Gladys had appropriated and was using as a pantry, he asked her where she'd found it. She was defensive and told him it was none of his business where she'd found it.

"I'd like to buy it from you, Gladys. I'm moving from my old apartment to a new place, and I'd like to have one of those in my bathroom. I'm fixing it up, and of course you know, what you have here is for men only." Rodney liked to show off his superior knowledge to Gladys.

"It's not for sale. I'm using it to store my food. It keeps the bugs and the mice out. I know it's for men only, men standing up only. I know a thing or two. Don't patronize me." Rodney had always wondered why a woman who was as intelligent as Gladys and had such an excellent vocabulary preferred to live under the Verrazzano-Narrows Bridge. She was a mystery to him, and his inability to figure Gladys out was one reason he kept coming back to see her and talk to her. What other homeless person in New York could correctly use the word "patronize"?

"What if I bring you a special metal box that's designed to keep food dry and safe from the weather? They make boxes just for that, and they are not as heavy as the urinal. You won't be able to move that heavy thing around with you."

"I don't ever intend to move again. This is my spot, and I am staying here until I die."

"What about if I bring you some Thunderbird *and* the special food box?" Rodney knew her weaknesses. "By the way, who is R. Mutt? Did you put that on there?"

"None of your business, damn it. It's my business who R. Mutt is, and I'm not going to tell you anything about it." Gladys in fact had no idea who R. Mutt was or why it was painted, along with 1917, on the side of her porcelain pantry. She'd assumed 1917 was the year R. Mutt had written his name on the thing. "It belongs to me now, and R. Mutt no longer has any claim on it. So don't go off and try to find him and offer to buy it from him. It's mine now. R. Mutt be damned." Sometimes Gladys lost touch with reality, even with her own reality.

Chapter 15

odney Granger was a do-it-yourselfer, a fix-er-upper kind of guy. He thought he was good at carpentry work, painting, and plumbing, but his work was more than a little bit sloppy. After considerable cajoling and a few bottles of Thunderbird, Rodney had been able to convince Gladys to part with her porcelain bathroom fixture.

Some of Rodney's fancy friends were putting bidets into their Manhattan bathrooms, but Rodney wanted nothing to do with a bidet. He wanted a urinal. A confirmed bachelor, he was confused by the women's movement that was currently sweeping the country and the world. He wanted to establish his maleness amidst this overwhelming and, to him, suffocating atmosphere of feminism. What better way to do that than with a urinal? To install a urinal in one's apartment was, for Rodney, the definitive statement about masculinity. He only wished he had the nerve to put it in his living room. He wanted to be able to brag about and show off his "men's only" plumbing fixture. Public bathrooms were full of urinals, but few people had them in their own homes.

As he struggled to transform his rented apartment in Greenwich Village, Rodney inevitably ran into problems with his bathroom renovation. He had planned a space for the urinal to be attached to the wall. But when it came time to hook up the plumbing and piping part of it, to actually make it functional, he wasn't able to do it. The urinal was an antique, and the pipes in Rodney's apartment were incompatible with the hookups on the outdated fixture. A professional plumber would have had no trouble overcoming the fact that the urinal had a slightly different size opening for its pipes, but Rodney thought he could figure it out on his own. He promised himself he would figure out how to hook up the thing, but he never got around to it. He never hooked up the urinal but left it in place. He put duct tape over the top of it and made a sign for it that said "DO NOT USE."

Rodney was a sociable young man and liked to have parties. It was the late sixties, and things in New York and every place else in the country were loose. Most of those who came to party at Rodney's apartment in The Village honored the sign on the urinal and didn't use it, but a few friends and acquaintances who used his bathroom were so inebriated or so stoned, they didn't bother to read the sign or decided to ignore it. Occasionally, somebody poured a drink into it, and occasionally, somebody used it for the purpose for which it had originally been intended.

Rodney wasn't much of a housekeeper, but he did try to keep the urinal clean and periodically put new duct tape over it. Eventually, he ended up draping a sheet over the urinal to try to hide it so no one would use it. Of course, everyone who came into his bathroom lifted up the sheet to see what was underneath. Rodney had never bothered to remove the painted name and date on the side of the fixture. A few people over the years asked Rodney who R. Mutt was and if the urinal really dated from 1917. When Rodney moved out of his apartment in 1972, he left the urinal behind.

Two women rented the small apartment after Rodney moved out, and they complained bitterly to the landlord about all of the "improvements" Rodney had made to the space. The women insisted that repairs and repainting be done before they would move in. The urinal was the first thing to go. The landlord hired a plumber to renovate the bathroom, and the plumber took the not-very-clean urinal away and threw it into the pile of junk behind his shop.

A hippie couple, who had opened a knick-knacks and second-hand store in Asbury Park, New Jersey, saw the urinal in the junk heap at the back of the plumber's warehouse and liberated it from the rest of the trash. Sunshine Morning, who had been named Barbara Ann Jackson at birth, was the female half of the couple. She thought the urinal was "quaint" and would be a good addition to their shop at the New Jersey shore. In spite of trying to belong to the counter-culture and ostensibly eschewing the sins of capitalism, Sunshine was a CPA and an excellent businesswoman. She was very organized, to the point of being compulsive. She had changed her name, but she was still the superb record keeper she had always been. Sunshine photographed each item that she and Evening Moonlight, her male counterpart and business partner, put into their store. She kept meticulous records and filed everything away in a refurbished antique oak filing cabinet that she kept in the office at the back of their store, Cool Doodads.

A few weeks after the urinal went on display at Cool Doodads in April of 1973, a woman from Bala Cynwyd, Pennsylvania saw it and had to have it. She also deemed it "quaint" and thought it would be perfect for her garden. Buyer and sellers agreed that the find was destiny for the woman from Philadelphia when she told the owners of Cool Doodads that her name was Roberta Mutt Van Devries. And, she had been born in 1917. Mrs. Van Devries put the urinal into the back of her station wagon and drove home to her six-bedroom house on the Main Line. She planted rosemary in the urinal, and it had pride of place in her herb garden for twenty years.

When Roberta died, her daughter Marjorie Van Devries Cannon, dug the unusual and "quaint" pot out of the dirt in the now long-neglected herb garden. Marjorie cleaned it off and moved it to a storage unit in Tulsa, Oklahoma where she now lived. Once in Tulsa, the urinal sat in the storage unit with pieces of her mother's furniture, oriental rugs, objets d'art, and other things the daughter didn't know what to do with but couldn't bring herself to get rid of.

Marjorie religiously paid the monthly fees on the storage unit for ten years. She'd promised herself many times during those years that she would clean out the storage unit and try to sell a few of the more valuable items. But she never got around to it. Then her marriage ended, and Marjorie fell on emotional hard times. She had the money to pay the rent, but after her divorce, the rent on the storage unit was one of the things Marjorie stopped caring about. She was depressed and couldn't muster the energy to do much of anything, let alone clean out a storage unit that was half-way across town, in another part of Tulsa from where she lived. For six months, the storage facility sent her overdue notices about the rent. She ignored these, along with most of the other things in her life.

Years before the show *"Storage Wars"* made an appearance on television, Leonard Bundy, a junk dealer from Dallas, bought sight unseen the contents of abandoned storage units in all parts of the South, including Oklahoma. Roberta Mutt Van Devries's daughter's storage unit was one of these. Bundy purchased the contents of the abandoned Oklahoma storage units, including Marjorie's unit. He loaded his newly-acquired wares into an 18-wheeler and drove it back to Dallas.

Bundy had a showroom of sorts, which he called Texas Open Market Treasures, where he displayed and sold the spoils of his storage unit finds. Bundy knew his valuables, and he quickly separated the wheat from the chaff. He found buyers for the top-dollar items. He took to the landfill the worn-out clothes and other things that had been destroyed by bugs, mice, and mildew. Anything he thought might bring a dollar or two, he put into his showroom. It was a messy, not-very-well -organized hodgepodge of everything anyone had ever thought was worth putting into a storage unit. There were bargains to be had, but buyers had to sort and sift through piles of things they didn't want to find the occasional prize.

Chuck Grimaldi found the urinal partly hidden under a mound of ugly furniture. He had just rented a condo in Irving, Texas and was hoping to furnish it on the cheap. He'd found a scuffed table and some wooden chairs that didn't match. The urinal caught his eye. He thought he could use paint thinner to remove the "R. Mutt 1917" from the side. It carried a price tag of only $3.00, and Chuck thought he could find a place for the urinal in the bathroom of his newest bachelor pad.

Chuck was a procrastinator, and he never got around to doing many things he'd promised himself he would do. The urinal sat in a closet, waiting and waiting to find a place in Chuck's home. Chuck's first wife had left him two years earlier, and Chuck was now spending most of his spare time on the internet, trying to find wife #2. Chuck was smart, handsome, and charming. He had a good job. But he had personality issues that had been variously described as borderline personality, bipolar2, and adult ADD-ADHD. Chuck thought he was fine, but he put forth a great deal of effort to keep his anger and duplicitous behavior concealed from others. He eventually met a beautiful and successful woman through an online dating service. He was hoping to keep his dark side hidden long enough to convince Marilynn Murray to become the second Mrs. Grimaldi.

The couple bought a townhouse in an upper-middle-class neighborhood of Arlington, Texas. Chuck moved out of his condo in Irving and threw away his terrible furniture. But he couldn't bring himself to part with the urinal. It had symbolic meaning for him. It represented, in some convoluted and complicated way, his manhood. He doubted that the sophisticated and particular second Mrs. Grimaldi would allow it to be installed anywhere in their fancy townhouse, but he would store it in their garage. One could always hope.

Marilynn Murray and Chuck Grimaldi were married in an elaborate garden ceremony at a museum in Ft. Worth. It turned out that Marilynn was not only smart and attractive; she was also from a wealthy family. It was Marilynn's first marriage, so she produced the extravagant wedding and reception she'd been planning all of her life. She wore an expensive and elegant traditional wedding gown, and the wedding was a huge success.

The marriage, however, was not a success. Marilynn wanted children. Chuck did not. Marilynn wanted Chuck's numerous half-finished home improvement projects in their townhouse completed, so the place would be reasonably habitable. Marilynn wanted Chuck's junk gone from the garage and the basement. She especially wanted to get rid of the ugly urinal Chuck loved so much. He kept threatening to have it installed in the master bathroom. He knew this sent his wife into a rage, and he enjoyed provoking her. They argued all the time. Marilynn spent more and more time at work. Chuck started seeing an old girlfriend he'd broken up with before he and Marilynn were married. Things went from bad to worse, and in spite of spending a considerable amount of money on counseling to try to keep the union intact, the couple separated after having been married for five years.

They continued to fight over the ownership of the townhouse and its contents. Marilynn paid off the large mortgage. She'd had her name put on the deed. She stayed in the townhouse, and Chuck moved into his girlfriend's condo. He had taken his clothes and books and a few other things he cared about and left the rest of his stuff behind. He stopped paying his half of the taxes and other expenses on the townhouse.

When the divorce was finalized, Marilynn was awarded the house and everything in it. She rented a truck and hired a day worker from the parking lot of Home Depot to help her lift the heavy things. She and her helper carried everything that had belonged to Chuck out of the house and the garage and loaded it into the truck. They drove it to Dallas which was thirty minutes away. They unloaded it all into a dumpster. Marilynn was finally free of her former husband and every single piece of his crappy stuff.

Before the junk in the Dallas dumpster made it to the landfill, an eccentric old woman with very long gray hair had been delighted to find and rescue several of the items she considered to be treasures. She struggled to get the urinal out of the dumpster and into the back of her pickup truck. She was old, and the urinal was heavy. But she was stronger than she looked, and she was finally able to load her prize on board. The porcelain facility was on its way to Marfa, Texas. It would be the perfect addition to the old woman's collection of artistic supplies.

The Present...
Marfa

Chapter 16

Jinx Carruthers' body was being sent to the state medical examiner's office in Austin. A complete autopsy and toxicology screen for drugs and alcohol would be done. I sent a quick email to Augustus Gemini, suggesting that perhaps it wasn't safe for Ellery to come back to Marfa. It seemed to be turning into a pretty dangerous place. I decided I was going to have to be the one to go to Melody's house and tell her about Jinx. Who else would do it? I intended to ask Consuela to go with me when I went over that afternoon. In the past, I might have driven to the Saint George for lunch, just to get the scuttlebutt and be able to grill the waiters about what they knew. Not today. It was unusual for me to feel so down. When Consuela asked me what I wanted for lunch, I couldn't think of anything that sounded good to me. I could tell she was concerned. Hardly anything interfered with my appetite, but today I wasn't hungry at all.

"Can you eat some chicken broth with those tiny egg noodles in it? It will take only a minute to prepare, and it will be very soothing. You need to eat something. I will bring it to you in your office, if you'd like to eat here. "

"I'm not really hungry today, but that sounds fine. I'll try to eat some soup."

"I know you're upset by everything that has been going on lately, Ms. Margaret, but you must be thankful that you have been spared."

"The authorities will probably think I'm a suspect since I haven't been poisoned. I don't care about that, but I'm so worried about Ellery. And I feel terrible about Mr. Carruthers. I hadn't even bothered to introduce myself to him."

"Don't feel guilty about that. He wouldn't allow anybody to introduce themselves to him. He screamed at everybody who came to the door, and then he chased them away."

"I need to find out if Melody gave Jinx any bottles of her soy milk. I'm guessing that she did, and that's what killed him. I think she buys, I mean, bought, food for the man. I know I have to go over and talk to her, but I just don't have the heart."

"Eat the chicken broth and take a nap after lunch. I'll go over there with you."

As I was eating the soup, my cell phone rang. It was Deputy Whitefeather at the sheriff's office with news about Melody's cat.

"Ms. Lennox, you were right about your neighbor's cat. We have determined that it was poisoned and that the poison was a combination of strychnine and cyanide. We are finished with our examinations and would like for you to pick up the animal today. We don't usually do this kind of testing, and we don't have facilities for storing animal bodies. What time can you come to pick up the cat?"

Deputy Whitefeather had just loaded one more thing onto my day that I wasn't prepared to deal with. "I'll be there at 2:00, if that's okay with you."

"I'll see you at 2:00." She hung up the phone. Deputy Whitefeather didn't waste her time with idle chitchat.

Consuela was standing by the desk in my office, ready to take my lunch tray back to the kitchen. She asked me, "Where are we going at 2:00?"

I sank back in my desk chair with a sigh. "To the sheriff's department to pick up Melody's cat's body. Deputy Whitefeather just confirmed that the cat was poisoned, and she wants me to pick Girdle up today."

"It doesn't surprise you, does it, that the cat was poisoned?"

"Not at all. I'd figured that out from the beginning. I can deal with everything except Melody. I don't know if she will be drunk or sober when I go over there. The cat needs to be buried right away. I don't know what to do. Melody thinks she wants to have some kind of a service for Girdle, but if she's on a several day binge .... And, I don't know where she wants to bury the cat. I'm sure whatever I do will make her angry."

"You can't worry about trying to please Melody. Drunks will always blame other people for something that isn't right in their lives. You can count on that. We will take the cat over to Melody's house, and I'll have my nephew meet us there and dig a grave. If Melody is too drunk to tell us where to dig, we will make the decision about where to bury her cat. We will have the service later, sometime when she is sober. Does that sound like a plan?"

"Thank you, Consuela. It's been a bad day." I was curious. "How many nephews do you have?"

"I have many nephews. They do everything for me. Now it's time for you to rest. I will wake you in time for us to get to the sheriff's office before two o'clock."

I parked illegally in front of the sheriff's office. Consuela went inside and came out after a few minutes, carrying a small box. Thank goodness the cat was inside a box, and I wouldn't have to see the poor thing. I silently thanked Deputy Whitefeather. The box didn't even smell. Consuela kept the box on her lap during the short ride home. Her nephew Roberto was waiting for us when we got to my garage. He was a young man of about seventeen and had bright eyes and a bright smile. He shook my hand. We would be taking the golf cart to Melody's house.

"Let's get this over with." I warned Roberto about what we might have to confront at Melody's.

"He's done work for Melody in the past, so he won't be shocked by whatever condition she's in." Consuela was in charge now.

Roberto climbed onto the second seat of the golf cart. He had a shovel and his work gloves. Consuela held the box and sat in the passenger seat, up front with me. We pulled into Melody's driveway, and Consuela handed me the box. "I'll go in and bring her outside. It will be better that way." I sat with Roberto in the golf cart and tried to prepare myself for any one of a number of Melodys who might come out the door. What would I say to her if she were sober? What would I say to her if she were drunk?

Consuela knocked on the front door, and we all waited with baited breath. No one came to the door, and we collectively decided that Melody was probably passed out inside.

Consuela tried the door, and it was unlocked. She stuck her head in and yelled for Melody. There was no answer. I nodded to her, and she went inside. She was gone a few minutes and came back out shaking her head. "She'd not there. The house is empty. When was the last time you saw her?"

"Yesterday afternoon. She was out cold on her couch when I left. She'd been hitting the vodka very hard. Look in the garage to see if her car is gone." The car was gone, and I was certain that Melody had left town.

"Well, she's not here now." Consuela wanted to get this over with as quickly as I did. "I suggest we go to her back garden and pick a spot for Girdle. Roberto can dig a grave, and we will bury the cat. We'll mark the site and tell Melody about it later. We can explain to her that the remains were going to begin to smell, and we couldn't wait to ask her what to do. How does that sound?" Roberto and I nodded in agreement.

I hobbled through Melody's overstuffed house and tried not to breathe until I was outside again on her back patio. We chose a nice place for Girdle in Melody's herb garden. There was a bare spot beside a large patch of rosemary, and it seemed like the perfect burial site. Roberto began to dig, and I sat in a chair with the box on my lap. Consuela went through Melody's house one more time, to be sure she wasn't there. She wasn't. We put the box into the ground, and Roberto shoveled dirt on top. We mounded the dirt over the grave so Melody would know immediately where to find Girdle. Consuela picked a small branch off an evergreen shrub and stuck it in the mound of earth. We all stood silently beside the grave for a minute and then returned to the golf cart. We debated whether or not to lock Melody's door and decided to leave it unlocked. She always left it unlocked.

All three of us were subdued after burying the cat. I thanked Roberto, and he kissed his aunt on the cheek and left in his beat-up SUV. It was past time for Consuela to leave for the day. She had to be home in time to meet her kids when they got off the school bus. I know she felt guilty about leaving me in such a down mood.

"I'll be fine, Consuela. I'm going to take a shower, get dressed up, and drive myself to the Saint George for dinner tonight. I want to hear what everyone is saying about Jinx Carruthers. Thank you for everything you did for me today."

"I hate to leave now, but I have to go home. I'll make a special breakfast for you in the morning."

"It's okay. I'm feeling down now, but I'll bounce back. I always do." I hated to see her go and hated to be alone. I usually enjoy my alone time, but today I just felt sad. I dressed in my nicest black winter pants and a black cashmere sweater set. I wore a scarf I loved. I put on my favorite pearls. I called to be sure my special table would be available. I was stepping out for the evening, and I was hoping that would cheer me up. I put on my long leather coat. It was December, and it was cold outside tonight. I thought I smelled snow in the air. Marfa doesn't get snow very often, but it does snow occasionally. Maybe tonight was the night.

I drove to the Saint George, and everybody was glad to see me. They made a fuss, and that cheered me up a little bit. I ordered lots of food and had a glass of red wine. I don't usually have wine when I'm driving the golf cart, but tonight I planned to eat a great deal of food. I decided it wouldn't hurt to have one glass of medicinal red wine. I ordered soup and salad and shrimp cocktail. Then I ordered Delmonico steak rare, mashed potatoes, and Brussels sprouts. Finally, I ordered chocolate cake for dessert. Of course, I couldn't eat it all, but the wait staff was happy to wrap up the leftovers for me to take home.

They were full of news about Jinx Carruthers. He had been poisoned with a deadly dose of strychnine and cyanide. Even though the autopsy hadn't yet been completed, word had already filtered back from Austin that poisoning was the cause of death. The CSIs had taken the cereal bowl and the cereal that Jinx had been eating when he died. The milk in his cereal had been full of both cyanide and strychnine. I was now certain that I knew what had happened to the missing soy milk.

It was well known among people in town, although not to me, that Melody bought food for Jinx and left it outside his door. She bought nonperishable staples in cans and boxes whenever she went to the grocery store, and the word was that she literally kept Jinx alive with her care packages. He never left his house to shop for groceries and had no other visible means of feeding himself, other than Melody's kindness. Everybody was multifaceted, and I would try to remember Melody's thoughtfulness to Jinx the next time I found her passed out drunk on her couch or on mine.

My waiter told me Melody had gone to Jinx's house earlier that morning when the sheriff's department had executed their warrant. She'd known about Jinx's death as soon as anybody did, other than the sheriff, and supposedly she had left town in her pickup truck not very long after she heard he'd died eating his bowl of cereal with milk. Maybe she was upset, and maybe she was afraid. Maybe she was afraid somebody would blame her for Jinx's death, or maybe she was afraid she would be next.

My waiter put my take-home boxes in a shopping bag, and I drove back to North Austin Street. My neighbors were falling like flies. They were disappearing, and they were dying. I locked my door and put away my food. It had been a long, sad day, and I had a hard time making my mind stop racing. Exhaustion sometimes does not result in a good night's sleep. I finally drifted off before three in the morning and slept until eleven the next day.

Chapter 17

*I*t had snowed during the night, just enough to cover the ground and make Marfa into a winter wonderland. I had planned to get up early to drive the soy milk I'd rescued from Ellery's pantry to the lab in Alpine but decided to wait a few days. There was the snow, which was nothing for someone who had lived in Washington, D.C. for years and driven everywhere during and after countless terrible snowstorms. But before I made another trip to the lab in Alpine, I wanted to try to account for those missing three bottles of soy milk and take them with me. I was certain that Jinx Carruthers had used one of the three bottles on his cereal, and that's what had killed him. But I was hoping to get into Jinx's house after the crime scene investigators were finished with it and look for the bottles of soy milk Jinx hadn't used.

And I was emotionally drained from burying the cat, worrying about Ellery, and wondering what in the world had happened to Melody. I thought she was the target of the poisoning, but I could not imagine why in the world she would be. She herself had said she didn't know anybody, but actually, she knew a few of the neighbors. She knew me. I reminded myself that because she had no family, she had named the Chinati Foundation in her will.

I had to ask myself the dreaded question. Had Melody also been murdered? Would we find her body someplace? I had warned her about the milk and told her to be careful about whatever she ate and drank. But I don't think she believed me that someone had targeted her for death. If poisoning had failed, whoever was after Melody might resort to some other means.

Consuela brought a lovely brunch to my bedroom. She was spoiling me, and I loved every minute of it. She sat down with her own cup of coffee at the small table in my sitting room, and we talked over the situation.

I asked Consuela what had to be uppermost in both of our minds. "What do you think has happened to Melody? Do you think she has met with foul play, or do you think she's run away?"

"Because her car is gone, I think she beat it out of town. I think Jinx's death scared her, and she's gone into hiding. Or, she may have had some kind of a distorted notion that someone would blame her for his death." Consuela was thinking along the same lines as I was.

"I warned her to be careful about what she ate and drank, but I'm not sure my warning registered with her. She was so upset when I told her about Ellery. She's very fond of Ellery. She knew she had given soy milk to both of her neighbors, and I think Jinx's death convinced her she was the intended victim." I was glad that Consuela and I were both on the same page with our thinking, but it was all so upsetting.

Consuela couldn't understand it either. "Why would somebody want to kill Melody? I can't even imagine what the motive might be. Her life is so circumscribed. She does her sculpture, but other than that, she doesn't do much of anything...except drink. She doesn't have any friends. She comes over here and hassles you, but she doesn't really have a social life. You said she came here for Thanksgiving."

"I think she's a true eccentric, and I think her drinking has turned off most of the people she's tried to make as friends. I know it has turned me off. I dread her knocking on my door. I know addictions are the worst of beasts, and I feel sorry for Melody. She can be a pest, and she can be very direct, bordering on being downright rude. But she's not so annoying that anybody would want to murder her for it."

"What about her work? Is any of it valuable enough to kill for?"

I rolled my eyes. "It's hard for me to answer that question. Her work does not resonate with me, but Ellery told me once that she gets excellent prices for her sculpture pieces. She supports herself selling her work, so somebody likes it. I think her hairstyle and her wardrobe choices are more indicators of her eccentricity and her philosophy of life, than they are of poverty. She buys milk and food for her neighbors. Ellery can afford his own food, and maybe Jinx could have too. But Jinx didn't buy his own food. He never left his house. According to my sources at the Saint George, Melody provided Jinx with everything he ate and drank."

"Maybe somebody knew that, and Jinx was the intended victim. But I doubt it. He was in his nineties. He didn't appear to have anything in his house worth stealing. Why in the world would anybody want to kill an old man? I think his death was a bad mistake. Melody is the one who was supposed to die, but who knows why anybody would want to kill her either? Who knows if she will ever come back to Marfa? Her life style is such that she might have decided to set up her 'studio' someplace else."

"And leave all that junk behind? It doesn't look like it's worth anything to me, but she's gone to a lot of trouble to get it, digging it out of dumpsters all over Texas and carting it back here to her house. She probably has plans for at least some of that stuff. It's valuable to her, for whatever reasons we can't understand." I had been trying to get a grip on why Melody gathered all of these found objects, her artistic materials. It puzzled me, and I had to keep myself from slipping into the belief that she was just a hoarder. She had taken considerable risks to acquire her junk. She had driven great distances without a valid driver's license. Her stuff was clearly important to her.

"Did Melody have a cell phone? Can we call her?" Consuela was practical and approached problems in a logical way.

"I never saw her with a cell phone, but she must have one. She doesn't have a landline. I doubt if she is eccentric enough to cut herself off completely from the world. She would have asked to borrow my phone, I think, if she didn't have one of her own. She wasn't shy about imposing on others. She never called me; she just came over and knocked on my door. Sometimes she didn't even knock and walked right in."

"Do you want me to go over there and look for a cell phone? I looked around for her purse when we were there to bury the cat. I think she took her purse and whatever was in it with her when she left. I could go back and do a really thorough search for the phone." Consuela didn't look eager to search Melody's house. To actually go through all of it would be a prodigious and overwhelming task. It was almost frightening to contemplate searching vast mountains of mysterious and ordinary objects.

"I have a better idea. I'm going to contact Augustus Gemini and ask him to check Ellery's cell phone to see if he has a number for Melody. Ellery has lived here longer than I have, and if anyone has a phone number for Melody, it would be Ellery."

I texted Augustus and asked him to call me at his convenience. I knew he didn't like to talk on the phone, but I had too much to tell him to put it all in an email or a text. I wanted him to know the latest details about Jinx Carruthers' death and about Melody's disappearance. I felt all of this was pertinent to Ellery's poisoning. I composed a text and sent it to Augustus. Consuela went back to her cleaning and cooking, and I tried to write, although I knew there was no way I was going to be able to focus on anything else right now, except what was happening in my immediate neighborhood.

My phone rang within a few minutes, and it was Augustus.

"Augustus, thank you for getting back to me so quickly. How is Ellery? I have news here in Marfa related to his situation."

"Ellery is doing better, but he continues to be very weak. It will take him a long time, I'm afraid, to come back from this. He's just incredibly lucky he didn't die. His doctors have assured me that he did not suffer any permanent organ damage, and I have to believe them. He is such a talented genius. I'm so terribly afraid this health crisis is going to diminish his ability to be creative."

"Sometimes, tragedy enhances creativity, Augustus. Don't fret. Ellery is alive. He's young and he'll bounce back. I will make certain of it."

"We will work together on that, my dear. I will do all I possibly can. What's going on there?"

"There has been another death from cyanide and strychnine, and this time it isn't a cat. Melody's next-door neighbor on the other side from me, Jinx Carruthers, died a couple of days ago from drinking soy milk on his cereal. Melody bought six bottles of the milk and gave three bottles to Ellery and, I'm almost certain, gave three bottles to Jinx. Ellery took one on his trip to Terlingua, and I have rescued the other two from his pantry, unopened. I think Jinx got three bottles of the soy milk, too, and he opened one for breakfast to put on his cereal. He's dead and his body is currently undergoing an autopsy at the medical examiner's office in Austin."

"How do you know all of this?"

"My sources at the Saint George Hotel and my housekeeper Consuela. I lived at the Saint George for three months while my house was being renovated, and I know almost everybody who works there. I still eat there several times a week, and it's a small town. The staff at the hotel knows everything that's happening in Marfa. They knew there was strychnine and cyanide in Jinx's cereal before the ME in Austin even began to do the autopsy. My housekeeper also has family members who give her a lot of inside information. Consuela has all these nephews who work in every field of endeavor in Marfa. Nothing escapes Consuela's family's scrutiny."

"Wow! Another neighbor poisoned! I understand now what happened with the milk, but this is really very scary.

Melody bought six bottles of soy milk; somebody poisoned them; and she gave three bottles to Ellery and three to Jinx. Ellery was lucky; Jinx was not. How old was Jinx?"

"I think he was in his nineties. He was a real recluse, and the word is that Melody bought all of his groceries for him. He wasn't the target, though. I'm sure the poison was intended for Melody, but I can't begin to imagine why anybody would want to kill her. In any case, now she's disappeared. Her car is gone, so I am assuming she drove herself out of town. Her purse is also gone. Supposedly, she left right after Jinx was found dead, and nobody has any idea where she is."

"It sounds like going into hiding was a smart thing for her to do. She has to know the poisoned milk was intended for her. She's a drunk, but I don't think anybody believes for a minute she's a murderer."

"Since her car and purse are gone, we think she left of her own volition. At least we don't think anybody kidnapped her. I hope she runs far away and stays hidden. I called you because I wondered if you'd found Ellery's cell phone. If Melody has a cell phone, she took it with her. I wanted to try to call her, but I don't have a number. She doesn't have a landline, and I don't either. Nobody has a landline anymore, it seems. I just want to call Melody and leave a voice mail for her. She won't pick up. Of course, she may have thrown her phone away or dropped the locator chip in the river or beat her phone to death with a hammer. I don't know how electronically savvy she is, but if she really doesn't want to be tracked down, she should have dumped her phone."

"I do have Ellery's phone. It's at my hotel. I will check to see if he has a number for Melody, and if I find anything, I'll text it to you. I wanted to talk to you anyway, about

Ellery's convalescence and his release from the hospital. When I toured your house at Thanksgiving, I noticed that nice casita in the back. You have done a wonderful job with all of your renovations, by the way, including the fix-up on that guest house. This is a big favor to ask, but I was wondering if you would be willing to let Ellery stay in your casita until he's back on his feet. I've hired a private duty nurse, an R.N., to take care of him. I will hire additional help when he's out of the hospital. I promise, there will not be any extra work for you. I know you have recently hired a housekeeper. You've mentioned that her name is Consuela. I don't want there to be any extra work for her either. I would just feel better if Ellery and the health care workers weren't by themselves at his house for the next week or two. There's safety in numbers, and if he were at your house, I think there'd be less likelihood that he would be in danger from whoever is poisoning people in Marfa. It would only be for a few weeks, until he is able to function. He's in pretty rough shape right now and can't begin to take care of himself. He really likes you, and I think he would feel comfortable staying with you."

"Of course, I would love to have him stay at my house. The casita will be the perfect place for him and his caregiver. Does he need a hospital bed? I can have it set up and ready for him. When will he be discharged?"

"I will take care of everything. No worries. Thank you so much. I remember exactly the layout of the casita, and yes, he will need a hospital bed. I will arrange for it. I will feel so much better if he's with you and not all alone with the nurse in his own house. I don't think he would be willing to go anywhere else, but I think he will be willing to stay in your casita. He knows he won't be under foot out there.

There is a small kitchen in the casita, and the nurse can make his meals. He doesn't have a very good appetite right now anyway."

"We'll work things out. I will love having him here. There are two bedrooms in the casita — plenty of room for the nurse to stay there with him. My pool is supposed to be completely finished by the end of next week, and Consuela is a wonderful cook. When Ellery's appetite comes back, she will love cooking for him. She makes everything, not just Mexican, but her chicken enchiladas are to die for."

"Great. It's settled then. The hospital wants a detailed discharge plan before they will let him go. Since they still think I'm his brother, they are looking to me to organize that plan. I will fly him to Marfa on my plane next Monday. I'll let you know everything that's going on. I'll have the bed and everything he needs delivered to the casita and ready for him by Monday. And, I will text you Melody's phone number, if I can find it in Ellery's phone."

"Thanks for your help. All this poisoning and death have turned everybody's lives upside down. I can't do anything about Melody, but I am trusting she will be able to take care of herself. I am happy to be able to do something for Ellery and look forward to having him here."

"Try not to look shocked when you first see him. He looks terrible. He was skinny to begin with, but now he is emaciated. He doesn't even look like himself." Augustus Gemini's voice caught as he described Ellery's condition. I could tell Ellery's brush with death had affected Augustus more than he wanted to admit.

"I promise not to look shocked. I will be so happy to see him, my delight will be the only emotion he will notice. I promise to help nurse him back to health."

"We need him back working, making music. The film industry needs him. The world needs him. I hope he will be able to pull himself out of his depression. He's almost catatonic at this point." Augustus's voice caught again. He had been really shaken by Ellery's poisoning and slow recovery.

"I will do whatever I can to help. Just let me know."

"Margaret, I know you will, and I know he will be in good hands. When I bring him back, I will stay for a few days at Ellery's house until I get things settled. I have to arrange for nursing shifts, to give the caretakers a break. I have to deal with his mail and pay his bills, and all of that. We will make it work. I just hope he has the strength and determination to get better. If he continues to be depressed, I have someone I can bring from L.A., a doctor I've used myself, who works with creative people. The very creative and artistic are different, and they need a different kind of counseling. We don't want to turn Ellery into an accountant." It was Augustus's small joke.

"As if that were ever going to be possible." I laughed a little.

"You'd be surprised. Some psychiatrists just want to load their depressed patients up with meds so they can function at a low level. Ellery has such a special gift. His kind of functioning is very different than that of most people."

"I understand. Just tell me what I can do." We hung up. I was so touched by the concern Augustus had for Ellery. I knew Ellery was special, but Augustus had known him much longer and in a much broader way than I had. Augustus almost seemed to worship Ellery's musical abilities. I was thrilled to be able to do something to help Ellery and was delighted that Augustus had felt as if he could call on me. Consuela had never met Ellery, but she'd heard so much about him in the past few weeks, I'm sure she felt as if she already knew him.

I realized Ellery would be with me for Christmas. This would give me something to look forward to and plan for. It would be fun. Consuela had hung the live wreaths with big red bows at the doors and windows of the house. Now I would decorate the casita a little bit, at least with a small tree and some wreaths. Maybe that would cheer Ellery up and put him in the Christmas spirit. I had more gifts to buy. Christmas was just two weeks away. I wondered if Ellery would be well enough to go to the Saint George with me for Christmas dinner. I would make attending that dinner a goal for the future.

Chapter 18

*I*n spite of the warning Augustus Gemini had given
me about Ellery, I was completely shocked by his appearance when he arrived at my house the week before
Christmas. I almost succeeded in hiding my dismay, but
from the sad look in Ellery's eyes, I could tell I'd revealed too
much. I hugged him gently and kissed him on the cheek.

"Welcome to the casita, Ellery. I am thrilled to see you
and to have you here. I hope you will be comfortable. If there
is anything you need, all you have to do is ask. I probably
have whatever it is, and in fact, I probably have several of
them. So don't be shy about asking."

Ellery gave me a very small and very weak smile. His
vigor was gone. Where does vigor go when a person loses
it? Surely we could find it again, somewhere. My ideas about
brightening Ellery's days with Christmas decorations and
Christmas cheer went out the window. My hope that in a
week he would be able to go to Christmas dinner with me

at the Saint George, dropped off my wish list. Ellery was barely alive.

I would not have recognized him if he hadn't arrived with Augustus and a nurse. He was in a wheelchair, and his hair was turning white. It wasn't as white as mine, but he was only in his thirties. His coloring was what frightened me the most. It was as if all the blood had drained from his face and arms, leaving a ghost behind. I had to get myself under control. My crying or feeling sorry for him was not going to be helpful. I had to accept what had happened and embrace the Ellery that had come back to us. It wasn't the Ellery that any of us had wanted to see, but at least he was a living, breathing Ellery. And it was the best Christmas gift anyone could hope for.

"Having you here, Ellery, is the best Christmas gift I could ever have imagined. Thank you."

He smiled his fragile smile again. "Merry Christmas, Margaret." It seemed to take every ounce of energy he possessed to utter those three words.

I squeezed his hand. "You need to rest. It's been a long day." I met Ellery's nurse, Doug Petrie, who seemed like a pleasant, competent fellow. I told Doug not to hesitate to ask me if he needed anything. I told him my housekeeper was making a roast chicken for dinner, and I would send food out to the casita for Doug and his patient. "I know you like chicken and mashed potatoes, Ellery."

"I used to." It was a small attempt at humor, and my eyes welled up with tears that he was trying so hard. Ellery began to nod off in the wheelchair, and Augustus and I slipped out of the casita.

Before we were back inside the house, I broke down and cried.

"I warned you that it wasn't pretty. Are you up for all of this? I certainly understand if you aren't." Augustus had warned me, but it was so much worse than I'd imagined.

I got myself under control. "Of course I'm up for this. I wouldn't have it any other way."

"I could have taken him to L.A., to my house, but I knew he would much rather be here. My place is big, but it's a mad house. People are coming and going all the time. I don't have an office, so I run my business out of my home. It's crazy there. He would never get any rest. And Marfa is home for Ellery. He can look out the window of the casita and see his own little blue house, right across the street. Just try to keep Melody away from him for a few weeks, until he's stronger."

"Melody is gone." I reminded him. Augustus had sent me Melody's phone number. I'd called it many times, and she had never answered. I'd left messages. I had considered going over to her house and calling her phone. I thought she might have left it there. It could have fallen behind something or been kicked under the couch. Maybe I would hear it ringing in the house, but of course the battery would have died long ago.

"She's never come home after her neighbor died? And you've never been able to reach her on her phone?"

"No. I've not heard one word. I've called her repeatedly, and the calls go right to voice mail. I gave her my cell phone number and asked her to call me. Did you check Ellery's phone? She might have tried to reach him. She wanted him to dig a grave for her cat and was upset that he wasn't here to do it."

"I did check his phone. She called him several times about digging the grave, but she's not called at all since Carruthers died. You can't worry about Melody, you know. You have enough to worry about right here at your own house. My opinion about Melody is that she's scared and she's running. She knows whoever poisoned the milk meant to kill her, and she has no idea who or why. Several musicians from Ellery's jazz ensemble also called and left messages. They hadn't heard from him since they were all together in Terlingua and were concerned. He's missed several of their practices."

"Of course they are worried about him. What should we do about that?"

"Nothing. We are not going to do a thing about it. I don't want anybody to know that Ellery is here at your house. In case he was the target, or one of the targets, of the poisoned milk, he might still be in danger. As long as nobody knows he's here, I don't feel the need to hire any security guards. Doug knows the situation, and I will be doing all the shopping and making all the trips to the grocery store. Doug is going to stay inside and out of sight. A strange man wandering around in the neighborhood might raise suspicion. People are used to seeing me around here, so I can come and go as I please."

"But you are staying at Ellery's house. Doesn't that put you in danger, too?"

"I don't think it does, but I am being very careful about everything. Be sure you tell your housekeeper not to talk about Ellery staying in your casita."

"I will be sure she knows what to do. Changing the subject, what are you doing for Christmas, Augustus? Do you have plans in L.A. or are you staying here?" For the first time ever, I saw a somewhat wistful, even sad, look in his eyes.

"I don't have any plans, really. I've been preoccupied with work and trying to arrange for Ellery to leave the hospital.

There are lots of Christmas parties in L.A., and I'm invited to way too many of those...."

I interrupted him. "The reason I'm asking is because I would love to have you spend Christmas with me." I had given some thought to going to San Diego to see my daughter, but she's swamped with work. She has a trial coming up the first week in January and doesn't have the time right now for me to visit. "I was going to invite Ellery to go to the Saint George with me on Christmas Day, but he's not anywhere close to being well enough to do that. They have a fabulous Christmas dinner, or so I hear, and I've reserved a table for two. I would be thrilled to have you join me. What do you say?" I could tell he was pleased with the invitation.

"Thanksgiving and now Christmas. Pretty soon I'll be family." He smiled.

"Augustus, I hope you know you already are. Wonderful. It's a date."

"I have to go to Ellery's house to open his mail and pay some bills. I know he takes care of a lot of that automatically and online, but there are some things that have to be paid the old fashioned way, with a check. But I'll be back for that roast chicken. What time do you want me?"

"Consuela will put the chickens in the oven at 3:30, and they should be done by 5:30. Everything else will be ready by then, too. Consuela is making mashed potatoes and gravy and fresh asparagus. I'm making my own grandmother's special egg noodles cooked in chicken broth. It's a very old school dish, but you will absolutely love it. The broth is homemade, and the noodles are homemade. The broth is on the stove right now, and Consuela and I are going to make the noodles this afternoon. My grandmother used to cut the noodles very, very fine. I have never been able to cut them as finely as she did, but I try. I've always wondered if she had a special knife or just how she managed to do it. Anyway, mine taste the same, or almost the same. Consuela has a fruit salad to go with the chicken and a vanilla panna cotta for dessert. It will be Ellery's welcome home feast, but he won't be at the table." I sighed.

"It sounds like the food of the gods. I'll see you at 6:00." Augustus gave me a quick hug and was out the door.

Consuela had been working in the kitchen. She could see that I was feeling down. "I stayed out of the way so you could get Ellery settled in the casita. He must still be very ill. You were white as a sheet when you came back to the house."

I almost started to cry again. "He looks just terrible. He doesn't look anything like the same person who left Marfa three weeks ago. I'm very worried about him. We will have to work hard to bring him back to life. He seems as if he has lost the essence of himself. How can that be?"

"We will pray for him and we will feed him and we will love him. That is what we will do, and that is what will make him well again. We will do our very best." She looked at me with concern. "You still have not been able to reach Melody?"

I shook my head. "Augustus thinks she's on the run. She's probably using a prepaid phone and has thrown away her own phone so no one can track her."

"Does he think you are in any danger?"

"I don't think I am. Why would I be?" I could see that Consuela was worried. Her forehead wrinkled up and her eyebrows drew closer together, but she didn't say anything about her concerns

"You and Mr. Augustus will have a nice dinner tonight. He can take one of the chickens and some of the other food to the casita. I have laid out containers and all the serving dishes to make it easy for you. She showed me what she had organized so Augustus could take the meal to Ellery and his nurse. She'd even found the perfect basket to put it all in.

"You are the best, Consuela. Thank you."

"We will make those noodles now, and then you will have a nice rest before dinner."

My nap was a success. The noodles were a success. The dinner was a success. Augustus carved one chicken and took dinner to the casita for Ellery and Doug. He came back and carved our chicken. I served the other dishes, and we sat down to eat in the kitchen. Consuela had set the table with green placemats, red napkins, and my Christmas dishes. She wanted to cheer us up. Augustus brought a chilled bottle of Pinot Grigio, and we had a lovely dinner together. He raved about the homemade noodles, and the panna cotta was perfect. Augustus made coffee and cleaned up the dishes.

Augustus had a serious look on his face. "I need to ask you about something. It has to do with the shoe you discovered in the bushes behind your house, the shoe you think belonged to the woman who was found dead beside the railroad tracks."

With all the other things that had been happening in the neighborhood, I had completely forgotten about the woman who'd been thrown off the train and about the shoe I'd found. A couple of weeks earlier, I had sent Augustus all the pictures I'd taken of the shoe, the coins, and the Euros. I wondered, with all the other things he'd been doing, especially with everything he had done for Ellery, how he'd had time to think of that shoe. "You were going to ask your 'shoe guru' to look at the pictures. You said she could tell where the shoe was made and everything about it."

"She can, and she did. My question for you is, where is the shoe now, and can you get it back from whoever has it?"

I had decided I would probably never see the shoe or the coins or the Euros again, ever. That's why I'd taken the photographs of everything, because I knew once I'd given it all to law enforcement, it would forever be stored somewhere in an evidence locker. I'd kissed it all goodbye when I'd given it to the Texas Ranger. "I gave it to the Texas Ranger who's investigating the case. I haven't heard a peep from him since he drove off with the shoe in his car. I never expect to see any of that again, although, technically, I guess the shoe and the money in the shoe do belong to me. Don't they?"

"Yes, they do, and I think you should try to get some of it back from Mr. Texas Ranger. Or at the very least, we need to have a talk with him. I'll tell you why. My shoe expert knew immediately that the shoe was made in Taiwan, not in mainland China. She knows the location of the factory that made the shoe. These shoes were manufactured for sale inside the country of Taiwan only. They were not made for export. So the woman who was wearing them purchased them in Taiwan, not in the United States. I can give you all that information if you want it, but it isn't important. The shoe is two years old. It looks older because it has been worn constantly since the owner of the shoe put it on. Whoever owned the shoe didn't have another pair of shoes to wear."

"Taiwan? Is that significant?"

"I think it might be. Especially in light of what else my shoe expert discovered. She told me that from the beginning, she thought something was off about the polka dot design on the fabric of the shoe. It took her a few minutes to figure out what was bothering her about the polka dots. She got out her magnifying glass and showed me everything she was talking about. I can show you...in the pictures on your phone, if you want me to. The dots were regularly and perfectly placed on the shoe fabric, except for one dot. My expert had only the photograph you sent, but cell phones these days take pretty darn good pictures. She could tell that one of the dots on the shoe fabric was not in quite the right location."

"Why is that important? What does an irregular pattern of polka dots on shoe fabric have to do with anything?"

"My shoe expert is a shoe expert. She's not an expert in the tradecraft of spies. But she thinks the dot that is out of alignment is not a polka dot on the shoe fabric. She thinks it is a micro dot that was embedded into the shoe. She thinks that the microdot might contain some kind of secret intelligence, information the woman who was killed might have been trying to smuggle to someone. I told my expert the woman had been murdered. We are speculating here, of course, but because of the microdot, we think she might have been murdered because of the information she had in her shoe. Or, I guess it was really *on* her shoe."

My mouth was literally hanging open. I had lived in Washington, D.C. for decades, and spies were tripping all over each other in that city. I'd always imagined that half the population of the nation's capital was spying on the other half. In my wildest imaginings, I'd never thought I would move to Marfa, Texas, and find myself in the murder capital of the world or in the presence of spy shoes with microdots on them. I looked at Augustus with disbelief written all over my face. "Augustus, really. I respect your expert, but what in the world...?"

"I know this sounds preposterous, especially in light of what else has been happening around here. It is quite like *The Twilight Zone*, isn't it? But hear me out on this. Let's say the woman who was killed was from Taiwan. We know Taiwan and China are always at odds, always enemies. But they are all Chinese. If the woman who died was a Taiwanese spy, maybe she had been spying in China. Maybe she was carrying information she'd gathered about something secret that was going on in China, something she'd found out about. Something nefarious is always going on in China, of course, but maybe the woman was a spy and had discovered an important secret, something that could impact the United States and Taiwan and other countries. Maybe that secret information she'd found was stored on the microdot. Maybe she was trying to get the information, via the microdot, to someone or some place in the United States."

"Pretty far-fetched, even for you, dear heart."

"What do you mean, 'even for me'?"

"You are in the movie business, the business of make believe. You live in La La Land. Augustus, this is far out, very far out."

"We have to find out where the woman came from and how she got on that train. I have some theories, but we will probably never be able to prove any of them."

I was exhausted. I had to go to bed. All of this was fascinating and would make a great thriller, but it would have to wait until tomorrow. "I have to go to bed, Augustus. I don't want to be rude, but I can't keep my eyes open another minute."

"I'm done in as well. Sorry, I shouldn't have started talking about all of this tonight when we're both so tired. But, I am very concerned about who knows you found the shoe. Does anyone besides the Texas Ranger know you were the one who found it? I wonder if anyone believes the shoe is still in your possession. If there's a microdot embedded in the shoe fabric and if the microchip has important intelligence on it, someone might be willing to kill to get that shoe and that microdot."

"First of all, nobody except the Texas Rangers know that I'm the one who found the shoe. Do you think somebody besides law enforcement knows one of the shoes was missing? Maybe they think Melody found the shoe. Everybody in town knows she's a scavenger. Everybody knows she collects whatever junk she can find. Would whatever is on that microdot be the reason somebody tried to kill Melody and ended up killing Jinx Carruthers and Melody's cat?"

"I don't know the answers to those questions, but ever since I heard from my shoe expert, I've been asking myself all the same things. There's more, but it will keep until tomorrow. Please watch your back. If anyone realizes you're the one who picked up the shoe, they might think you still have it. You could be in danger."

Augustus took our coffee cups to the kitchen sink. He gently pushed me in the direction of my bedroom. He gave me a hug, turned out the lights in the kitchen and the living room, and let himself out the front door. He was going to spend the night at Ellery's house.

As tired as I was, my mind was now spinning. I wished I hadn't had any coffee. I was going over and over everything Augustus had said to me. I was lamenting that I would never get to sleep. The next thing I knew, it was morning.

Chapter 19

*C*onsuela didn't wake me when she came in to work like she usually did. She knew I'd had an exhausting day the day before, and she let me sleep. When I finally woke up, she'd already been to the casita and introduced herself to Ellery and Doug. I had told her that Ellery liked oatmeal, and she'd made a large pot of stone-ground Irish oatmeal, the kind you cook a long time, not the instant kind. She'd taken a week's supply to Ellery, and she had a large bowl ready for me, with cream and brown sugar. It was warm and comforting and just what I needed on this wintry morning.

I didn't want to worry Consuela with the news about the microdot on the shoe, although I knew that sooner or later I'd end up telling her all about it. I was feeling guilty that Melody might have been targeted because someone was trying to find the dead woman's missing shoe. Because it's what she always did, everyone expected Melody to pick up

stray objects she found on the ground and in the bushes. But
she hadn't found the shoe this time. I'd found it and picked
it up, before she'd had the chance to get it. Had whoever
poisoned the milk, believed that Melody had found the shoe?
I was the new kid on the block, or more precisely the new
old person on the block. No one would ever dream I was the
one who had picked up the shoe.

I was out of my league with the microdot thing. The
technology was something out of a spy novel. I didn't know
how information got on to or off of a microdot, and I didn't
think I needed to know. I was intrigued that the woman
had the dot in the fabric of her shoe and that she might
have been killed for it. There were so many unanswered
questions about that poor soul who had been thrown off
a freight train. I doubted the Texas Rangers had any idea
what they were dealing with. They would have been more
interested in the coins and the Euros that had been inside
the shoe than they would have been in the fabric on the shoe
itself. The microdot had literally been hiding in plain sight. I
would have to talk to Augustus again before I did anything
or called the Texas Rangers.

I was silent as I ate my breakfast. Consuela was very
tuned in to my moods. "Are you all right, Ms. Margaret?
You are very quiet this morning."

"I'm worried, very worried about Ellery. And there is
something else I need to talk to you about. Dinner last
night was outstanding, by the way. The chicken was perfectly done, and Augustus loved the panna cotta and the
noodles. But that's not what I wanted to tell you. Augustus
is concerned for Ellery's safety. We all think the poison was
intended for Melody, but until we can be sure of what is
going on, Augustus doesn't want anyone to know that Ellery

is staying here. He wanted me to ask you not to talk about it. He won't even allow Doug to go out of the house, for fear of arousing suspicion. As far as anyone in Marfa knows, or as far as anyone anywhere knows, Ellery is not here. Apparently some of his jazz group buddies have called him to find out if he's okay. He's missed some of the group's practices, and that's not like him. I don't know what we're going to do about that."

"You know you can trust me not to say anything, but I'm worried that you are putting yourself in danger."

"Nobody wants to hurt me, at least I don't think they do."

"So, why does anybody want to hurt Melody? That's very puzzling to me. She's an artist who makes weird sculptures that supposedly somebody, somewhere likes to buy. She's a drunk and won't cut her hair. She's very peculiar, but those aren't reasons for anybody to want her dead."

Augustus had let himself into the back door while we were talking. "You are exactly right, Consuela. These are the questions that are stumping all of us." I realized Consuela had never met Augustus. I introduced them, and they shook hands. I could see they were on the same wave length. Augustus praised the roast chicken and the panna cotta. Consuela was pleased with the compliments. Augustus realized he could talk freely about everything around Consuela. He could tell she was smart and had a lot of insight into people. He brought her up to speed on the microdot in the shoe fabric. Consuela's eyes got very large when she heard the story, and she was as disbelieving as I had been when I'd first heard about the shoe.

"I'm concerned that Ms. Margaret is in danger." Consuela was always my champion.

"As long as no one knows she found the shoe, she'll be all right. I have to wonder what's going on with the Texas Rangers. Can they keep their mouths shut? They don't even know that they should keep their mouths shut. That's a concern for me." Augustus didn't think the Texas Rangers knew what they were dealing with.

"I think you need to talk to them immediately. They need to know what they have on their hands. I think they ought to keep possession of the shoe. It would be dangerous for Ms. Margaret to have it here." Consuela paused, "I hope I haven't spoken out of turn."

"Not at all. I'm delighted to hear your point of view. Margaret and I have been so concerned about Ellery, we have kind of lost our perspective on things. You bring clarity to the situation. I think you are right about talking to the Texas Rangers. They need to know about the microdot. The question is, what is the best way for them to be told about what they have? I don't think it ought to come from Margaret or from me. I think the Texas Rangers need to find out about the microdot from the FBI, and I think I can make that happen. In fact, it would be better all-around if the FBI took possession of the shoe. Maybe the Texas Rangers don't need to know anything at all about the micro dot on the shoe. I'm going to make some phone calls to some people I know." Augustus turned to leave. He had his work cut out for him now, and he wasn't wasting any time. "I promise I will tell you everything when I get back. There is more to tell you about the coins and about the Euros, but that will wait. I'll be back for lunch...if that's okay?" Augustus was gone.

My swimming pool was being filled today. Cold weather had delayed the laying of the tile around the deck and the edges of the pool, but it was finally completed. The pool people were telling me it would be ready to heat by tomorrow tonight and ready to swim in by the next night. Because of my arthritis, many kinds of exercise were no longer options for me. But swimming in a heated pool was the best therapy I could possibly choose. I had always loved to swim, and immersing myself in the warm water would be heavenly. I could hardly wait. Having the pool ready and waiting for me on Christmas day would be a great Christmas gift to myself. I would probably not swim on Christmas day, but knowing the pool was ready made me happy.

Consuela knew how much I was looking forward to swimming in the pool. The sun was out today, and it was almost warm enough to sit outside for lunch. I had a patio heater, and we turned it on. Consuela, under my direction, had made curried Moroccan chicken salad from the leftover roast chicken. She'd made chicken salad sandwiches on sourdough toast with bacon, lettuce, and tomato. She had navy bean soup with carrots, onion, celery, and ham. Consuela was going to eat with us, and we waited for Augustus. He arrived and joined us on the patio. Consuela served the hot soup and the sandwiches as we watched the pool people clean up the patio and put the finishing touches on the pool-cover installation.

When she delivered soup and sandwiches to the casita, Consuela had warned Doug not to come out onto the patio while the pool people were at the house. I could see Doug and Ellery looking out the window of the casita, watching what was going on. I was thrilled that Ellery was taking an interest in something, in anything. I hoped he would want to get into the pool when it was heated. Swimming would build his strength and his confidence.

Augustus was full of news which he told us, as promised, in between devouring two sandwiches and two bowls of soup. Apparently, talking to the FBI could build up an appetite. "Don't ask me exactly who I called, but I will give you a hint. I'm in the movie business, as you know. I have contacts, and when a movie is in production, I bring in experts of all kinds to advise us. We aren't perfect, but I am more than a bit of a perfectionist when it comes to getting it right. I don't want to make a mistake in the architecture we show on exterior scenes. I don't want a mistake made in the background music. For example, in one very well-known and very well-done TV series, there was choral music in the background of a scene shot in a church. The song they were singing was a version of an old spiritual. But the arrangement they were using was written in the year 2000. That would have been fine, except that the television show was set in the 1980s. It was a discordant note, to say the least, in an otherwise nearly flawless production. That is never going to happen in any of my movies. I spend a lot of money to be sure I don't make mistakes like that. I insist on having the best consultants on everything I do. I hire legal consultants. I hire people who used to work for the FBI, usually retirees. I pay them well. They do a good job for me. But I digress."

Consuela and I were all ears, and we weren't about to open our mouths, yet. Augustus continued. "As we speak, the FBI in L.A. is taking a statement from my shoe expert. The agents on the case were not willing to tell me much, but I happen to know, from another source, that the FBI is over-joyed to have found out what happened to that microdot. They have already taken possession of the shoe. The Texas Rangers gave it up without a fight." Augustus chuckled. "I also happen to know that the body of the woman who was thrown off the train in Marfa will be in Washington D.C. by tonight. The case is now being investigated by the feds. Mr. Grumpy Texas Ranger, the one who gave you a hard time, Margaret, is apparently a very good investigator. He lacks people skills, according to those who know him, but he is smart. He was very helpful when the FBI moved in to take over the case."

"So, the FBI is now in charge of the murder of the mystery woman. Do we know anything at all about a connection between the shoe and the poisonings here in Marfa?" I wanted more information. I already knew everything Augustus had told the FBI.

"I made those points with my contact—about Ellery being poisoned, Melody's cat, and Jinx Carruthers' death. They are looking into it. I will know more this afternoon."

Consuela still wanted to know if I was in danger. "Does the FBI think Ms. Margaret is at risk? She was the one who found the shoe. Does anybody else know about that?"

Augustus had been concerned about that, too. "The Texas Ranger, Jeremiah Drayton, isn't the chatty type, and apparently he never told anyone who'd given him the shoe. He never said a name to anyone. He wrote up his report and put the shoe, the coins, and the Euros into the evidence locker. He was not that concerned with the shoe, of course, but he thought somebody might be interested in the money. So he kept it all to himself. There wasn't any way to identify the woman's body. She looked poor, like an illegal immigrant. Because she appeared to be a foreign national and in spite of the money in the shoe, the case has already been demoted to a cold case. No one at the local or state levels is looking into anything regarding the woman now. The Texas Rangers are understaffed, just like law enforcement is everywhere in the country these days.

They allocate their resources to cases they think they can solve. The woman from the train wasn't one of those, so they closed down the investigation. Drayton has been told, in no uncertain terms, that he is not to talk about the woman, the shoe, or the money. He's not a bad guy, Margaret, according to the FBI. He's cooperating, and he has promised never to mention your name. Your name was in his report in the murder book, but the FBI asked him to remove his original report and rewrite it, leaving out your name in the revised version. The feds now have that first report, and Drayton's scrubbed account is the one in the murder book. Any connections you might have had to the case have been completely removed."

"That's all great, Augustus, and I am grateful to be shielded from any involvement. But somebody must know. Somebody tried to poison Melody. How can these things not be connected?"

"I know. I know. It's a mystifying situation. I told my contacts about the poisonings here in Marfa, about Melody, about her being a scavenger, and about everything. They are looking into all of it, but they are positive that Jeremiah Drayton didn't tell anyone about the shoe."

"Everybody in town, or at least everybody who works at the Saint George Hotel, knew about the woman who was thrown off the train. Somebody from the coroner's office must have told somebody that the woman was missing a shoe. Everything else about the case has become local gossip. Because Melody does what she does, somebody must have assumed she'd found the shoe. That's all I can figure."

"I know it's a small town, but I didn't know that the details of the murder and the murder scene are common knowledge. I will let my source, who is a conduit to the FBI, know that there are many leaks from the local coroner's office. You may not be as safe as I'd hoped you would be, Margaret."

Consuela's wrinkles appeared again on her forehead. I wasn't as worried about my own safety as she was, but I worried about Ellery. I hoped nobody thought he had anything to do with this strange mystery.

Chapter 20

ugustus went back to Ellery's house. I ordered a few things from Amazon and paid for overnight delivery. I hadn't counted on having Augustus with me for Christmas, and I wanted to buy him and Doug a couple of gifts. I wanted Augustus and Doug to have something to open on Christmas morning. I'd already bought a stocking for Ellery, and I ordered stockings for Augustus and Doug. I had sent my daughter's gifts and her stuffed stocking to San Diego.

My "go to" stocking stuffers were old school and always included a big beautiful orange to put in the toe of the stocking, soft cloths I'd discovered that did a wonderful job of cleaning the lenses of reading glasses, extra charging cords for electronic devices, a bar of goat's milk and basil soap that I loved, a jar of homemade raspberry jam I special ordered from a farm in Ohio, a travel sewing kit, and a really nice corkscrew. The earmuffs I used to put in the stockings when I'd lived in a colder climate and the office supplies I'd included in pre-computer days had fallen by the wayside. I wrapped a few of my published books as gifts for Augustus. He would like it that I had written them and had put a personal, signed note to him in the front of each one. My gifts for Ellery and Consuela were already wrapped.

Augustus was grilling steaks for all of us tonight. Consuela would put the baked potatoes in the oven and do the vegetables and dessert before she left. I was pacing back and forth, anxious for Augustus to return and give us more news. Consuela was also edgy, I could tell. She didn't want to leave before Augustus came back. Tomorrow was Christmas Eve, and Consuela's kids got off from school early this afternoon. The day after tomorrow was Christmas Day, and she planned to take the mornings off during the week her kids were home for Christmas vacation. I was going to miss her making my breakfast, and I know Doug would miss her, too, even though I knew he had enough oatmeal to last for a while. The casita had a small kitchen, and Augustus had assured me Doug was perfectly capable of cooking for Ellery.

Finally, Augustus came through the door. He had a serious look on his face, and I knew he had news that we might not want to hear.

Consuela brought a pot of hot tea and a pitcher of cream to the kitchen table. She had a container of honey, some sugar cubes, and a plate of Christmas cookies decorated with colored icing and red hots, already on the table. We all sat down, and Consuela and I looked at Augustus.

"She was a spy, probably for the United States, probably for the CIA. She had been working undercover in mainland China, at a factory that makes microchips for all kinds of computers. Don't ask me about the details because I don't know exactly what she did or precisely the kinds of microchips the factory produced. She had a very low-level job at the factory, doing something on an assembly line. The products she worked on are various kinds of electronic microchips, vital parts found in just about everything you can think of. The electronics that this factory produces apparently go into everything important that we use on a daily basis — computers, phones, train engines, car engines, electronic monitoring equipment in hospitals, furnaces, Wi-Fi communications, and all kinds of equipment that public utilities use to keep the electricity flowing to businesses and households all over the world.

"The Chinese are our enemies as well as our competitors. A few years ago, they tried to poison our pets with their toxic dog food. They also produced some bad baby food that was sold in the U.S. and in China. Apparently, they have now upped their game, and they are producing faulty microchips for all the things I just listed, plus for things that can kill people like pacemakers and all kinds of medical devices. They are sabotaging everything we use, everything that contains these faulty electronic microchips. We have outsourced so much of our manufacturing that we've lost control over our future. We have, by default, turned over our quality control to them. Maybe it is because so few people in the United States speak Chinese. There are no doubt many reasons why we have failed to adequately monitor them. Too many things are made in China. We haven't been keeping track of all of it. It's the classic fox watching the hen house thing. Do you understand what I am telling you?" Augustus was angry. I'd never seen him angry before.

"The brave Taiwanese woman had been gathering information about this colossal sabotage of products made in China, products destined to be sold in the USA and in every other country that buys things from China. She was doing work that was vital to the national security of the United States and other countries around the world. She periodically brought this evidence out of China as microdots on her shoes. This was to have been her last mission. She thought the Chinese had discovered what she was doing, and she believed she was being watched. She had communicated these concerns to her handlers in Taiwan or Japan or wherever, and they'd decided she needed to be brought back to the United States. Her final report was on the shoe you found, Margaret.

"She was being smuggled out of China and into the United States with a group of illegals. She had spent days inside one of those shipping containers with a bunch of illegal immigrants who were being brought into the U.S. This container full of human trafficking victims made it undetected through the port of Los Angeles. The container was put on a freight train headed for Dallas. But somebody betrayed her. According to the people who were with her inside the shipping container, when the freight train reached Tucson, two men the others believed were Chinese agents, opened their container and took her out. The people she had traveled with and who were left inside the container, never saw her again. The two men who took her were almost certainly Communist Chinese thugs. Some of the others thought they'd heard her scream at one point, but they were locked inside the container until it reached Dallas.

Augustus was on a roll. I could tell he was terribly disturbed by everything he had to tell us. "A team from the FBI met the train. They knew which container the woman was supposed to be in, and they arrested all the people who were inside that container. But their main reason for stopping the shipment of illegals and arresting them wasn't there. After they interviewed the others who were in the container, they realized she'd been removed when the train stopped in Tucson. But nobody knew where she was. The FBI thinks she was questioned and tortured somewhere aboard the freight train. They think she died while she was being interrogated. When the train got to Marfa, they threw her away like a discarded piece of garbage.

"Now at least they know where her body is. She was brave, and she did her job brilliantly. Those who knew her and worked with her are devastated, but finally they know what happened to her. They are very grateful to you, Margaret, for finding the shoe and for making it possible to identify the Jane Doe who has been lying in the Austin, Texas morgue all these weeks. It is a very sad story, but you are the hero. She's a hero, too, since she never told the men who were torturing her that the information she had gathered was one of the polka dots on her shoe. She died before they found it and before they forced her to talk."

Augustus was shattered, spent from the phone calls he had been making all day and spent from telling us what had happened to the poor woman who'd been thrown off the train behind my house. I was completely drained just listening to the story. It was past time for Consuela to leave for the day, but she had been too captivated by Augustus's account to tear herself away. She got her purse and her coat, and without a word, she left to go home. There was nothing to say.

Augustus looked at me and sighed. He put his head down on the table. I let him rest and kept my mouth shut. Finally he looked up. His eyes were red. He was worn out, too.

"The world is a dangerous place, Margaret. I insulate myself from it most of the time because, as you have pointed out to me, I deal in the world of make believe. I help write fictional screen plays and make movies. My world is not real, and I guess there is a reason I choose to live in the land of fantasy. The real world has become so complicated and so mean, it's just too difficult for me to deal with."

Augustus was always so upbeat and so funny, it was painful for me to see him down and discouraged. Augustus was tough, but he was also very sensitive. "That's why we have turned this all over to the FBI. That's why there is such a thing as the FBI. This is their job. You did all the right things and called all the right people. It is not your concern anymore." I was trying to make him feel better.

"But I don't think I have made you or Ellery any safer with my phone calls and all the other things I've been working on. I may have made things worse. Now everyone is on alert. Too many people are thinking about and talking about that shoe. I think I have insulated your involvement from the discovery of the shoe, but who knows what will happen in this town. Everybody knows everything, almost before it's happened. I always try to do the right thing, and I'm glad the FBI now knows what happened to the woman from Taiwan. I'm afraid the high profile nature of this incident is going to have too much unpredictable fall out."

"Of course it will, Augustus. Someone may come after me, or Ellery, or you. And we will have to deal with that when the time comes. I am okay with everything you have done. Even if it means I am at greater risk, it's okay. Do you hear what I am saying? I wouldn't have had you do anything differently. I am glad I found the shoe, and I'm glad it found its way to where it was supposed to go."

"My whole effort was to try to protect you and Ellery."

"I know that, and I appreciate it. You did what was right,

so stop beating yourself up about this. Open that nice bottle of wine you brought with you. The potatoes are in the oven, and there's a salad in the refrigerator. The steaks are ready for grilling, and everything else is done. You and I are going to have a nice dinner. Put on some music, whatever will cheer you up and soothe your nerves. We should be celebrating that the lost shoe has finally found its home and done its job. Our Taiwanese hero has not died in vain. Let's rejoice in and be grateful for her sacrifice and be thankful that all the people who would have been injured or died as a result of the Chinese computer-chip treachery will now be saved. Ellery lived. Melody didn't die. There is a lot for us to be thankful for."

Augustus looked at me and smiled. "You are a glass all-the-way-full person, aren't you? The pool people set up a timer so your pool will begin to heat. Tomorrow night, you will be able to swim, if you want to. I'll turn on the grill now. Dinner will be ready in twenty minutes." Augustus lifted his glass. I lifted mine. Consuela had set up our small table in front of the fireplace in the living room. She had turned on the Christmas tree lights. She was determined that we were, in spite of ourselves, going to get into the Christmas spirit and enjoy ourselves.

The Past...
Philadelphia to Marfa

Chapter 21

*A*nnabeth Dryden had always loved art history. It
was her major during her undergraduate years at
Rutgers, and she went on to earn both a master's
degree and a PhD in art history at the University of Pennsylvania. Annabeth also loved Georgia O'Keeffe. The young
art student made three pilgrimages to New Mexico to see the
George O'Keeffe Museum in Santa Fe and to visit both of
O'Keeffe's homes, Ghost Ranch and the house in Abiquiu.
Annabeth had also visited the Stieglitz family compound at
Lake George in upstate New York, where O'Keeffe and Stieglitz had spent the summer and fall seasons. Even though the
Stieglitz family no longer owned the property, Annabeth had
prevailed upon the current owners to allow her to walk around
the grounds so she could absorb the atmosphere of the place
where the much-adored O'Keeffe had once lived and worked.

Georgia O'Keeffe died in March of 1986 at the age of
ninety-eight. Annabeth's PhD dissertation focused on how

the artist's work had changed and evolved over the years. O'Keeffe's life experiences influenced her work, as is true for all artists. Likewise, the different geographic locations where she lived had inspired changes in the subject matter and in the style of her art. Annabeth was particularly fascinated with the way Georgia O'Keeffe's physical disabilities had influenced her work towards the end of her life, as she'd aged and begun to lose her eyesight.

An in-depth study of Georgia O'Keeffe inevitably involved an in-depth study of Alfred Stieglitz. Annabeth was intrigued with how O'Keeffe's relationship with Stieglitz had shaped her artistic identity. Stieglitz had "discovered" O'Keeffe, and he'd done a great deal to enhance and promote her early career as an artist. But Annabeth was a feminist, and as she learned more about the relationship between O'Keeffe and Stieglitz, she grew to dislike Stieglitz and the way he had treated and abused this protégée who later became his wife. Understanding their relationship became the core of her graduate thesis, and by the time she had completed the work for her PhD, she knew a great deal about Alfred Stieglitz, his photography, his studio, his cadre of artistic friends, and his personality.

One story about Stieglitz that had particularly caught her attention concerned an event that took place before O'Keeffe moved permanently to New York City. Georgia and Alfred were corresponding, and Stieglitz gave O'Keeffe her first gallery exhibition in New York City in 1916. She spent her summers in New York City, but she had not yet decided to leave Columbia, South Carolina and live in New York year around.

In April of 1917, the French artist Marcel Duchamp had presented a men's urinal as an entry in the first exhibition of the Society of Independent Artists at Grand Central Palace in New York City. The United States had just entered the First World War, and the world was in turmoil.

Providing this background about what was going on in the art world during the period was important to Annabeth's discussion of O'Keeffe. The PhD student included the anecdote about Duchamp in her dissertation. She discussed the rejection of the urinal, which he had named *Fountain*. The controversy and confrontation surrounding *Fountain* exemplified the conflict among the various factions within the modernist art movement at that time. Chaos and transition were impacting the art world as well as other aspects of twentieth century life. This was the artistic environment into which the young Georgia O'Keeffe thrust herself in 1918. This was the creative world O'Keeffe became a part of when she moved to New York City to pursue her painting career.

Annabeth's doctoral thesis was titled *Georgia O'Keeffe's Journey: How the Places She Lived and the People She Knew Impacted and Transformed Her Art*. The dissertation's appendix included a copy of the photograph of Fountain signed, "R. Mutt 1917." Alfred Stieglitz's photograph of the urinal had appeared in an issue of the short-lived, avant-garde art magazine, *The Blind Man*. When Annabeth defended her dissertation in the late 1990s, she could not have known that in 2004, *Fountain* would be selected, by a panel of 500 distinguished artists and historians, as "the most influential piece of artwork of the twentieth century."

A copy of Annabeth Dryden's PhD dissertation was kept in the library at the University of Pennsylvania. Another copy was on file in the archives of the College of Fine Arts.

Darnell Anthony Jackson, formerly "Zeus Noonday Miracle," was the offspring of Sunshine Morning and Evening Moonlight. He was brought into the world by a midwife in a bathtub above his parents' store in Asbury Park, New Jersey in 1975 and named accordingly. Zeus was always a problem child. He was intelligent, but his behavior never conformed anywhere close enough to the norm for him to succeed in school, to play on an athletic team, or to get along in groups with other children. He was the product of the union of two people who were devoted to living an alternate lifestyle. In the 1970s, most of the rest of the world regarded his parents as "hippies."

It may have been the lax parenting style engaged in by his parents, Sunshine Morning and Evening Moonlight. It may have been the copious amounts of marijuana his mother had smoked during her pregnancy. Or, it might have just been the genetic cards that Zeus was dealt that contributed to his personality problems. Whatever the cause, Zeus Noonday Miracle was different from the beginning, and not just because of his unusual name.

Never married, his parents had split up when Zeus was a small child. His mother had tried to provide for her son by continuing to run her shop Cool Doodads in Asbury Park. Zeus's father was long gone. Sunshine Morning still had her CPA, and although being an accountant did not in any way fit with the revolutionary image she had of herself, she worked part-time for H&R Block during income tax season to put food on the table for her son and herself. Asbury Park had gone downhill, and Cool Doodads had become a junk shop. Few customers shopped there anymore.

Zeus's attitude and behavior were such that he was not able to attend the public schools. His mother found a place for him in an alternative educational environment, and he had a questionable measure of success in that setting. His one saving grace, academically, was that he loved to read, and this helped him earn a high score on the standardized SAT test, the College Board Examination. Because of his high scores on the tests and in spite of his lack of interpersonal skills, he was admitted to the University of Pennsylvania. He was granted a scholarship because of his mother's financial straits. Before he began his studies at Penn, he dropped the name of Zeus and all the rest of it and legally changed his name to Darnell Anthony Jackson. He struggled to fulfill the distribution requirements demanded by the University of Pennsylvania's College of Arts and Sciences. Before the second semester began, he transferred to the College of Fine Arts where the required math and science courses were less rigorous.

Darnell had decided he was an artist, and he took classes in painting, sculpture, and art history. Unable to complete his assignments on schedule, Darnell was placed on academic probation after his freshman year. During the first semester of his sophomore year, he didn't attend any of his classes. Instead, he chose to hang out in the college archives and read old master's theses and PhD dissertations. To say he lacked focus and direction would be an understatement, and when his mother died of kidney failure at age fifty-three, Darnell dropped out of college. He intended to live on the inheritance he thought he was going to receive from his mother's estate, but in fact she had very little to leave to her son.

Darnell had decided college was not really for him anyway, and he chose to return to Asbury Park to run Cool Doodads and live above the shop, as he and his mother had done while he was growing up. She had held things together for the two of them, and she had demanded very little of her lazy child. Sunshine Morning had been a good businesswoman, and when she and Evening Moonlight had opened Cool Doodads, she had decided to buy rather than rent the building. Over the years she had never failed to pay the monthly mortgage, and when she died, she almost owned the shop and the living quarters above it free and clear. Darnell had never helped his mother, either with the business or with the household chores. Consequently, he had no idea what was required to cook and clean and do his own laundry, not to mention what it took to run a business. All of it was too much work for the irresponsible Darnell Anthony Jackson.

The business was failing, and Darnell hated being tied down running a stupid store. He decided he was going to sell the building and the business, buy a motorcycle, a big Harley, and travel. He would live on the road, unencumbered by a store or a business or material possessions. He would be footloose and fancy-free. He found a buyer for the building, but one of the conditions of the sale was that he had to clean out and get rid of all the Cool Doodads junk.

Letting go of the stuff was easy, but Darnell got hung up on his mother's files. She had kept them meticulously in an antique oak filing cabinet. Somebody had once offered him a pretty good price for the filing cabinet, so he knew it was worth something. He was trying to turn everything he could into cash, so he decided to clean out the filing cabinet and sell it, too. But he couldn't let it go until he was certain there was nothing of value left in it. He imagined that his mother might have kept some money in her files, so he had to compulsively go through every file before he threw it away. He eventually found three dollar bills in one file, the refund a customer had never come back to collect. Being the reader that he was, he got bogged down going through the files as he read through each one.

His mother had photographed every piece of junk she'd bought or found to sell at Cool Doodads. She had kept her photos in the files. She had made a file for each category of treasures she had in her inventory. Whenever something was sold, she had precisely recorded each sale and put a copy of the sales receipt in the file with the picture of the item. When Darnell read through the file labeled "Plumbing Fixtures," he came across the photograph and the sales receipt for the porcelain urinal his mother had sold to a Philadelphia matron in April of 1973. The picture of the urinal rang a bell with Darnell, although he couldn't remember why. He knew he'd seen a picture of the urinal someplace before, but he wasn't able to recall where he'd seen it. He thought he'd read something about the urinal when he'd been a student at Penn. He remembered it because it had been such an odd story, and the whereabouts of the urinal remained shrouded in mystery.

Something in his subconscious told him to save the file, that it was significant, that the urinal might be important for some reason. He saved only the one file on plumbing fixtures and got rid of everything else, including the store and the old oak filing cabinet his mother had loved so much. He rented a small storage unit and left a few things in it. He bought his fancy motorcycle and set off to see the world. Because he was not a good money manager, he ran out of money sooner rather than later. He turned to a life of odd jobs, burglary, and shoplifting to keep from becoming completely homeless.

It was not until several years after *Fountain* had been declared the most influential piece of art of the twentieth century that Darnell became aware of the value of the urinal which had once been sold in his mother's shop. When he didn't have the money to stay any place else, Darnell often slept in the public library of whatever town he happened to find himself. He'd always liked to hang out in libraries, and he had figured out ways to hide himself from night watchmen and security guards inside the miles of book shelves. He liked to read, and some nights he would stay up almost all night, reading old newspapers and magazines.

It was during one of these late nights that Darnell came across an article in the Sunday edition of *The New York Times Magazine* from 2005. The article was about *"Fountain,"* the Alfred Duchamp urinal that had caused such a stir when it had appeared, or had tried to appear, at an exhibit in New York in 1917. Darnell read the article, and when he saw a photograph of the famous plumbing fixture, he realized that he knew exactly what had happened to that missing, famous, and priceless piece of utilitarian art. He realized that he might be the only person in the entire world who knew what had happened to *Fountain*. At least he knew where the piece of controversial sculpture had been in April of 1973, and, he knew exactly where it had gone after it had left Cool Doodads. He also thought he remembered that he had read something about *Fountain* in somebody's PhD dissertation he'd come across when he'd been wiling away his time reading in the archives at the College of Fine Arts at the University of Pennsylvania.

If he could track down the piece of junk his mother had sold to a woman who lived in the Philadelphia suburbs, he would be a very wealthy man, richer than he could ever imagine. He would never have to shoplift from Walmart or Safeway again. He would never have to sleep in another library. He would be rich beyond his wildest dreams. Darnell finally had a purpose in life. He was going to find the historic and illusive *Fountain*. He had a street address and a phone number in the Philadelphia area. He would drive his Harley to Bala Cynwyd, Pennsylvania and retrieve the sculpture from Roberta Mutt Van Devries.

Chapter 22

*D*arnell Anthony Jackson rode his motorcycle to
Bala Cynwyd. He had done some research about the
property at 68 Bluestone Road in that Philadelphia
suburb. Searching online documents, he found that in 2000,
the property had been transferred from Roberta Mutt Van
Devries's estate to Henry B. and Vanessa L. Crimmons. In 2012
Henry and Vanessa Crimmons had sold the house to Samuel R.
Malick and Josiah J. Delacourt. As of 2019, Samuel and Josiah
appeared to be the current owners of the property. When
Darnell checked to see who had lived in the neighborhood in
the 1980s and 1990s and still lived there, he discovered that
Roberta Van Devries's next door neighbors, the Calloways, had
bought their house at 72 Bluestone Road in 1982 and had not
moved away. At least the deed had not been transferred from
the Calloways. They would be older, but they would remember
Roberta. The Calloways could be a source of information
for Darnell.

He drove around the property at 68 Bluestone Road and saw the yard needed a lot of work. Samuel and Josiah were not into their landscaping. The grass was cut, but the bushes had not been trimmed for years. There was an elaborate and expensive swing set in the back yard, but no one had paid any attention to the gardens in a very long time. Darnell decided he would present himself to the homeowners as a gardener. He wanted to get to know the neighbors who lived at 72 and figured the best way to do that was to have a job doing yardwork for the people who lived next door at 68.

Darnell had flyers made up and business cards printed in the name of "James Donovan Yardscapes." He bought three prepaid cell phones. One was the phone for James Donovan Yardscapes, and the other two were for references. He listed two fictitious names with the numbers of the cell phones on the flyers. These would be two references for his prospective clients to call to check on the quality of the yardwork he did. He would, of course, answer all three phones if and when the potential client called. If the client called to check on the quality of his work, he would be able to give himself a glowing recommendation.

It took a couple of weeks, but Darnell finally convinced Samuel and Josiah they could afford his landscaping services. Darnell could be a bit of a con man when he wanted to be, and he was putting his all into the search for the urinal. Sam and Jos were a gay couple with two adopted sons. They were both busy lawyers and had hectic, even frazzled, lives, trying to work and raise a family. Neither Sam nor Jos was very organized, and their house was a mess. They were devoted and enthusiastic parents and spent a lot of time doing things with their kids, but they spent hardly any time at all taking care of their house or their yard.

They were almost grateful when Darnell appeared at the door and made his proposal to clean up their landscaping. He offered his services at such a reasonable rate, they couldn't say no. Darnell knew almost nothing about yardwork, but he knew his way around a library. He had studied up on pruning and planting. It was May, so he would put in some colorful annuals and give the guys a lot of bang for their buck. He would be long gone once he had the information he wanted.

Darnell rented an old pick-up truck and had signs for his business made up for the doors. He cut back the overgrown brush and put in some ground cover. He pulled a decade's worth of weeds from the flower beds and spread some mulch around. He planted red and pink impatiens along the walkway that led to the front door of the house. In just a few days, he'd made a major improvement in the yard at 68 Bluestone Road.

He was watching the house at 72 very closely, and after a couple of weeks, he knew when Mrs. Calloway came and went in her very old navy blue Mercedes 450 SEL. He had never seen Mr. Calloway and decided the man must be deceased. If Mrs. Calloway was a widow, she would be lonely and even more eager to talk to him. One afternoon, when he knew she was going to be home, Darnell purposely cut his hand with his pruning shears. He wrapped a rag around the cut, which was bleeding profusely, and walked next door. Mrs. Calloway seemed like a nice woman, and he thought she would be concerned about his injury and ask him to come inside her house. He knocked on her back door.

"Oh, my goodness. What's happened to you? That looks terrible." Irene Calloway was alarmed when she saw all the blood.

"It's not as bad as it looks, but it is making a mess. I'm James Donovan, and I work for Samuel and Josiah. I do their yard work, and it looks like I've been very clumsy today. They aren't home, and I need to do something about this cut."

"Come in, come in. I'm so glad to meet you, James. I'm Irene Calloway. Let me find some antiseptics and some bandages to get you fixed up." Mrs. Calloway went to her first floor bathroom and gathered the supplies she needed to clean and bandage his injury. Things were going as planned for Darnell. "I've been watching you over there, cleaning things out and pruning and putting in the annuals." Irene Calloway had said exactly what Darnell had hoped she would say. He knew Mrs. Calloway had been watching him, and he knew she cared about her own yard. She had a regular landscaping service that came twice a week, and her garden was beautiful.

"I'm so thrilled the boys finally decided to do something about their terrible yard. It was such an eyesore. Most people in this neighborhood are so particular about their gardens and the way their yards look. It was embarrassing that they wouldn't do anything about theirs."

"I love working in the dirt. There's something almost magical about planting flowers or bulbs and then watching them grow and come to life." Darnell knew what to say to win over this older woman who loved her flowers.

"You are so right. Some people love to garden, and others don't. I've so enjoyed educating myself about plants and bushes and herbs over the years. I love it, but Sam and Josh have other priorities. "

"Somebody had an extensive garden over there at one time. I can see where the plants were very carefully laid out. It's a shame all that was neglected and allowed to go to seed."

"I couldn't agree with you more. The last people who lived there tried to keep the garden going, but they were just too busy. Both Henry and Vanessa, the Crimmons, worked full time, and they had three kids in private schools. I think it was a stretch for them to pay all those tuitions. They just didn't have the time to work in the garden themselves or the money to pay anyone else to do it for them. Then the boys moved in. I adore them and their two little ones. They are terrific parents and neighbors, but they are just the worst about taking care of the house and the yard. I don't want to gossip, but I guess I am." Mrs. Calloway laughed as she scolded herself.

"Who planned and put in the herb garden? It must have been a long time ago, but some of the herbs are still producing. It's amazing. Mint and rosemary take over everything, wherever they are, it seems." Darnell liked to show off his knowledge about herbs. He'd picked up everything he knew on the internet and in the library.

"That was Mrs. Van Devries, Roberta, who planted the herb garden. She worked in her gardens all the time. She was just so avid. She taught me a lot. I was so sad when she got too old to take care of things anymore. I guess it happens to all of us, but she was such a creative person. She always had an eye and unusual ideas for how she wanted her garden to look. I admired her. I miss her."

"Tell me about Mrs. Van Devries. She sounds like an interesting woman who was a very devoted gardener. Did she have a family?" Darnell's wound had been bandaged, and Irene had brought him a glass of iced tea. He wondered how much longer he could keep the woman talking. Because she lived alone, Darnell knew she was probably eager for company and welcomed someone to talk to.

"Her husband was an investment banker. Very staid and very formal. He was also very rich. Roberta was more of a free spirit. I could never see them as a couple, really, but you know what they say about opposites. He died ten years before Roberta died. They had one daughter, Marjorie. She grew up in the house, but she went off to college in 1982, the year Vincent and I bought this house. We saw her occasionally when she was home for vacations, but she was busy with her own friends and activities. Then she married and moved to Tulsa, Oklahoma. I got to know her a littler bit better after Roberta died. Marjorie was here cleaning out the house, and she used to come over once in a while."

"It must have been a big job, cleaning out the house by herself, without any help. It's a large house."

"It was a big job for her. I tried to help her out when I could. I was younger then and could still lift and do things. Marjorie's husband never came to help. He was a very self-centered man, and I don't know why she married him in the first place."

"It was very kind of you to help her go through her mother's things. It's an emotional journey, and it is also a lot of physical work, sorting out what to keep and what to get rid of."

"Roberta had some very valuable antiques and rugs, and Marjorie kept most of the good stuff. She gave away a lot of things to the Goodwill and other charities. She and I had a heck of a time getting that, pardon my French, urinal, out of the garden, though." Irene Calloway almost blushed.

"Urinal? In the garden?"

"Oh, yes. It was one of Roberta's prizes. She had it buried in the herb garden, so you couldn't see what it really was. I mean, you really couldn't tell that it belonged in a bathroom. She had it planted with rosemary, and the rosemary did beautifully, year after year. It never froze, even during our

worst winters. Roberta always laughed when she said it was
because of the 'special pot' it was in. I don't know about
that. She was a bit eccentric, our Roberta. She told me how
she had discovered this porcelain convenience at some shop
in New Jersey, and you would have thought she'd found
the Mona Lisa. Roberta's maiden name was Mutt, you see,
and the plumbing fixture that she turned into a planter had
'R. Mutt' written on the side of it. It also had 1917 painted
on there. Roberta was born in 1917. She scraped away the
dirt around the side of the porcelain once and showed me
her name and the date, painted right on it. It really was her
name, and it really did say 1917. She said it was destiny that
she bought the fixture and had it in her herb garden. She said
good fortune had painted her name and birthday on it, long
before she'd laid eyes on it."

"So Marjorie didn't leave the planter behind when she
moved her mother's things out?"

"Oh, no. We really should have left it in the ground. It was
almost impossible to get out. Marjorie knew how important
that planter was to her mother, and she insisted on digging it
up and taking it with her to Tulsa. We tugged and tugged at
that thing. It was heavy, and full of dirt. I thought we would
never get it out of the ground. But Marjorie was determined
to have it. I asked her what in the world she was going to do
with it, and she said she would figure out something." Mrs.
Calloway was clearing up the bandages and other things she
had used to attend to Darnell's wound.

"Do you stay in touch with Marjorie Van Devries?"

"Her name is Cannon now, Marjorie Van Devries
Cannon. But she's divorced. She still lives in Tulsa. I get
a Christmas card from her every now and then. She had
some emotional problems after her divorce. She was very

depressed and wasn't taking care of herself. She didn't pay her bills and didn't take care of other things. She said she had financial problems, and I always wondered why that was. Everyone thought her parents were rich as Croesus. She inherited all their money as well as the money from selling her parents' house. Maybe her husband gambled and lost all of her money. Who knows? Anyway, she may have gone back to using her maiden name, but the last time she sent me a Christmas card, the return address still said Cannon. She's had a serious problem with depression, you know. Depression can do strange things to people. Very sad. Never had any children."

"She still lives in Tulsa?"

"Yes, as far as I know. I do know she got to keep the house when she and her husband divorced, and she stayed right there. I feel sorry for her."

"I've kept you way too long, Mrs. Calloway. Thank you for fixing up my hand so nicely. And I enjoyed hearing about the neighbors and about the gardens."

"James, it has been my pleasure. Please come over again and gossip with me. I know where all the bodies...and the porcelain conveniences...are buried." Ms. Calloway giggled at her joke and shook Darnell's hand that wasn't bandaged. He went out the back door. He had the information he needed. He was ecstatic. He'd thought it would take him weeks and weeks to find out what he wanted to know, but it had taken only one session with a lonely and talkative older woman who loved to garden. He might still have a long way to go before he located the Duchamp urinal, but he thought he was off to a great start.

Darnell returned his pickup truck to the rental agency that afternoon; made a stop at the library where he kept his duffle bag of clothes, hidden on a shelf behind the books by Chaucer, which nobody ever read anymore; and left for Tulsa on his motorcycle. Irene Calloway and Samuel and Josiah would never know why the landscape guy, who charged such reasonable rates, had suddenly disappeared. He hadn't even stayed around long enough to pick up his last paycheck.

Chapter 23

*I*t wasn't difficult to find where Marjorie Van Devries Cannon lived in Tulsa. She was listed online in the white pages. The house was a split level in an older neighborhood, and it was in serious disrepair. The roof needed work, and the vinyl siding was covered with mildew. The trim on the house was desperately in need of paint. The yard was a mess. The house screamed neglect.

Darnell wondered if Marjorie still had the urinal. He figured she would be in her sixties by now. After he had done his reconnaissance around the house, he knew she hadn't planted rosemary in it, and she didn't have it in her yard in Tulsa, Oklahoma. He had a plan to find out what had happened to the urinal, and it did not involve doing any yard work for Marjorie.

Darnell wanted to get inside Marjorie's house to look around. He broke into her garage one night, but the urinal wasn't there. He was afraid to go into the house itself for fear of waking her or setting off an alarm. He would have to wait until she wasn't home and then break in to do a thorough search. Looking for something inside somebody's house can be a noisy task. The problem was, Marjorie never left her house. Irene Calloway had said she had a problem with depression, and that certainly seemed to be the case.

Darnell had observed, when he was poking around in her garage, that the tags on Marjorie's Ford Taurus had expired eighteen months earlier. He wondered if she was aware that the registration on her car was out of date. Darnell had been watching the house, and he knew that Marjorie only drove her car to the drug store to pick up medication. She would be gone for forty-five minutes at most. She had her groceries delivered, and she ordered a lot of stuff from Amazon. She was almost always at home. He would have to use his creativity to find a way to get inside her house to look around.

If the urinal/planter had not meant so much to her mother, Darnell figured Marjorie would have gotten rid of it by now. Because it had her mother's name on it, kind of, Marjorie had probably kept it. He hoped that it was here. But where was it? Only Marjorie would be able to tell him that, and he had to figure out a way to make her give him the information. He decided he would have to confront her in person. He was not a violent kind of guy by nature. He was more passive than active in everything he did, but the stakes were high for him now. He was on a treasure hunt, and if he had any hopes of finding the urinal, he would have to rise to the occasion.

Marjorie didn't seem to have friends or acquaintances who were likely to stop by the house for a visit. This was a good thing for what Darnell had planned. He decided he would break into her house at night and drug her while she was sleeping.

He knew nothing about drugs or how to immobilize anybody, but he fell back on his ability to do research and learn how to do things by reading up on them on the internet and in the library. During his years on the road, Darnell had acquired some expertise at shoplifting and burglary. He had his own set of lock picks. After studying what to do, Darnell broke into a pharmacy after closing hours and helped himself to several hypodermic needles and the drugs he thought he needed to restrain Marjorie Van Devries Cannon.

Darnell had never done anything like this before, but he'd done his reading and thought he'd found out what he needed to know. He had read up on police procedures and knew he didn't want to leave any fingerprints, hair, or any other DNA evidence behind. He knew he had to wear a ski mask, a head covering and latex gloves when he interrogated Marjorie. He already had a black knit ski mask with small eye slits, the kind of mask that revealed as little as possible of his face. He bought a shower cap to contain his unruly hair and a box of plastic gloves. In addition to the hypodermic needles and drugs he had stolen, he armed himself with rope and duct tape and a gag for Marjorie's mouth. Darnell decided he was ready.

Darnell broke into Marjorie's home without any problem. Her place was a mess. Marjorie neglected her housework, and there was paper clutter everywhere, on every surface in sight. Darnell briefly considered drugging Marjorie and searching the house while she was unconscious, but he had a feeling what he was looking for wasn't there. It was a split level and didn't really have a basement. He would have to find out from Marjorie herself what she had done with the urinal.

He crept up the short flight of stairs to the bedroom level of the house and waited outside the room where Marjorie slept. He could see she spent most of her time in her bedroom. There was the smell of unwashed sheets and the smell of someone who didn't bathe regularly. If her father had been such a rich guy, Darnell couldn't understand why his only daughter was living like this. Irene Calloway had wondered the same thing. Had her ex-husband made bad investments with her money and lost it all? Did the woman have a gambling addiction? Had she squandered all of her parents' fortune on internet poker? Or on internet stock speculation? She didn't seem to have a drinking problem. Did she have money sitting in idle bank accounts and was just too depressed to pay her bills and take care of her daily needs?

He crept closer to her bed and one of her arms was hanging over the side. He had the needle ready, and he jabbed it into her arm. She went limp, and he knew the first step in the interrogation process had succeeded. She was not a large woman, so Darnell was able to drag her, even in her unconscious state, to a straight-back chair that was already in the bedroom. He threw the dirty clothes that were piled on the chair onto the floor. He stuck the gag into Marjorie's mouth and wound the duct tape once around her head. He would have to remove the duct tape to allow her to speak and answer his questions, so he spent most of his time and effort securing Marjorie's legs and arms to the chair. She would never be able to get way unless he cut her loose from her bonds.

Then he waited. He didn't know exactly how long the dose of tranquilizers he'd given her would keep her unconscious. How many hours would it be before she woke up and could talk to him? He brought another chair into the bedroom from Marjorie's dining room and sat there facing her, waiting for her to wake up. It took a while for her to come around and realize what was happening. When she finally saw the man in the ski mask, a shower cap, and latex gloves, she thought he was there to rape her. She began to cry. She whimpered through the gag and the duct tape.

Darnell wanted her to shut up. "I don't want to hurt you, Marjorie. If you promise not to scream or make any unnecessary noise, I'm going to remove the duct tape and the gag. I need some information from you. I won't let you go until you've told me what I want to know. Nod your head if you promise not to scream." Marjorie nodded her head, and Darnell ripped the duct tape from her mouth.

Marjorie began begging him not to hurt her. "I'll tell you anything you want to know. Just please don't hurt me. How do you know my name?"

"I'm looking for something that I know you have, or at least I know you used to have it. You brought something your mother used as a planter in her Philadelphia garden to Tulsa. Your mother used it for herbs. Do you remember that porcelain planter?"

Marjorie's eyes were wide with fear, but she whispered, "Yes, I remember it."

"Where is it, Marjorie? As soon as you tell me where it is and I have it in my hands, I will let you go."

"I don't know where it is now. I really don't. It was in a storage unit I rented for years. I was always going to go through the unit and clean it out, but I never took the time to do it. Then I lost everything that was in it because I didn't pay the rent. I was really depressed. I had the money in the bank to pay the rental fees, but I was confused and sleeping all the time. I wasn't keeping up with any of my bills. I kept putting the bills in a pile, and then I would forget about them. I didn't pay the monthly rental on the storage unit for a year or so. If you don't pay, they get rid of the stuff in your unit so they can rent it to somebody else. When I was able to get myself together again to pay my bills and take care of myself, I called them. They told me I hadn't paid, and they'd cleared my stuff out. I was sorry for a little while, but there wasn't much of anything in there I really wanted anyway. My mom's planter was in the storage unit, so I don't know what happened to it after the storage place got rid of it all."

"So you are telling me, you didn't pay your storage fees, and you lost everything that you had paid to store for all those years? Why would you do that?" Darnell had thought his search was at an end, and now he realized things had become more complicated.

"Please let me go. I don't know where the planter is. Why do you want it anyway? It was a piece of junk. It was valuable to my mother because it had her name and the year of her birth painted on the side. Please let me go."

Darnell was quiet for a few minutes while he was deciding what to do about Marjorie. "What was the name and address of the storage facility where you rented your unit? When was the last time you paid the fees? When did you call and ask about your stuff and they gave you the news that your unit had been cleared out?"

"I can't remember the name of the place, but it was way out on the Gilcrease Expressway, kind of out in the country. Or at least it was out in the country when I moved my mother's stuff in there years ago. I haven't been back. I paid the fees for about eight years, until after my divorce was final. That would have been about 2009 or 2010. I must have called in 2010, or maybe it was 2011. They'd cleaned out my unit by then."

"You can't remember the name of the storage facility? Do you have any receipts or anything that might have the name on it? What was the number of your unit?"

"I probably do have receipts from when I was paying the rent, but I couldn't possibly find them in this mess. But I remember my unit number was 68, the same number as my parents' address on Bluestone Road, the address of the house where I grew up. I had my choice of units, and I chose #68. That's all I know. Please let me go."

"I will let you go after you've remembered the name of the storage facility. I have to have that name. Would you remember the name of the place, if I found it in the phone book?" Darnell knew phone books were not like they used to be, and the storage facility could have changed its name a couple of times since 2010. He looked around the house for an old phone book. He found one from 2007 and began going through the yellow pages. He read off the names of storage facilities that were located on the Gilcrease Expressway. Finally Marjorie thought he'd read one that sounded familiar.

"That's the one, I think, B & A Storage Park. I remember writing checks to them. Yes, that's the name. The address must be in the phone book, too. So now you have everything you need. Please untie me and let me go."

Darnell thought he had the information he needed, but he was suddenly overcome with rage that he didn't have the urinal itself. He'd counted on having it in his hands by now. He was furious with Marjorie Cannon for not taking care of her bills and for failing to keep the urinal safe. He grabbed the lamp from the bedside table and hit her across the face with it. She began to scream, and he hit her again and again with the lamp. The light bulb in the lamp broke and cut her face. Blood began to pour down her neck. Then the ceramic base of the lamp shattered, and the sharp pieces of the base cut even more deeply into Marjorie's flesh. He had told her he wouldn't hurt her, but she hadn't delivered the goods. He'd promised not to harm her, but only if she told him where the urinal was. She hadn't told him. He hit her again. She'd fainted by now, and blood was flowing from her face. He wound more duct tape around her head and mouth and pushed the chair over on its side.

Darnell was now out of control, and he thought about killing the stupid woman. Nobody cared about her anyway. He decided not to kill her, but he would leave her tied up here in her bedroom. She may or may not ever get free of her bonds and be able to call for help. He would be long gone, anyway. He would leave her here to either die or save herself. He threw a few more things around the bedroom to make it look like a robbery. His adrenalin was surging, and he was still furious when he left the split-level. He walked to his motorcycle which he'd hidden in the bushes three blocks away. No one would ever be able to trace this home invasion to him. He had no connection to Marjorie Van Devries Cannon, none at all.

He couldn't get back into the library to sleep for the night. He really didn't want to pay for a motel for just a few hours, but he was so tired. The burst of adrenalin that had given him the urge to batter Marjorie with the lamp had passed. It left him spent, and he needed to rest. He found a Motel 6 on Deerborn Parkway and got a room for the few hours that were left of the night. He would retrieve his duffle from the library the next day. Depending on what he learned at the B & A Storage Park, he might have to spend a few days in Tulsa. He fell asleep immediately, enjoying a real bed rather than a library shelf for the first time in weeks.

Darnell's violent encounter with Marjorie had left him with no guilty feelings at all. It was remarkable that this man who espoused non-violence and was the progeny of two people who belonged to the "Peace and Love" generation could have displayed such a horrendously brutal side of himself. He had always floated from one thing to another, without focus, without intensity. His life was rootless and airy. But he had become a man obsessed—obsessed with finding great riches. He was driven for the first time in his life. Driven by greed and by his own narcissism, he saw no reason to put any limits on his behavior. His compulsion to find *Fountain* had allowed him to free his dark side. He felt no guilt for anything he had done. He had no regrets. He only looked ahead to finding his great prize.

Chapter 24

*T*he next morning, after he'd retrieved his belongings from the library, Darnell drove to the address he
had for the B & A Storage Park. The storage facility
was no longer there. It had been replaced by a new, large,
and very nice-looking assisted living campus. There was a
small sign along the road where B & A Storage Park used to
be. It said the name had been changed to TOK Mini-Storage,
and the business had relocated to another address, at 39528
North Barberra Avenue. Darnell rode his motorcycle to TOK
Mini-Storage. He was becoming discouraged. This wild goose
chase was turning out to be much more complicated than he'd
ever imagined. But he was not giving up. The more he thought
about what he would find in the pot at the end of the rainbow,
the more determined he was to continue his search.

He pulled into the parking lot at TOK Mini-Storage
and struck up a conversation with the woman who was on
duty in the office. "I'm in the process of relocating from

Philadelphia. My problem is, I've sold my condo in Philly but haven't yet found a place to live here in Tulsa. I'm still looking and haven't seen anything I want to buy. I need to move my stuff out of my Philadelphia condo before the settlement and store it somewhere. I'll be driving a U-Haul, and your facility here is convenient to where I hope to find my new place. Can you give me a price list of monthly rates for the different sizes of storage units?"

"The sizes of our units and the monthly rates are posted here." She pointed to a printed list on the wall beside her desk. She wasn't chatty, and Darnell was going to have to work to get any information out of her. The nameplate on her desk said her name was Gloria.

He looked at the list on the wall. "I need some help deciding what size unit I'm going to need. I don't really know whether I need the 8 X 10 or the 8 X 20. How do I determine that?"

"It depends on how many rooms you plan to move." Gloria reached for a stack of brochures that sat on a nearby shelf. This is a pamphlet that will give you some guidelines about how to estimate how much you'll be bringing to put in storage."

Darnell took the brochure and looked it over. "You know, I watch that show *Storage Wars* on TV all the time. It's fascinating. You really get into the characters, the different buyers who are bidding on the units. And, I've gotten so I try to figure out what's in the units, just like the bidders are trying to do."

"Yeah, everybody who comes in here talks about that show. I don't watch it myself. It's too much like being at work, if you know what I mean."

"How long have you worked here, Gloria?"

"I've worked here about six months. It's just a temporary position until I finish my course at the Vo-Tech. I'm studying to be an LPN."

"Good luck with that. Nursing is a good field these days."

"Thanks, I like to help people. It makes me feel good."

"How long has TOK been in this location? The units look pretty new. I lived in this area years ago, before I took the job in Philly, and my family used to deal with a company called B & A Storage Park. Did TOK buy them out or what?"

"The guy who used to own B & A Storage Park died, and his daughter didn't want to run the business. She got a great offer from a company that builds and runs assisted living places all over the country. They're nice ones, and I hear it's expensive to live there. Anyway, she gets this great offer on the property, but she's got a hundred storage units full of all these people's stuff. How do you go about getting rid of all that mess? Anyway, some young guy bought this land way out here on North Barberra and built these units. The people who were renting the units from B & A had three months to move their stuff out themselves or have it moved by the new company, TOK. Most of them just let TOK do the moving. The owner of TOK moved the stuff out of almost every one of those B & A units. Can you believe it? Boy am I glad I wasn't working here then. The people who were here during the big move are still talking about what a nightmare it was. People's stuff got mixed together. Stuff got put in the wrong units. Lots of stuff got lost. They are still sorting out some of it."

"Wow, that's quite a story. I'm curious about what happens when somebody doesn't pay the rent on their unit, when they abandon it. Is it like on TV? Do people come and bid on the stuff in the units?"

"No, there's nothing quite that glamorous going on around here. No TV cameras and no celebrities. The owner has a man from Texas who comes and cleans out the stuff for him. The junkman takes whatever is in the unit as his payment for cleaning it out. The owner gets rid of the stuff in the abandoned unit, so he can rent it out again. The Texan gets the contents for his open market, or whatever he calls it."

"This guy from Texas, has he been cleaning out the units for a long time?"

"I don't know. Like I said, I've only worked here six months. I think he has, though. My opinion is that they should have an auction and make some money on the stuff that's in the units, but nobody's asking me. I guess the previous owner at B & A liked the arrangement he had with the man from Texas because he always came within a day or two of when he was called. He would show up the next day or the day after that with a crew of workers, and they would have the abandoned units cleared in a few hours. That's a lot less hassle for the owner than having an auction and all of that. Who knows what that Texan got when he cleaned out the abandoned units? He might have struck it rich a time or two. Anyway, the man who now owns TOK liked the arrangement the old guy'd had with the Texas junk man, so he decided just to stay with that. The Texas guy still comes every few months or whenever he's called. "

"What's the name of the company from Texas?"

"I have no idea."

"What city in Texas is the junk man from?"

"Dallas?" Her tone of voice let him know she wasn't sure, and Darnell wondered if she'd said Dallas because that's the first place that always comes to mind when somebody mentions Texas.

"The name of the guy from Dallas, Texas, is it in the computer?"

"Probably, but that's not part of my job. I just book rentals, get credit card numbers, and fill out a lot of paperwork."

"Who does that job? Who makes the arrangements to get rid of the stuff in the units?"

"The owner, I guess. Why do you want to know all of this? Are you from *Storage Wars*?"

"No, I was just interested in what happened to the stuff in the units when people don't pay their rent."

"I told you. The guy from Texas comes with his 18-wheeler and loads it up. That's the whole story. It works for the owner, and it's not part of my job." Gloria was now getting bored or annoyed or both, and Darnell needed to move on. He doubted that the records for B & A Storage Park from 2010 were still on the computer, but he would be back tonight to try to find out.

The storage facility office closed at 8:00 p.m. but people who had the code to the main gate could have access to their units 24/7. Darnell found a diner where he could get something to eat, and then he went back to his motel to sleep. When it was dark, he drove back to North Barberra Avenue, parked his motorcycle in a grove of trees, and walked to TOK. It was fairly easy to scale the fence. Storage facilities were more worried about a big truck full of someone's hijacked valuables driving out of the place than they were about one guy climbing over the fence to get inside. Getting into the office was even easier than climbing the fence. Darnell put on a new pair of latex gloves. As far as he knew, his fingerprints weren't in any system, but he wasn't taking chances. He would leave no traces that he'd ever been inside the TOK office.

The computer was already on, of course. There were no passwords required to get into the files he wanted to see. If he'd been looking for credit card information, he imagined the security was better and would require him to put in a password. As it was, he just looked in the documents file, and there it was, as big as could be, Texas Open Market Treasures. It had its own file and Darnell opened it. He had been in the office less than five minutes when he had the information he needed. He'd thought he would have to search the computer to find Marjorie Cannon's file for unit #68 from 2009. But luck was with him tonight, and all he had to do was look in the Texas Open Market Treasures file.

Leonard Bundy had been picking up the contents of the abandoned units for more than twenty years. The date of every one of his pick-ups was recorded in the file. The numbers of the units he had cleaned out on each trip were also listed. Easy peasy! Right there in the computer file was an entry that said Leonard Bundy had cleaned out Unit #68 on December 17, 2009. He had cleaned out five other units that day, and he'd left the B & A Storage Park premises at exactly 4:32 p.m.

Darnell now knew exactly where *Fountain* had gone, and he knew approximately when it had gone on sale at Texas Open Market Treasures. He was almost afraid to believe it had been so easy. Just when he couldn't pat himself on the back hard enough, he saw trouble. Trouble had arrived in the form of the blinking red and blue lights of a cop car, waiting outside the automatic gate. Darnell figured he had inadvertently done something that had triggered an alarm. Had he missed a camera or a motion detector? Maybe it was his search on the computer? Maybe somebody had seen a shadow moving around in the office. Most likely he had tripped a silent alarm somewhere. There was probably a way for somebody to open the gate remotely to allow the cop car to enter. Darnell had to get out of the office and out of the TOK storage facility ASAP.

Darnell thought he knew his way around computers, but he had no hacking skills. Hackers could hide, after the fact, whatever it was they'd been doing on somebody else's computer. Darnell didn't have a clue how to hide what file he'd been looking at. If anyone wanted to know exactly what he'd been researching, he had led them right to Texas Open Market Treasures. He quickly opened two more files and typed in some gibberish. He didn't really know how to confuse the computer or whoever would be looking at the computer. He pushed some control and delete keys, hoping he'd thrown off whoever would be trying to figure out what he'd been up to.

Darnell let himself out of the office and stayed low as he crawled through the skimpy bushes that somebody thought made the office look like it was landscaped. There were no cars in the parking lot, and there was no place to hide. The cop car was now inside the perimeter of the storage facility. Darnell had to get out, and the only way to escape was to climb back over the fence. It had been easy climbing in when no one had been watching and he hadn't had any time pressure. Now he was going to have to make a run for it and climb over the fence again, but the cops would see him for sure. Or, he could try to hide in the rear of the storage facility and hope the cops wouldn't find him when they searched the place. He decided he couldn't take that chance. He would have to make a run for it and go back over the fence.

Darnell wasn't in terrible shape, but he wasn't in great shape either. He had struggled a little bit climbing over the fence to get in, but now he was stressed and afraid he wouldn't make it back over in time. He made his way to the rear of the storage units, as far as possible from where the cop car was parked. He ran for the fence to get a head start on his jump. He grabbed the metal of the chain link fence and tried to pull himself up. But he lost his grip and fell backwards, back onto the concrete of the storage lot. He fell on his left shoulder, and he felt it tear and twist. It burned like a thousand fires. He got to his feet and ran at the fence again. He tried to jump up but couldn't grab hold of anything with the arm or hand on his injured side. The excruciating shoulder pain made his left side useless. He was going to have to depend on his right arm alone to help him climb over a fifteen-foot-high chain link fence.

He was almost over the top of the fence when the spotlight from the cop car shined its light on him. Somebody shouted, "Police! Stop or I'll shoot." Of course Darnell was not about to stop, and someone did shoot. As he dropped to the ground on the other side of the fence, Darnell's right hand was hit by a bullet from the cop's gun. He picked himself up and ran as fast as he could away from the fence. He didn't know how far away he had to run so that another bullet wouldn't hit him. He found himself on the wrong side of the storage facility property from where his motorcycle was hidden, so he had to run all the way around the perimeter to get to his ride. His left arm was hopeless, and his right hand was dripping with blood.

He made it to his bike. In spite of having serious injuries to both of his upper limbs, he roared away down North Barberra Avenue. As soon as he could, he got off the main road and wandered around, in neighborhoods and out into the countryside, until he was sure he'd shaken his pursuers. He was thankful he was staying at a motel and not in the library tonight. Blood all over the library would have caused a problem. Blood in the motel room would also cause him trouble, but it would be easier to clean up the blood at the motel. His shoulder was so painful, he was afraid he was going to be sick or pass out. He'd been hit with a bullet in his right hand, but he couldn't feel that at all. The pain in his shoulder was so intense it overwhelmed any pain he might have felt from the gunshot wound.

When he was almost at his motel, he stopped alongside the road and took off the black hoodie he'd worn to hide his face when he broke into the storage facility office. He gritted his teeth with pain as he twisted his shoulder around to get his arm out of the sleeve of the hoodie. He wrapped the hoodie around his hand to keep blood from dripping all over the parking lot of the motel and on the carpet in his room. He was frantic to get out of Tulsa. He'd been involved in two incidents in this city that could cause him big, big trouble. If everything had gone the way he'd intended for it to go, he could have grabbed his duffle from the motel room and been on his way to Texas by now. But things had not gone his way, and he would not be able to leave Tulsa tonight.

He locked himself in his motel room and went into the bathroom to examine his injuries. His shoulder was killing him. He was sure it was dislocated, but it might also be broken. He didn't know. He struggled to get out of his shirt and looked at himself in the mirror. His face was ashen, and he told himself that his pallor must be due to the pain from his shoulder. He could tell it was dislocated because of the pain and because of the way it hung down his side at an odd angle. He had seen shows on TV where an EMT or a doctor had done something quickly to a shoulder and snapped the dislocated bone back in place. If only he could go to the ER or some "doc in the box" and have somebody do whatever that was to his shoulder. But he also had a gunshot wound, and because of that, he was afraid he couldn't go anywhere to get treatment. Medical professionals had to report gunshot wounds.

Darnell unwrapped the hoodie that had kept him from bleeding all over everything. He ran his right hand under the warm water in the bathtub. Once the blood was washed away from the wound, he could see that the bullet had gone all the way through the palm of his hand. There was no bullet left behind that would have to be removed. This was good news. Maybe he could make his hand look like he had injured it working on machinery or using some kind of cooking equipment. Maybe he could make the gunshot wound look like a knife wound. He could tell the doctor he'd been chopping wood and cut his hand with an axe. He could bind up the wound and tell the doctor to ignore it when he went into the doc shop about his arm. He thought he could take care of the hand himself, but he needed help with his shoulder. He had to do something. He couldn't stand the pain.

He got his computer out of his duffle and looked on the internet for the closest twenty-four-hour emergency medical center. He didn't want to go to a regular hospital because he thought they probably kept better records. He wanted a fly-by-night place where they would just fix the shoulder and let him leave. He found a place about six miles away and called to see if they really were open all night. He said he thought he'd dislocated his shoulder falling off a ladder. He asked how long the wait was to be seen. They told him the wait was about forty-five minutes, and he decided he could put up with that to get relief from his shoulder pain. He tore one of the pillow cases from his bed into strips and bandaged his hand. The bleeding had slowed down. If the doctor asked, he would say he had been on a ladder, cleaning leaves out of his gutters. When he fell, he'd tried to grab something to keep from falling and pierced his hand on a sharp piece of metal sticking out from the gutter. Maybe the doc would buy it.

Darnell stopped at a pharmacy on his way to the emergency center and bought real bandages to rewrap his hand. The strips of sheeting looked pretty tacky, and the doctor might want to unwrap the awful looking bandage and put on a neater one. Darnell wasn't very good at putting a bandage on himself, and he didn't think the real bandages looked much better than the strips of sheeting. His hand was starting to throb now. He needed to get the shoulder taken care of and get back to his hotel room to lie down.

He had to wait only thirty minutes to be seen by the nurse practitioner. The only M.D. in the place was delivering a baby in the next treatment room. The pregnant woman, who looked very young and was probably undocumented, spoke no English. She had waited until the last minute to come in to give birth. The nurse practitioner was upset and let it slip that the young woman was only fourteen and that she was having a difficult first delivery. The doctor would have sent her to the local hospital if there had been time. As it was, she probably needed a C-section, and this doc shop was definitely not equipped to do that procedure. The woman was screaming. The nurse practitioner was distracted by the drama in the next room, but he was able to realign Darnell's shoulder. Snapping the bone back into its socket had caused so much pain that Darnell thought he was going to faint. It was a tremendous relief when the practitioner had finally manipulated the shoulder back into place. The severe pain stopped, and Darnell could breathe again. The nurse practitioner didn't ask about his hand. He told Darnell to wait for a prescription for pain meds, but Darnell quickly and quietly left the medical facility before the nurse came back.

He was out of the doc shop and on his way back to his room at the motel. He swallowed four Ibuprofen, took a long hot shower, poured rubbing alcohol on the wound in his hand, rewrapped the bandage, and fell naked into the bed. He slept for twelve hours.

Chapter 25

The next morning, his shoulder was not as painful, but it was still very stiff and sore. Darnell washed and sterilized his gunshot wound again and put on a clean bandage. His hand was more painful today, and it was red and swollen. He packed his duffle bag and checked the motel room for blood. He threw the now-bloody black hoodie into a dumpster behind a grocery store. At the nearby diner, he ordered the "Farmer's Morning Special" which consisted of four eggs cooked any way you wanted them, bacon, sausage, grits or hash browns, toast, three buttermilk pancakes, a large juice, and a large coffee. He asked himself if he was pushing too hard. Maybe he should take it easy for a few days. He felt it was urgent to get out of Oklahoma, but once he was in Texas, he wondered if he ought to get a motel room and rest. He'd been injured, and although he didn't like to admit it, he was suffering from the pain of both injuries.

When he had finished his meal, he filled the motorcycle with gas, got back on the highway, and didn't stop even when he'd crossed over the border into Denison, Texas. He kept on until he'd reached the town of Sherman. Finally, he felt he was safely out of the reach of Oklahoma law enforcement authorities. He looked for a Motel 6. His whole body was stiff and sore, and he needed to lie down and sleep. He acknowledged to himself that he wasn't an experienced criminal. He was a petty thief. He thought he was smarter than most career criminals, but he didn't have the experience or the street smarts. He would have to be more careful in the future.

Dallas was very close, and he could keep on going and be there in less than an hour. But Darnell was at the end of his strength and stamina. His hand was throbbing painfully. Although he knew very little about medical matters, he was sure it had become infected. He had no idea what he was going to do about that, but he knew he had to do something. He began to feel dizzy. Dizzy and motorcycles are never a good mix.

Darnell found an Econo Lodge and asked for their least expensive room. He got a bucket of ice and locked his door. He was going to have to find a doctor and get some antibiotics, but he couldn't deal with that right now. He was dead on his feet and not thinking clearly. He thought he would feel better if he took a shower. Sleeping in libraries, where they didn't have showers, was not good for one's personal hygiene. Darnell wondered if he was getting too old for life on the road. He put a clean bandage on his swollen hand which was now twice its normal size. His gunshot wound had become a serious problem. He took some Ibuprofen for the pain and went to sleep.

When Darnell struggled to wake up, it was dark outside. He was shivering and looked around for extra blankets. He took another hot shower to try to get warm. He felt sick to his stomach and knew he had to do something about his hand. He went back to bed and woke up again at four in the morning. He was burning up with fever. He called the motel office and told the person on duty he needed a doctor.

"I'm very sick with a fever. You need to call a doctor for me."

"You don't have Ebola, do you? We don't want any more Ebola here in Dallas. If you have Ebola, I have to call the health department ASAP."

"I don't have Ebola. I had an injury to my hand and didn't take care of it like I should have. Now it's infected, and I'm afraid I've developed a systemic infection."

"What's this 'systemic infection'? Is that like Ebola infection?"

Darnell had a good vocabulary because he read so much. He forgot that other people didn't know as many words as he did. "'Systemic' means it's throughout my whole body, an infection in my blood."

"Then it is like Ebola, in your blood. Oh, my God? I will call the fire department. The motel will have to be shut down."

"Listen to me! I don't have anything you or anybody else can catch. I have an infected hand that has made me feel really bad all over my body. Call a doctor who will come to see me, here in my motel room. I need antibiotics. I don't have Ebola or anything like Ebola." It had been years since a man had died of Ebola in Dallas, but clearly the incident had made a big impression on this guy.

"Doctors don't make house calls anymore. You have to go to them. I don't know anybody that I can call."

"I feel too bad to go anywhere. If you don't want me to die here in my room, you will find me a doctor and have him come to me."

Darnell thought about calling 911. He thought about calling an Uber and having the car take him to another all-night medical clinic. Things like health insurance had never been on Darnell's radar screen, so of course, he didn't have any health insurance. He had stiffed the doc shop in Tulsa and left before they could make him pay. He'd almost forgotten that he was also on the run from them. They'd been so preoccupied with the woman who was having the baby, they probably had forgotten all about him by now. He was worried about how he would pay either a doctor who came to the motel or a doctor he went to see in a clinic. But he was more concerned that whatever doctor looked at the swollen hand would recognize it for what it was, an infected gunshot wound.

Darnell unwrapped the bandage carefully. His hand had become a huge ball of pain. The odor from the soiled bandages let him know the infection was festering. He decided to soak the hand in hot water. Maybe that would get rid of some of the smell. He sat on the toilet seat in the tiny motel bathroom with his hand in the sink. The wound felt better after he'd soaked it, but it didn't look any better. He poured more rubbing alcohol over it and put on clean bandages. He was running out of rubbing alcohol and gauze to wrap his hand. He would have to go to the store and steal or buy more. He took another dose of pain pills and went to sleep.

When he woke up the next time, he was frightened. If he'd felt well enough, he could have broken into a pharmacy after hours and stolen the antibiotics. What he usually did was to look on the internet to find out what he needed and then steal it from a pharmacy. He realized he was dehydrated and his blood sugar was low. If he could get himself in better shape, he might be able to go someplace and steal his medical supplies. He ordered a pizza with everything and a two-quart bottle of Coke. When it arrived, he ate the whole pizza and drank most of the Coke. He felt a little better. He soaked his hand again and used his last bandage to wrap it. He put on his cleanest clothes, which weren't really clean at all, and drove his motorcycle to the nearest Walmart.

He paid for the rubbing alcohol and the bandages. They were cheap. While he was in the store, he checked security at the pharmacy and tried to figure out how to break into the store after it had closed. This Walmart was not a twenty-four hour store and that was a good thing for Darnell's purposes. He needed a store that closed at night, and he was lucky this Walmart was just a few minutes from his motel. He would be going after antibiotics in the pharmacy. The narcotics would be locked up after hours in a special section of the pharmacy, but nobody bothered to lock up antibiotics. He knew what he needed to steal, and he knew he had to do it quickly, before he had another sinking spell and couldn't function.

Darnell was good at shoplifting and breaking into mom and pop type stores and grocery stores. He was not experienced at overcoming elaborate security systems and complicated alarms. If he wasn't able to get into a place with his lock picks, he got in by breaking a window or using a crowbar to pry open sliding glass doors. He wasn't subtle about his break-ins. But he didn't have a digital device to crack the code on an electronic lock. He was seat of the pants, old school, and pretty clumsy. But he was good at hiding. He decided to hide inside the Walmart store until it closed. If no one discovered him in the store, he thought he could get into the pharmacy and steal what he needed.

He moved his motorcycle from the parking lot to a spot in the woods behind the store. After the Walmart closed, a lone motorcycle would stand out in an otherwise empty parking lot. He waited until fifteen minutes before closing time and went back inside. He'd decided the best place to hide himself was in the area where the camping equipment was displayed. There were several tents set up on the floor, and there was big stuff for sale in the outdoor activities department that he could use to conceal himself. He found a pile of sleeping bags and carried them, a couple at a time, into one of the tents. He built a sleeping bag wall and lay down behind it to wait. He hadn't planned to fall asleep, but he did. It was three in the morning when he woke up.

It wasn't difficult to access the pharmacy. He'd seen the employees come and go the back way, through a door off the hall that went to the bathrooms. That door was locked but easy to break into. It took him a while to find what he wanted, but he eventually put his hands on the Augmentin. He helped himself to plenty of large doses and also helped himself to some other things he saw in the pharmacy. The strong painkillers would all be locked up, but he found a few other things he thought he could use. He had a plastic bag full of drugs and medical supplies when he exited a door at the back of the Walmart. Unfortunately, he set off the alarm when he left through the rear fire door. He should have been more careful, but he had messed up on his exit strategy.

A security guard came running towards him as Darnell took off across the parking lot in the direction of the woods where his bike was hidden. He was fighting a systemic infection and had a badly damaged hand. He was in no condition to run anywhere, let alone run for his life. The Walmart security guard carried a gun. It was Texas! The guard fired his gun at Darnell as he retreated towards the woods. The security guard was not a very good shot, however, not as good as the policeman in Tulsa had been. The guard fired several shots at Darnell and missed. But being shot at for the second time in three days rattled Darnell, and he couldn't remember exactly where he'd hidden his motorcycle. He knew it was in this part of the woods, and he'd been careful to secure it under some brush. Right at this moment and in his panic about the gunshots, all the brush looked the same to him.

Darnell had enough insight to realize he wasn't at the top of his game, either physically or mentally. He knew he had to get out of the area before the security guard found him. He thought he had a few minutes because he figured the security guard would call the sheriff or the local police for reinforcements before anybody began a serious search for him.

All he wanted to do was lie down in a pile of bushes and go to sleep, but he made himself keep looking for the motorcycle. He finally found it, and with his last ounce of strength, he pushed it along a dirt path he thought would take him out of the woods. Finally, he thought he was headed in the right direction, away from the Walmart parking lot. It seemed to take forever to get out of the woods and onto a regular road where he could start his bike. He was disoriented and wasn't sure what direction to take to get back to the motel.

He put the address of the motel into his phone, and Google Maps told him where to go. At last, he made it back to the Econo Lodge, but he was at the end of his rope. He dumped the drugs he'd stolen onto the bed and found the Augmentin. He took three times the recommended dose. He knew when he did this that it wasn't a smart thing to do.

But he did it anyway. He needed a big fix on the infection, and he needed it fast. He was filthy from rolling around in the dusty Walmart camping display and looking for his motorcycle in the woods. He took a shower and put a clean bandage on his hand.

He was hungry again, but decided he needed sleep more than he needed food. He had stolen a digital thermometer when he'd been in the Walmart pharmacy, and he took his temperature. It was 103.8 degrees. Darnell knew that wasn't normal and wasn't good. No wonder he was confused. He set the alarm on the bedside table to wake him in four hours so he could take another dose of Augmentin. His life now depended on it.

Chapter 26

fter three days of taking massive doses of Aug-mentin, Darnell thought he had kicked the worst of the infection. His internet research had told him it was important to keep taking the antibiotics for ten days, but he'd cut back on the dose. He was now taking a large but normal dose, religiously every four hours. He soaked his hand in warm water and Epson salts (also stolen from Walmart) several times a day and kept the wound clean. He took his temperature to be sure it was staying down. He ordered food delivered to his motel room.

When he had checked into the motel, he'd put down the required one night's deposit in cash for his room. He had no intentions of paying for the additional four nights he had stayed at the Econo Lodge, and he needed to get out of town before somebody knocked on his door and made him pay. Darnell had expected the motel's manager to come to the room before this, asking for more money, but no one had come asking for payment. Darnell decided the guy in the motel office really was afraid of catching Ebola. He knew Darnell was sick, and Darnell figured the manager didn't want to come to the room for fear of contagion. Darnell had put false names and addresses on all of the paperwork he'd filled out when he'd registered for his motel room. No one would ever find him after he'd left. He was a vagabond.

He always parked his motorcycle as far from the motel office as possible. He had rubbed mud over the motorcycle's license plate so the clerk, if he bothered to look, couldn't be sure what the letters and numbers were. Darnell reminded himself that he needed to steal another motorcycle license plate at the earliest opportunity. When he was traveling on the road, he would use his own legal license plate. When he parked his bike at a motel, he used the stolen plate.

The people in the motel office knew he'd been sick and was having food delivered. As long as they believed he was too ill to leave his room, it wouldn't occur to them that he might be leaving. He packed his duffle and slept for a few hours. In the middle of the night, he was ready to go. He left the door of his room locked and climbed out the back through the bathroom window. It wasn't easy, but he had to do it that way.

After his trip to Walmart and in anticipation of sneaking away from the Econo Lodge without paying his bill, he'd left his motorcycle at the edge of the parking lot again, as far as possible from the motel office. He snuck behind the rooms of the motel and made a dash for the bike. He threw his duffle on the back. The bike's engine was loud, and he didn't want to wake the man in the office who was probably asleep. Darnell pushed the bike down the road before he started it. In a few minutes he was away—away from Sherman, Texas and away from the Econo Lodge. He was on his way to Dallas and on his way to being rich.

He put the address of Texas Open Market Treasures into his phone, and Google Maps once again told him where to go. Texas Open Market Treasures was actually located in Mesquite, Texas. Darnell promised himself he would get a room at a motel in Dallas for a few nights, rather than sleep in the library. He had to take care of his wound, and he needed hot water and a bathroom to do that. When he made it to Mesquite, he drove to Texas Open Market Treasures. He left his motorcycle in the parking lot, and when the junk store opened, he went inside to look around.

The business was in a warehouse, and the treasures were presented in a huge open space. There were no shelves or display cases. Everything was piled on the floor. The merchandise was arranged in rows. There had been some attempts to keep things separated into categories. There was a row of furniture, a row of clothing, a row of books and smaller things. It was semi-organized, but it was messy. Stuff was heaped into stacks with similar items. Customers had to dig through the mounds of things to find something good. The haphazard arrangement must work for Leonard Bundy; he'd been in business for years. There was an old-fashioned cash register at the back, and TOMT was an all-cash business. There were not many of either of those left in the world. Darnell was betting that Leonard didn't overpay when it came to filing his income taxes with the IRS.

Darnell was also betting they didn't keep many records here at TOMT. This might be where his search hit a wall. This might be where the trail went cold. He decided he would apply for a job at Texas Open Market Treasures. If he was ever going to figure out what had happened to *Fountain* and where it had gone when it had left this warehouse, he would have to be on the inside. If there were any sales records anywhere, the only way he was going to have a chance to look at them was to be an employee.

Darnell left the store and drove to a Walmart in Fort Worth. If he was going to apply for a job, he needed new clothes. He visited laundromats when he was on the road to wash his underwear and other clothing, but when his things got too dirty or too ragged, he just threw them away and shoplifted new ones. If he was going to be working at TOMT, he didn't want to steal from a Walmart close to the store. That's why he traveled to Fort Worth to steal his new wardrobe.

He'd done this before. He filled a shopping cart with everything he needed and pushed the cart close to the front door. He waited for a handicapped person to enter the store. Then he "accidentally" stumbled and pushed his cart into the person with the walker or the cane or the wheelchair. If the person was using a cane or a walker, they usually fell. Darnell was ready and full of apologies and pretended he felt so terrible that he'd run into someone with his cart. He helped them up and made a big fuss. He offered to take them to the hospital. He was the nicest guy in the world, so sorry, so sorry. Employees from the store usually came rushing to help the person who had fallen, partly out of genuine concern and partly out of fear that the injured person would file a law suit.

By the time Darnell's part in the drama was done, he'd managed to ease his cart out the door. As the concerned store manager, employees, and other customers rallied around the disabled victim, Darnell faded from the scene. He was outside in the parking lot without having had to show a sales receipt, which of course he didn't have, and have it checked against the contents of his cart. He always parked his motorcycle in as obscure a part of the lot as he could find. He quickly transferred his ill-gotten goods into bags, which he had also stolen. He strapped the bags to the back of his bike, and in minutes he was out of there and on the road again.

He'd been caught a couple of times at the door. When that happened, he just abandoned the cart, walked out the door, and ran like hell through the parking lot to get to his motorcycle. Sometimes his ruse worked, and sometimes it didn't. It worked this time in Ft. Worth, and he had all new clothes. Now he needed to find a place to stay and take a shower. He would show up the next morning, dressed for success, and talk his way into some kind of a position with Texas Open Market Treasures.

Turnover at TOMT was high. Leonard was getting up in years and was somewhat forgetful. Darnell was intelligent enough and enough of a con man that he could figure out what Leonard needed. Darnell would become whatever that was, and he got the job. It wasn't a great job, but Darnell wasn't in it to build a career. He was in it to find out what had happened to the urinal Leonard Bundy had brought from a Tulsa, Oklahoma storage facility to this store in Dallas almost a decade earlier.

Darnell knew *Fountain* had arrived at TOMT just before Christmas in 2009. He didn't think there would be a high demand for that particular plumbing fixture. How many people were named Roberta Mutt, after all, and how many of them had been born in 1917? He figured the urinal must have sat around the warehouse for a few weeks or months. Darnell needed to find someone who had worked here when the urinal had been sold.

There were two long-time employees, people who'd been working at the warehouse since 2009. One was Leonard Bundy's nephew, Alger Duncan. Darnell didn't think Alger was all there mentally. He figured Bundy employed Duncan out of the kindness of his heart, if Leonard Bundy actually had a heart. Alger did odd jobs, changed light bulbs, swept the floors, and was a kind of a gofer for Bundy. The other employee who'd been with Bundy for almost a decade was a rough, tough character who did the heavy lifting. Bundy always took him along on road trips to load and unload the 18-wheeler. Neither one seemed like a good bet to remember selling a urinal ten years earlier.

There was so much stuff in the place. How could anybody remember anything about the inventory? There were no sales records and no lists of items on hand, past or present. Darnell wondered what his meticulous record-keeping mother would have had to say about the state of the books at the warehouse. Darnell doubted that the books being kept for TOMT had any resemblance to what actually transpired there.

Darnell realized his chances of finding out where *Fountain* had gone when it had left TOMT, were slim to none. But, Mesquite, Texas wasn't a bad place to be, and the work he did for Leonard Bundy wasn't difficult. Darnell was in charge of keeping the goods in categories and the piles neat. Leonard wanted pathways kept clear between the rows of his piles of junk. The paths needed to be wide enough for customers to walk through without tripping on stuff and wide enough to allow them enough space to stand and look through the piles. As workers came and went, Darnell took over more and more functions for Leonard Bundy. In a few weeks, he had made himself an indispensable part of the TOMT team. It hadn't been difficult.

Once his hand was sufficiently healed, Darnell began sleeping in the local library. He was delighted when Leonard Bundy offered to let him sleep in an efficiency apartment above the warehouse. There were two tiny living spaces up there, and Alger Duncan lived in one of them. Darnell immediately accepted the offer to stay in the other apartment. Bundy told him he would take the very reasonable monthly rent out of Darnell's paycheck. It was one room with a hot plate, a small sink, and an ancient refrigerator in one corner. The place came with a daybed that also served as a couch and a few other pieces of furniture. Darnell would share the bathroom with Alger. Darnell liked Alger, and the two got along fine. The warehouse had Wi-Fi, Bundy's one concession to the modern era, and Alger paid for cable TV service.

Darnell realized, as he got to know Alger better, that Alger remembered some things from the past very well. Alger might be slow intellectually, but he had a vivid memory for selected events and people, some from a long time ago. When he told a story about something that had happened years earlier, it was as if he was reliving the incident with all of its emotional drama, impact, and immediacy. Darnell liked to hear Alger tell his stories, and Alger was thrilled to have the attention from his new friend.

Darnell hoped he might be able to use Alger's memories from the past. Darnell would try to tap into Alger's memory about the urinal from 2009. Maybe his search for the urinal was not as hopeless as he'd thought it was. Darnell was pinning his hopes on Alger and whether or not he could remember the urinal.

Darnell was careful about the way he delved into Alger's memory. He knew the man didn't remember everything, but he thought the urinal was such an unusual, even unique item, that Alger might remember it. Darnell got hold of a catalogue of plumbing supply fixtures. It was an old one, from years earlier. Before websites and the internet, catalogues selling merchandise used to overload everybody's mailboxes. With the advent of online shopping, many companies had stopped sending out catalogues.

One afternoon when there weren't many customers in the warehouse, Darnell sat in the office, leafing through the plumbing supply catalogue. Alger came over and sat beside him.

"What're you lookin' at, Darnell?"

"I've been looking at one of these." Darnell pointed to the men's urinal. "I've been wondering if you'd ever seen one of these come in to TOMT? It seems like everything else in the world has shown up here at one time or another."

"What is that called? I think we had one of those once."

Darnell's hopes soared. "It's called a men's urinal. You see them in men's bathrooms in restaurants, offices, and other public places. You hardly ever see one in a private bathroom in someone's home." Alger seemed to be studying the picture of the urinal in the catalog. Darnell let him have the book. Alger began to go through the pages, looking at all the plumbing fixtures. Darnell's hopes faded. Then all of a sudden, Alger spoke up.

"Chuck bought it. He said he had a bachelor pad, and it was only $3.00. He bought some really ugly furniture, too. I told him not to buy the furniture, that it was just junk, but he said it was only temporary."

"Who bought the urinal?"

"Chuck bought it."

"Okay, so Chuck bought it. But how did it get here, to the warehouse? It's an unusual item."

"Uncle Leonard brought it on one of his trips. He almost threw it out. He said nobody would buy one of them. He said it was an older style, very out of date. He said it was ruined because somebody had painted their name and some numbers on the side of it. It wasn't worth the time to try to get the paint off. Uncle Leonard said he would price it real low, maybe somebody would 'take it off his hands.' I asked him what it was for. I'd never seen one like that one before. He laughed at me and said 'it's so's us guys can take a piss, Alger.' I told him he didn't need to laugh at me, and he said he wasn't laughing at me, but he was."

"Who is this Chuck who bought it? Do you remember his last name?"

"No, his name is just Chuck. He used to come in here more. He hasn't been in here for a long time. He was always looking for the cheapest things he could find. He bought crappy furniture."

"Does your uncle know Chuck?"

"Maybe, I don't know. Uncle Leonard said, 'Whoever thought that piece of crap would be almost the first thing to go from the load? I guess if you put the right price on anything, somebody's going to buy it, just because it's cheap.'" That remark sounded to Darnell like something Leonard Bundy would say, and Darnell knew Alger didn't make things up. Darnell decided that when the time was right, he would try to pick Leonard's brain about Chuck.

Chapter 27

*D*arnell *figured he was probably never going to be* able to locate Chuck. The search for *Fountain* was at an end. He might have to wait until Chuck came into the warehouse again to discover the man's last name. That might be years from now, or it might be never. Darnell felt he had a pretty good place to live right now, and he had an easy job. He knew that in a few weeks or months, he would be overtaken by his inevitable wanderlust, but for now he was going to stay put in Mesquite.

Darnell and Alger occasionally made deliveries to people's homes. If you bought enough items from TOMT, you were offered the opportunity to pay a ridiculously high price to have your items delivered to your home or office. Darnell had figured out this was one of the ways Bundy made his money. He offered junky furniture for sale at really cheap and tempting prices. People thought they were getting a bargain and often overbought. Lots of people who lived in the suburbs and worked in the city had long commutes and therefore owned small cars. These were great for getting to and from work and great for gas mileage, but not so good for hauling stuff. Leonard Bundy would deliver the furniture his customers bought, but he charged through the nose for the service.

Darnell and Alger made deliveries for Uncle Leonard in a dilapidated van. Darnell did the driving, handled the paperwork, set up the appointments for the deliveries, and made sure the cheap goods were delivered to the right address. Alger helped load and unload the van. They went on delivery runs once or twice a week. One hot July afternoon, they were making three deliveries in the area of Irving, Texas. They were driving down Johnson Street which was just beyond Irving's downtown area.

All of a sudden, Alger shouted and waved as they were speeding down the road, "Hi Chuck!"

Darnell was so startled, he almost drove the van onto the sidewalk. "What did you say, Alger? What did you just say?"

"I was just saying 'Hi' to Chuck. You know, the Chuck you were asking me about, the one who bought the...the urinal." Alger giggled like a small child who had just said a dirty word.

"Why did you say 'Hi' to Chuck? Did you see him? Does he live near here?"

"Yeah, he lives right back there, a couple of blocks back. We just went by his house. I didn't see Chuck himself, but I saw where he lives. I waved to him at his house."

Darnell made a rapid U-turn and drove back to the spot where Alger had shouted a greeting and waved to Chuck's house. They were in a neighborhood of condominium buildings. "Show me the exact building where Chuck lives." Alger pointed to a yellow brick low-rise. "Did you go inside? Do you know which condo he lives in, inside that building?"

"Yes, I know where he lives. I helped Gizzard carry Chuck's furniture up to his condo." Gizzard had been one of Leonard Bundy's employees before Darnell had arrived at TOMT. Gizzard was long gone.

Darnell found a place to park the van, and he and Alger walked back to the condo building. Alger didn't understand why Darnell wanted to see Chuck, but he didn't have to understand. All he had to do was tell Darnell where Chuck lived. They pushed all of the residents' doorbells, and luckily somebody was home to buzz them in through the outside door. Darnell examined the names on the mailboxes in the vestibule, but they were mostly all last names. "Show me where he lives, Alger."

"But we don't have anything to bring Chuck today. He'll be mad if we come to his house and don't bring him anything."

"It'll be all right, I promise. Leave it to me. I'll do the talking. Chuck won't be mad."

Chuck's condo was on the third floor, #37. Darnell knocked on the door but no one answered. He knocked again. Still no answer. Finally a neighbor, an older woman, stuck her head out the door of the condo across the hall, "There's nobody home. They're at work. You can forget knocking. Save your knuckles."

"Is the person who lives there named Chuck?" Darnell wanted to know if Chuck was still in residence.

"No, Chuck hasn't lived there for more than five years or so. And, no, I don't know where Chuck went to, so don't ask me."

"Do you remember Chuck's last name?" Darnell had finally found someone who had known Chuck, and he wasn't going to let her get away without finding out everything she knew.

"No. There have been two other people who have moved in and out of there since Chuck lived here. At least one was an illegal sublet, I'm sure. Probably both were illegal. Chuck hasn't lived there in a long time. I already told you that."

"Who would know Chuck's last name or how I can contact him? Is there a building superintendent or manager?"

"These are condos. Everybody has to take care of their own problems here, calls and pays for their own plumber and everything else. I have no idea who would know Chuck's last name. It was some kind of an Italian name, though, I think. He liked to cook, and the place always smelled like onions and garlic. Yeah, he was definitely Italian. He didn't really look Italian, but he was definitely Italian."

"The person who lives here now wouldn't know anything about Chuck, would they?"

"No. Chuck was long gone before these people moved in."

"Thanks for the information." Darnell didn't want to leave his name or phone number. He didn't want anybody to know who had been trying to track down Chuck, the Italian guy. Darnell wondered briefly if Chuck was "connected" in any way to the mob. That would be just his luck, if Chuck was a member of the Mafia. Darnell would have to be careful and discreet as he tracked down Chuck's current whereabouts.

Darnell and Alger returned to the van and made their deliveries. Darnell could barely contain his excitement. He had a new lead on *Fountain*. He had another chance to find Chuck. He decided to search the internet first to try to find the records of deeds and titles to properties.

If Chuck had owned the condo, his name would be in the records. If he had rented the condo from the owner, his name would not be there. Darnell knew for sure that Chuck had purchased the urinal in December of 2009 or January of 2010. When he looked online, he found that the city's property records had been computerized beginning in January of 2010. Again, just his luck. He was counting on the probability that the person who owned the condo in December 2009 still owned it in January 2010.

A Gerald H. Bevins had owned the condo where Chuck was living in 2010. He'd bought it in 2003 and sold it in 2011. Gerald H. Bevins was an unusual name, so Darnell felt like he would be able to track him down, even if he was living in Montana or Alaska by now. Bevins had to know Chuck's last name. Darnell searched the internet and found a Gerald H. Bevins living in Plano, Texas. This had to be the same man who'd owned the condo where Chuck had lived. Darnell got Bevins' address in Plano and asked Leonard Bundy if he could borrow the van for a few hours. Darnell's plan was to drive to Bevins' house which was less than an hour's drive from the warehouse. He would question Bevins about Chuck's last name, and then he would go in search of Chuck.

Darnell always wondered if Chuck had left the urinal at one of the places he had lived between 2009 and the present. He might actually have had it installed in a bathroom, although Darnell seriously doubted that had happened. Chuck could have left it in a closet or a basement storage area in one of his apartment buildings. Another worry was that Chuck had thrown the urinal away during one of his moves. The only way to find out exactly what had happened to it was to find Chuck and ask him.

Darnell had no conscience, so once he had traced the urinal through Marjorie Van Devries Cannon, he never gave her another thought. He did not have any curiosity about what might have happened to her after he left her tied up in her bedroom. Darnell also didn't watch much television. He occasionally watched a show with Alger, but Alger wasn't into the news, so Darnell completely missed the remarkable story of the woman in Tulsa, Oklahoma, who had rescued herself from certain death.

> **TULSA DAILY REGISTER**...The man in the ski mask, the shower cap, and the latex gloves broke into her house in the middle of the night and tied her up with ropes and duct tape. He tortured her and questioned her about items she had inherited when her mother died. The woman answered all of the intruder's questions, and in spite of his promise that he wouldn't hurt her, he beat her savagely and left her for dead. He ransacked the woman's house and took a few things to make the break-in look like a robbery. He left the woman lying on the floor—unconscious and bleeding.

> When she woke up hours later, she used her last ounce of strength to crawl to her bedside table. Her landline phone, her only link to anyone who might rescue her, was sitting on that bedside table. She wondered if he had cut the phone line. Would her phone still work?

> The woman had an old flip phone in her purse, but she couldn't reach her purse. Even if she had been

able to get to her cellular phone, if the battery had died, that phone would have been no use to her.

After repeated attempts, she was able to turn over the bedside table. The receiver fell to the floor. After many frustrating tries, she successfully called 911. Because her hands were tied behind her back and because her feet and legs were bound to the chair, she had to use her bleeding tongue to punch the buttons on the touch tone phone.

The EMTs that arrived a few minutes later reported that the woman was almost dead from dehydration and loss of blood. She was taken to a hospital, but law enforcement officials will not say whether or not the woman survived her ordeal. Because the perpetrator of this vicious crime is still at large, the authorities will not give out the woman's name or the address where this incident took place. The attempted homicide is shrouded in mystery and secrecy. The investigation into this brutal assault is ongoing.

Darnell found Gerald Bevins' house in Plano without any problems. If Darnell had been a professional criminal, he would have staked out the house for a day or two, to see if Bevins had a family or if anyone else lived in the house with him. But Darnell was a reckless narcissist, not a professional, and he thought only of the riches he was trying to find. He was smart about some things, but he was not smart about everything. He knocked on Bevins' front door. When no one answered, Darnell decided to break in through the kitchen and wait for Bevins to come home.

While he had been working at TOMT, Darnell had stolen two guns. The guns were a set from a storage locker in Tennessee. Darnell had found them when he was helping unload the 18-wheeler. Neither gun had ever been fired, and both guns were arranged in an expensive wooden gift box. Their ammunition was in the box with them. Darnell was able to hide the box before Leonard Bundy found it. Darnell didn't know how to use a gun, but he planned to visit a shooting range to learn how to use the two from the boxed set.

Leonard always insisted that he had to be the first person to go through the contents of the 18-wheeler when it arrived at TOMT. Leonard wanted to look at everything before anybody else touched it, so he could cherry pick the valuable items before his employees unloaded the less valuable stuff and either arranged it inside the TOMT warehouse or put it in the dumpster to go to the landfill. Sometimes there were valuables in the haul, and sometimes there was only junk. Leonard was getting older, and he wasn't able to move as fast as he used to or keep an eye on things as closely as he had in the past.

In the months Darnell had been working for Leonard Bundy at TOMT, Darnell had been able to steal quite a few valuable things from Leonard's 18-wheeler loads. Darnell hadn't tried to pawn or sell any of it yet. He kept it hidden in his apartment. He figured Leonard knew all the dealers, honest and dishonest, within hundreds of miles of Dallas. These were the people who bought his really good merchandise. Leonard Bundy sold the valuables personally and pocketed the cash. Darnell knew none of the sales of the valuable items were ever reported as income on the books. Darnell planned to find a buyer in another part of the country, many miles away from Dallas, Texas, and sell the things he'd stolen from Leonard.

The guns were a different story. Darnell went to the gun range a few times. He'd gone often enough to learn how to load and unload both guns, how to operate the safety mechanisms, and how to stand correctly and aim the firearms. He had fired at paper targets a few times. He was a terrible shot, but he planned to use the guns more to threaten people into talking than to actually shoot anybody. He took both guns and the ammunition with him when he drove to Plano to talk to Gerald Bevins. Darnell loaded one of the guns and took it with him when he entered Bevins' house.

Darnell waited in a closet near the back door. The garage was attached to the house, and there was a door that opened from the garage into a back hall, off the kitchen. He waited three hours in the closet until Bevins finally came home. Gerald Bevins was a sixty-two year old man. He was overweight and not in good physical condition. Darnell again wore his ski mask, his shower cap, and his plastic gloves. He hadn't practiced holding his gun wearing the gloves, let alone firing it wearing the gloves. It was awkward when he came out of the coat closet and confronted Bevins. Bevins clutched at his chest and sat down on a bench in the back hall.

"Don't hurt me, please. I'm an old man. Take my wallet and anything else in the house you want. I won't put up a struggle. Please don't shoot me." Bevins was scared. Darnell's gun had already done its job.

"I don't plan to hurt you, Mr. Bevins. I just want some information from you. Listen carefully and answer my questions. When I find out what I need to know, I'll leave. You used to own a condominium at 3529 Johnson Street in Irving, Texas. You owned unit #37 in that building and rented it to a man whose first name was Chuck. What is Chuck's last name?"

Bevins looked confused. "That was years ago. I don't own that place anymore. Why do you want to know about that condo?"

"I am trying to find Chuck. I need his last name."

"Well, I lived there after my divorce. Then I sublet it to a friend of mine. But his name wasn't Chuck. I rented the place to my friend Alvarez Benito. I know he sublet it to somebody else when he moved out, but I don't know anything about anybody named Chuck. It was illegal, against the condo's HOA rules, to sublet the condo. But everybody did it anyway, and everybody knew everybody else was doing it. Nobody ever said anything. It was just business. The HOA wanted to vet the people who lived in the building, so they didn't allow subletting. They investigated me to kingdom come when I bought the place. They wanted a bunch of references and my financial records and all the addresses of where I'd lived before. It was all bullshit, but they finally let me buy the place. But how hard was it going to be to sell the place with all those ridiculous rules about who could live there? It was going to be impossible! So I sublet to my friend who needed a place to live. He sent the mortgage payments in to the bank and paid the utility bills which were still in my name. The bank didn't care who paid the mortgage, and the electric company didn't care who paid the bill, as long as it all got paid on time. I don't know your Chuck. So leave me alone."

"How can I find Alvarez? Does he live in the area?"

"He moved to Phoenix, but I don't know if he still lives there. We've lost touch."

The demon rage suddenly hit Darnell again. What he had thought was going to be an easy interrogation had become another complicated search. He was furious and couldn't control his anger. He was holding his gun to Gerald Bevins' head, and before he could think about what he was doing, he'd fired it three times into Bevins' ear. Bevins fell from the bench, and a pool of blood began to form under the man's head. Darnell had to step back to keep the blood from seeping under his shoes.

Darnell had a name, and now he had to get out of there. He was just about to leave the way he'd come when he looked out through the glass of the kitchen door. A woman was standing there, looking down into her purse for her house key. She hadn't yet seen Darnell. He had no idea who this woman was, but he figured it was probably Bevins' wife or girlfriend. Darnell realized he was going to have to kill her, too. He stepped back into the hall so the woman wouldn't see him until she was inside the house. As soon as she came through the door, Darnell stepped out from his hiding place and put the gun to her head. She didn't have time to say a word before he fired three shots into her ear.

Darnell locked the back door behind him. It might be days before anyone came to check on what had happened to these two. A locked door wasn't really going to slow anything down, but he locked it anyway. He had parked Leonard's van on a street two blocks away. He hurried to the van and drove back to Mesquite. He felt no guilt or remorse for what he had done to two people he didn't even know. All he felt was anger—anger that he was going to have to find and question Alvarez Benito to find out what Chuck's last name was. Then he was going to have to find and question Chuck. He was angry that this whole thing was getting so involved, that there were so many people between him and his big payoff.

Chapter 28

lvarez Benito no longer lived in Texas. Suppos-
edly, he now lived in Phoenix. Darnell was furious,
almost paralyzed into inaction by the thought of
having to go to Arizona to get the information he needed
from Benito. He had to think. There had to be a better way.
Darnell realized he didn't have a lot of time. When Bevins
and his girlfriend or wife were found, their deaths would
quickly become news. If Alvarez Benito heard the news, he
might be on his guard.

Darnell decided he would try calling Benito. Darnell went
to a pay phone in Fort Worth to make the 411 call. It was a
trek to find a working pay phone these days, but it didn't take
as long as it would take to drive to Arizona. He didn't have the
man's address, and but he would call information to try to get
his phone number. He was counting on the man still having a
landline, and Alvarez did. Darnell went to the trouble to find
a different pay phone to make the call to Alvarez.

"Hello, I'm trying to get in touch with Alvarez Benito who at one time lived in a condominium at 3529 Johnson Road in Irving, Texas. My name is Fred Sanders, and I'm calling about a class-action suit that's been filed by the HOA of the building at that address.

"This is Alvarez Benito, but I never owned any condo in Irving, Texas. What's this about?"

"The HOA has discovered that when the building was built, the insulation the contractor used contained asbestos. The HOA is filing a class-action suit on behalf of the condominium owners and all those who lived in the building at 3529 Johnson Street."

Alvarez wasn't owning up to having lived in the condo. He had lived there illegally, so he wasn't admitting to anything. "I told you, I didn't own a condo in that building."

"I know that, Mr. Alvarez. Gerald Bevins gave me your name. He wanted you to know about the class action suit. It's okay. We know about the rule against sub-letting. That's not the issue here. We don't care about that. Gerald told us that when you left, you rented the condo to another man, a Chuck somebody. Gerald didn't know the man's last name, but he said you would know it. We have to get in touch with Chuck, too, about the class-action lawsuit. Can you tell me his last name and his current address or phone number?"

"His last name was Grimaldi, but I don't know anything about him. He was a friend of a friend that I knew at work. He needed a place to live, and I wanted to move out of the Johnson Street place. I got fired from my job, so I haven't seen my work friend for quite a few years. I don't know where he is now or where he works. Also, I never actually met Chuck Grimaldi. I moved out of the condo, and then Chuck moved in. We never crossed paths. I know nothing about where

Chuck is now or where he lives or anything about him. What do I need to do to get my money?"

Darnell was anxious to get off the phone. He had the information he needed. "I will be in touch with Mr. Bevins, but he wanted you to know about the asbestos. There may be some compensation in this for you, but it will probably come through Gerald Bevins. I will be in touch if I need to know anything more from you, Mr. Benito. Thank you for your help." Darnell hung up on Benito before he could ask any more questions. Darnell was feeling good. He now had Chuck's last name, and he hadn't had to drive to Arizona or kill anybody else to get it.

Darnell searched the internet for Chuck Grimaldi. Darnell found that Chuck had lived in a townhouse in Arlington, Texas, but he didn't live there anymore. A woman whose name had also been Grimaldi lived at the same townhouse in Arlington. She still lived there, but it looked as if she now had a different name. The house had been bought in 2010 and was owned jointly for six months by Marilynn Murray and Charles Grimaldi. Then the deed was changed, and the house was owned for almost eight years by Marilynn M. Grimaldi and Charles R. Grimaldi. Then the deed was changed again to indicate that the house had been owned by Marilynn M. Grimaldi alone for less than a year. The townhouse was currently owned by Marilynn Murray alone. Marilynn Murray had owned the townhouse alone for five months.

It was complicated. It looked as if the two had bought the house together before they were married. Then they married. Then they divorced, and Marilynn got the house. Then she changed her name back to her maiden name. Darnell didn't care about any of this. He needed to talk to

Chuck Grimaldi, but Chuck didn't own any property now. He couldn't be tracked that way. Darnell was going to have to go after Marilynn Murray to find out where Chuck was. The phone call had worked so well with Alvarez Benito, Darnell decided to try it again. He called Marilynn Murray several times before he was able to reach her.

"I'm trying to reach Marilynn Grimaldi. I'm interested in buying her townhouse in Arlington, Texas."

"There isn't anyone by the name of Marilynn Grimaldi living here, and the townhouse is not for sale."

"I'm actually looking for a Chuck Grimaldi."

"He doesn't live here, and he doesn't own any part of the townhouse."

"Can you give me Chuck's phone number or new address?"

"No." Marilynn Murray hung up the phone.

It was clear the divorce had not been an amicable one. It had been finalized within the past year, so Darnell thought he might be able to find out some information about Chuck in court records. He searched online and found a divorce decree, but there was nothing about where Chuck currently lived. Darnell searched the internet and found a place of employment for Chuck. He didn't want to approach Chuck at work, but he decided to look into the company Chuck worked for. Darnell would try to find out what Chuck looked like and what kind of car he drove. He would have to follow Chuck home to wherever he was living now and confront him there.

Darnell also felt there was a chance Chuck had left *Fountain* behind when he'd moved out of the townhouse in Arlington. In case that is what had happened, he would break into the Arlington home and search for it. That would be an easy solution to his problem. He wouldn't have to see either

Chuck or Marilynn or anybody else, if he could just steal the urinal from the house.

Darnell watched the house and knew that Marilynn left for work every day at eight in the morning. He would break in just after she left. It was a large townhouse and had a basement and a detached garage behind it. Darnell didn't want to spend much time searching. He didn't want to have to shoot anybody else, and most of all he didn't want to get caught. He did a quick but thorough search of the town-house in Arlington, but he came up empty. The urinal wasn't there. He was going to have to go after Chuck and confront him facet-to-face.

Darnell was able to find out that Chuck worked as an insur-ance adjuster for a large insurance company. Darnell called Chuck's place of work and asked to be connected to Chuck's office. From Chuck's secretary, he learned what floor of the office building Chuck worked on. Wearing a wig and a beard, Darnell went to the floor where Chuck worked and was able to get into his office by pretending to be lost. He got a good look at Chuck Grimaldi and then waited in the building's parking garage for him to leave work. Darnell followed Grimaldi's car to an apartment house located near Arlington, Texas. Darnell had learned a lesson when Gerald Bevins' significant other turned up unexpectedly, and this time Darnell decided to watch Chuck's house before he burst in and began to question him. Sure enough, Chuck was living with a woman. Things had become complicated again. Darnell would have to wait until Chuck was alone.

Darnell still had his job in Mesquite. He had been spending too much time on the search for Chuck Grimaldi, and he couldn't stake out Grimaldi's house all the time. He had to figure out a way to get Chuck alone in his apartment for a few hours so he could grill him about what he had done with *Fountain*. Maybe it was at Chuck's current apartment, but by this time, Darnell didn't believe anything would be easy. He drove back and forth between Mesquite and Chuck's apartment near Arlington. He watched when he could and eventually discovered that every Wednesday night, Chuck's girlfriend went bowling with a group of women from work. Darnell would strike on a Wednesday night.

He watched Chuck's girlfriend leave the apartment, and then he knocked on the door. He knew Chuck was home, and Darnell quickly put on his ski mask, shower cap, and gloves. He had one of his guns in his hand. It was loaded, and when Chuck opened the door, Darnell pushed himself and his gun into the apartment. Chuck looked scared.

"What do you want? I'll give you my wallet. There's not much money in it and nothing of much value here in the apartment. But take whatever you want. Just don't hurt me."

"What did you do with the urinal you bought at Texas Open Market Treasures? I know you bought it there, and I know it was delivered to your condo in Irving."

"What? I bought that thing years ago. I left the urinal in the garage at my townhouse in Arlington. I wanted to put it in the bathroom, but the bitch I was married to wouldn't let me put it anywhere. She probably threw it out the minute our divorce was final."

"I've been there and searched the house and the garage. It isn't there. Where exactly did you leave it?"

"I told you; I left it in the garage. Exactly where is it? Hell, I don't know. In the garage someplace. In a corner, behind something. It's not my fault if it isn't there anymore. I don't live there anymore. We rent this place. We can't put in plumbing fixtures. I only paid a couple of bucks for the thing, so I left it behind when I moved out. My ex got the house and everything in it, except my clothes and personal belongings. That's all that crook of a judge would let me have. I don't know why it's not there. She might have gotten rid of it. Why do you care about that piece of junk?"

"I have one last question. What was painted on the side of the urinal?" After all of this, Darnell wanted to be certain he was pursuing the right urinal.

"Somebody's name was on it and 1917. I don't remember the name. It was painted on there in black paint. I always planned to take some paint remover and try to get that off the side, but I never got around to doing it."

Darnell's rage overtook him again. He could keep himself under control for a period of time, but when he realized the urinal had once again slipped through his fingers, he couldn't handle the news. Chuck had confirmed that he had been in possession of *Fountain*. Darnell's fortune had been within his grasp. Now he was going to have to go back to Arlington and question Marilynn Murray about what she had done with it. He didn't want to do that. He knew *Fountain* wasn't in the house anywhere, and it wasn't in the garage. She had probably thrown it away.

When he admitted to himself that this was probably going to be another dead end, Darnell lost it. He shot Chuck Grimaldi in the face six times and left the apartment. He suspected Marilynn wouldn't feel particularly sad when she got the word about her former husband's death. But she might be frightened. Darnell had to move fast before she heard about Chuck and got too spooked.

He drove the van immediately to her townhouse. Marilynn's car wasn't in the garage, so Darnell knew she wasn't home from work yet. She almost always worked late and ate dinner before she came home. He waited in the garage at the rear of the townhouse. When Marilynn's car pulled in, Darnell was there to confront her. When she stepped out of her car, he shoved his gun in her face.

"I don't want to hurt you, Marilynn, but you need to tell me what you did with that urinal Chuck had. He told me he left it behind in the garage when you got divorced."

Marilynn was frightened but defiant. "I got rid of the darn thing. I got rid of everything, and I mean everything, that belonged to that worthless Chuck Grimaldi. I put it in a dumpster, and I'm sure it is long gone by now. Why do you want that piece of junk? In fact, I drove all the way to downtown Dallas to get rid of his crap. I rented a truck, and I rented a guy to take it all out of town. If I could have dumped it on another planet, I would have."

Darnell realized he was going to have to drive Marilynn to Dallas and have her show him the exact location of the dumpster where she'd left the urinal. He was angry about having to do that, but it was his last chance. If he killed Marilynn now, he would never know where she had trashed *Fountain*. He might never find it anyway, and he knew the odds were against him. But he did know he was chasing the right porcelain plumbing fixture, and he had come this far. He was going to make her tell him where she'd left it. Then he would kill her. He thought he could maintain his cool until after she had led him to the right dumpster.

Darnell had parked his van a block away from Marilynn's townhouse. It was dark outside, and he pressed his gun into her back as he forced her to walk ahead of him down the deserted alley. Darnell warned her not to cry out or make any noise. When they got to the van, Darnell pushed her into the passenger seat. Then he hit her on the head with the handle of his gun and knocked her unconscious. It would be easier to restrain her if she couldn't move. He tied her up with plastic cuffs and duct tape. Then he wound the duct tape around and around Marilynn and the back of the passenger seat. She was not going to get away. Darnell got into the driver's side, and they began the trip to Dallas. Marilynn regained consciousness. At first they didn't speak. Marilynn didn't know she was about to die. She was frightened but not yet panicked.

"How long ago did you leave the urinal in the dumpster?"

"It was a several months ago. I had just changed back to my maiden name, and I wanted everything that had ever belonged to Chuck out of the house. I couldn't stand to look at his crap anymore. I rented a truck from the U-Haul down the street from me and went to Home Depot where there are people standing in the parking lot every day looking for work. I hired one of them, and we drove to the townhouse. I told him what to take out of the house and the garage and put into the truck. Then we drove to Dallas. My hired helper unloaded it all into a dumpster, and I drove him back to Home Depot. I didn't even know his last name, but I paid him well. I paid cash. I was just so glad to be rid of all of Chuck's stuff."

They drove around a little bit until Marilynn was certain she had the right place. She was trying to be cooperative and give Darnell the information he wanted. He hadn't bothered to put on his ski mask this time, because he knew he was going to kill Marilynn when he had learned everything from her that she could tell him. He hadn't learned much, but he believed her when she finally identified the dumpster where she'd left the urinal. She explained she knew it was the right one because she remembered it was behind the section of a shopping center that had an Applebee's restaurant. Darnell thought she was telling him the truth. It was dark, and no one was anywhere close to the dumpster.

Darnell was surprised he didn't need his rage anymore. He found he could now kill without being angry. Killing had become easy. Darnell would be coming back to this dumpster where Marilynn had discarded her ex-husband's urinal. Darnell didn't want to leave Marilynn's body anywhere close to this place, so he drove to a strip mall in Fort Worth. Marilynn was quiet during the entire drive, and Darnell thought she had to realize what was coming.

It was the middle of the night. When he'd found a secluded dumpster to hide her body, Darnell unwrapped the duct tape that held Marilynn in the passenger seat. He pulled her from the van and shoved her to the ground. He put two shots in her head at close range. Darnell hadn't wanted to shoot her in the van. Two bullet holes in the back of the passenger seat would be difficult to explain to Leonard Bundy. With a great deal of effort, Darnell got Marilynn's body over the side of the dumpster and into the garbage. He got back into the van and drove home to his apartment at TOMT. He was going to have to think about whether or not it was worth it to proceed in his search. Maybe it was time to give up. How in the world would he ever find the urinal now? Did he really want to search all the landfills in the Dallas area?

Chapter 29

arnell bided his time while he thought about what to do next. He wanted the murders in Plano and Arlington and Ft. Worth to be forgotten before he started out on another quest for his fortune. He had used one of his guns in Plano, and he had used the other gun to kill Chuck in Arlington and Marilynn in Ft. Worth. He didn't think the murders in the three cities would ever be connected.

The dumpster where Marilynn had left *Fountain* was about thirty-five miles from TOMT, and Darnell went back to the dumpster from time to time and looked around. There was an ATM in the mini-mall, near the Applebee's. Because of the ATM, Darnell was sure there were security cameras in the area but didn't know if any of the cameras were pointed in the direction of the dumpster. Even if they were, he had no idea how long the bank that owned the ATM kept their surveillance videos.

Although he knew in his heart that the search was finished, Darnell had a couple of loose ends he hadn't attended to, a few things he wanted to pursue. When he had interrogated Marilynn, she had not remembered the exact date that she'd put the urinal in the dumpster. In case he was ever able to come up with any security footage, Darnell had to know exactly what day Marilynn had discarded the urinal. Marilynn said she'd rented a truck to take Chuck's stuff to Dallas, and she'd mentioned that the truck was from the U-Haul close to her house.

Darnell was sure that somebody with better computer skills than his would be able to hack into the U-Haul records remotely, without ever actually going to the U-Haul office, to find the rental paperwork for the truck Marilynn had rented. But Darnell didn't have those skills. To find out what he needed to know, he would have to break in the old fashioned way. He thought he'd improved his talents as a burglar, but every time he broke into a place that had alarms, it made him nervous. He knew that modern security systems could automatically set off an alarm at a monitoring station when a phone line was cut. Motion detectors and heat detectors set off silent alarms. You might never know the police were on their way until it was too late. Darnell had been caught in that snapper in Tulsa and had paid a high price for setting off a silent alarm. Fortunately, the U-Haul office he was interested in was not that high tech. All he had to do to shut down the alarm system was cut a few wires, and he would be inside.

Remembering what had happened to him when he'd accessed the computer in the office of the Tulsa storage facility, he took more care as he looked through the computer in the U-Haul office. It wasn't like he had to go back years this time; he only had to go back a few months to find out what he wanted to know. He had planned his escape more carefully, too, and there was no fence around this office. Darnell wasn't great at finding things on a computer, and he spent more than an hour searching for the information he wanted. Finally, he located the truck Marilynn Murray had rented. She had picked up the truck at 8:06 on the morning of April 16th and returned the truck that evening at 6:37. April 16th was the day he was looking for, the day Marilynn had dumped Chuck's urinal.

Darnell was going to give his pot of gold one more shot. He checked out the ATM located near the dumpster behind the Applebee's and found it was owned by the TRC Bank of Dallas. Darnell thought he was a fairly good-looking guy. He thought it might be worth a try to get a date with someone who worked in the security department of the TRC Bank. He wanted to find out how long the bank kept its surveillance videos. He'd heard that most banks kept them for a year, but he needed to verify the information. He needed to find out if any of the nearby surveillance cameras were directed at the area around the dumpster.

Darnell began to visit the dumpster site at night. He drove his motorcycle, wore a hoodie, and kept his face obscured as much as he could. He didn't want to be caught on a surveillance camera, if it turned out any were pointed towards the dumpster. He knew the homeless liked to pick through dumpsters, and he was on the lookout for a homeless person who hung around the dumpster behind the Applebee's. Darnell couldn't visit the area behind the restaurant every night, but one night he caught an old man digging in the dumpster. The homeless man was frightened when Darnell approached him, and he started to run away. Darnell reassured the guy, and a twenty-dollar bill convinced the toothless man he just wanted to talk.

"Do you come to this dumpster every night?"

"I come here sometimes. Applebee's throws out a lot of food. I get pretty good meals here. It's none of your business."

"Does anybody else hang out here to get food?" Darnell knew the homeless liked to stake out their territories. If this dumpster was the old guy's turf, other homeless people probably didn't come here.

"I'm pretty much the only person who comes here. Why?"

"I'm looking for something that someone threw into the dumpster a few months ago. She threw it away on April 16th, sometime in the middle of the day. I'm looking for a men's urinal. You know, like they have in public restrooms, in men's rooms."

"I know what you mean. How much is it worth to you to know what happened to it?"

Darnell wasn't sure if this meant the homeless man had seen the urinal or if he was just fishing. "Have you seen it?"

"I might have. It depends. It depends on how much you want to know what I know."

"I'll pay you fifty bucks if you know what happened to the urinal, if you really did see what happened to it."

"Let me see the money."

Darnell took a fifty dollar bill out of his wallet. He held it up so the old guy could see it but couldn't get to it. "Tell me what you know."

"Granny Haircape took it. She takes all the good stuff out of my dumpster. Lucky for me she doesn't come very often, but sure enough, she took the urinal. I was going to try to get it out of the dumpster into my cart, but it was too heavy. Granny Haircape is a drunk, but she's strong as an ox. I watched her the night she came for the urinal. She checked it out during the day and came back that night to get it. She had a heck of a time dragging it out of there. I couldn't figure out why she wanted that old thing, but then, she always takes the weirdest stuff."

"Is this Granny Haircape somebody you know? Does she live around here?"

"I don't know her but I've talked to her. She says she's an artist. She says that all the time. She takes the stuff from the dumpster for her art, she says. Sometimes I think she's nuts, but mostly she's just drunk."

"Does she come here often? Does she live in Dallas?"

"Naw, she doesn't live in Dallas. She lives away some-place else. She comes here every month or two. She told me she drives to Dallas to get her 'art supplies.' She's about due. She drives a full-size pick-up and hauls her junk back to wherever it is she lives."

"Here's your fifty bucks. Can you meet me here tomorrow night? I want to talk to you about watching out for Granny. I'll pay you another fifty if we can figure out a way for me to talk to her. What's your name? I'm Jim."

"I'm Surry. I'll be here tomorrow night at midnight."

"Okay. One more question, do you know if there are any surveillance cameras that watch this dumpster?"

"Yep, there's a camera pointed directly at your face right now. I stay off to the side, see. But you are right in the cross-hairs." Surry started to laugh.

Trying to get out of the camera's eye, Darnell moved away from where he was standing. He moved closer to the tooth-less, homeless Surry. "Who runs the surveillance cameras? The bank?"

"Not the bank. There was a body dumped here a year or so ago, and I guess the city decided it was a high crime area. They put in cameras. After that, I had to be much more careful not to be seen. I watched them put the cameras in, though, so I know where they are and how to stay out of the way." Surry laughed again. He had outsmarted the cameras and the city.

"So you think it's the city that has cameras on the dumpster."

"I told you. I know it's the city. I saw them come here and put them in. I don't know how often they come and pick up the videos. Maybe only when something bad happens."

"You mean, somebody actually comes here in person and picks up the videos?"

"They come here and pick up whatever it is they have in the cameras. The cameras are very small, you know. And they're motion activated. You won't be able to find them unless I tell you where they are. And that's going to cost you."

"I know. Surry, what did you do when you were younger? You're smart and well-educated. What did you do before you started living on the street?"

"I was a school teacher. I taught high school in a small town in Illinois. It's a long story how I ended up here, and it isn't a good story. But it's okay. I have a place to go inside when it's cold. I've found a way to survive. My life on the streets is my own. I don't miss teaching. I wasn't very good at it anyway."

"I will pay you to show me how to get the videos from the surveillance cameras. That's all I need. I want to see the woman who took the urinal, Granny Haircape. I want to look at the surveillance videos to find out if I can see the license plate on her truck. If I can find that, I can find her address."

"Is that what you want, the numbers and letters from her license plate?"

"Yes, that's all I need. I can figure out where she lives with that information."

"I know her license plate. I memorized it. I was a math teacher, and I always notice and remember numbers. If you pay me another fifty dollars, I can tell you the license plate number. She comes here every so often."

"Here's the fifty."

"It's a Texas plate, expired almost two years ago. It's **MPC * 127**. That's Granny Haircape's license plate on her truck."

Darnell shook hands with Sully. He liked the old geezer with no teeth. He was glad he didn't have to shoot him.

Chapter 30

*D*arnell made plans to get into the Texas DMV database. He had come this far, and he was going to pursue it until he couldn't pursue it anymore. It sometimes occurred to him that he was crazy to do what he was doing, but he was going to keep on doing it. Breaking into the main office of the DMV in Dallas would be lunacy, but he thought he might be able to more easily access the computers at a less secure DMV facility, a satellite office. He thought he was getting pretty good at searching computers for information, but he had to admit that the skills he needed for breaking into alarmed buildings had not improved very much.

Breaking into a DMV was going to be his biggest challenge yet. Hiding in a Walmart after it closed and breaking into a storage facility office and a U-Haul rental place were all small potatoes compared to breaking in to a state agency office building. Darnell visited several DMVs in the Dallas area and chose the one he thought would be the easiest to get into after hours. He had learned that surveillance was an important part of planning, and he watched the building carefully when it closed for the day. He knew what time the doors were locked and found there was no guard who stayed behind at night after the employees left. Banks and institutions that had money and other valuables inside employed night guards, but apparently the DMV was not considered a high priority target for a break-in. There wasn't any money inside the DMV; everybody paid with a credit card now. The locks on the doors of this building were all electronic, and Darnell knew he couldn't break into those. He would have to find another way.

He didn't think he could hide inside the DMV until after hours like he'd done at Walmart, but he thought he could leave a window unlocked in the bathroom. This was not going to be an easy job, and he didn't know if there were motion detectors or hidden surveillance cameras inside the building. He had to assume there were interior surveillance cameras, so he would wear his ski mask. His face would be obscured. He would also wear his shower cap and his plastic gloves. Even if somebody knew he'd been inside the building, they would not know what he looked like, and he wouldn't leave any fingerprints. His weak spot was that he was not computer-savvy enough to hide what he would be looking for in the DMV computer.

He went to a parking garage at the Dallas-Ft. Worth airport and wrote down the numbers of several random license plates. He copied the numbers from different kinds of Texas licenses. He chose a couple of vanity plates and a couple of the special issue conservation "Keep Texas Wild" plates. When he got to the DMV, he would run all the plates.

It would take him a little bit longer, but searching for the owners of more than one license plate was a good way to obscure which one he was really looking for. He had learned to plan ahead and to be more careful. He thought it would pay off.

He made a visit to the DMV office an hour before closing time, and he sat for a few minutes with the other poor suckers who were sitting and waiting their turns. Then he visited the men's room, and when nobody else was in the bathroom, he unlocked the window. He looked out the window. Even though the bathroom was on the first floor, Darnell realized, if he was going to get into the bathroom from the outside, he was going to need a ladder. Bringing a ladder meant he would have to drive Leonard Bundy's van. Darnell didn't want to use the van again, especially at night. Leonard might be losing it, but he still tried to keep track of anything that had an impact on his bottom line. Bundy made sure Darnell kept a careful log of how many miles he drove for each delivery. Darnell had faked deliveries and doctored the log entries many times to hide from Leonard Bundy the fact that he was using the van outside work hours. Darnell didn't want to risk borrowing the TOMT van, so he rented a pick-up truck for the night. He would borrow a ladder from TOMT.

Darnell was ready for what he hoped was his last break-in. He didn't mind killing people as much as he disliked breaking into places. Murder was easy compared to burglary, at least for Darnell. He drove the truck as close to the back of the building as he could. He put the ladder up against the side of the building. The ladder was a little bit short, but he thought he could make it in through the window. At this point, he hadn't really thought about how he was going to exit. He did not consider how he would get out of the window and onto the ladder to climb down to the truck. He left the truck unlocked and the key in the ignition for a quick getaway. He'd stolen a set of license plates and put them on the truck. He was patting himself on the back for being smart about that. Getting into the building was risky, but it didn't take long.

The computers inside the building were still turned on. Accessing databases was fairly easy, but Darnell ran into a problem because Granny Haircape's truck registration had expired. It took longer than he'd planned because he had to find and then search the database for expired vehicle registrations. This snag made his job more complicated, and he was sure he was leaving digital fingerprints all over the place. He had to go back three years to find Granny's truck, but he finally got her address. Of course, he didn't know if she still lived in the same place. It was three years later, but he'd found Granny. She was Melody Granger, and she lived on Austin Street in Marfa, Texas. Darnell carefully wrote down the women's address.

Melody Granger had dug the urinal out of the dumpster more than three months earlier, and Darnell was betting she still had it. He made plans to go to Marfa. Marfa was a day's drive away. He couldn't take Leonard's van that far. He would have to spend more money to rent another car or a truck if he was going to bring the urinal back with him.

He finally thought he knew who had *Fountain*. He was closing in. He knew Granny might have gotten rid of it in the past few months, but he doubted she had. She was old, according to Surry, and old people like to hang on to things. They sometimes even forgot they had things. Melody was an artist, so she was probably a little flaky to begin with. Also according to Surry, she was a drunk. That would make her even less likely to get rid of her 'art supplies.'

It was time to leave the DMV. He had what he'd come for, although he was certain somebody would notice that he'd searched for several license plate numbers. He hadn't done a perfect job on the computer, but he would soon be out of the DMV building. He returned to the men's room and began to climb out the window. He realized it wasn't going to be as easy to get out the window onto the ladder as it had been to climb from the ladder into the window. But he had to get out. The sun would be coming up in less than an hour. He had to risk climbing out the window and getting onto the ladder, even though the entire setup was dangerously unstable. He couldn't risk going out a door and setting off an alarm.

He took the chance. The ladder fell, and Darnell fell...into the bed of the pick-up. He didn't fall very far, but he fell hard enough to know he'd broken his wrist. He heard the sound when the bone snapped. His wrist didn't look right, and it hurt like the dickens. He knew he was in trouble. This was not a dislocation. This was a break, and it was a bad one. Unfortunately, it was his right wrist, and he was right-handed. More terrible luck! He couldn't go to an ER, and this was going to take more than a bag full of antibiotics to fix. He struggled to turn the key in the truck's ignition with his left hand. Once he got the truck started, he was able to drive with his left hand, but the pain was getting to him.

He dropped the truck at the rental agency and picked up his motorcycle. With only his left hand available to keep him balanced and on the road, the bike was even more difficult to drive than the truck had been. He was precariously unsteady on the Harley, and he was in pain and tired from being up all night. He realized he had other bumps and bruises from when he'd fallen, but he didn't think any of them were serious. He made it back to his room at TOMT without an accident, but he had no idea what he was going to do about his injury. He was smart enough to know that he probably needed surgery. Leonard Bundy didn't provide his employees with health insurance, so Darnell would be on his own. He was going to have to take care of his wrist himself, just like he'd taken care of the bullet wound in his hand. For the moment, he took a massive dose of Ibuprofen and collapsed in his bed. Leonard was expecting him to work in the morning, but Darnell knew that wasn't going to happen.

Leonard was very unhappy the next morning when he saw Darnell's swollen wrist. "What the hell happened to you?"

"I fell off my bike. It was stupid. I skidded and the bike flipped. I put out my hand to catch myself when I fell. My wrist is broken."

"Stupid is right. You aren't going to be able to work until that wrist is better. What are you going to do about it?"

"I think if I wrap it really tight with adhesive tape, it will be all right. I might be able to work in a couple of days, as soon as the swelling goes down."

"You know, being injured is not allowed around here. I don't give you any health insurance for several reasons. One reason is to save myself money. Another reasons is so you will be careful and don't hurt yourself. And you didn't even get this injury on the job. You got it on your own damn time! I'm not happy about this, Darnell."

"I didn't think you would be, Leonard." Darnell was in pain, and he was cranky. He'd never liked Leonard Bundy anyway.

"Don't you get smart with me! I can kick you out of your apartment in a second, if I want to."

Darnell realized he needed a place to stay until his wrist healed. He would have to suck up to Bundy and make nice until he could leave this place for good and relocate to Marfa. "Sorry, Leonard, I wasn't trying to be smart. I'm in a lot of pain right now, and I'm not thinking straight. I need to get some tape and wrap this thing. I promise I won't be out of work long. I need today off, but I'll be back tomorrow."

"No more catting around on that motorcycle at night. No more taking chances and getting hurt. Okay?"

"Okay. I promise I'll stay in at night from now on. I can't drive the bike anyway, with my wrist hurt like this."

Leonard stomped off. He usually let his workers go when they were hurt and couldn't work. Darnell had seen this happen quite a few times in the months he'd been employed by Leonard Bundy, so he knew what he had to do. He drove Alger to the drug store in the van and gave him money to buy several rolls of adhesive tape. Back at TOMT, Darnell wrapped his wrist. He hoped wrapping it tightly would keep the swelling down. He knew he could be permanently disabled because he wasn't getting the care he needed, but he had no options. The unknown was how bad the permanent damage to his wrist would be. Again his quest for the Duchamp *Fountain* was delayed. Darnell wondered for the thousandth time how much of a fool he really was.

Chapter 31

*A*s soon as his wrist had healed sufficiently, Darnell rented a car and drove to Marfa. He hated to spend the money on the car rental, but with his injury, he didn't trust that he would be able to control his motorcycle well enough with his one good hand to drive it on the highway for eight hours. And he couldn't make himself wait any longer to get to Marfa to find Melody. He'd convinced himself that she was now in possession of the key to the wealth that would define his future.

Leonard was angry when Darnell asked for time off to make the trip to west Texas, and he let Darnell know he wasn't happy about it. Darnell wanted to check out Granny Haircape's situation in Marfa before he relocated there and made a commitment to pull out all the stops to get *Fountain* away from Melody Granger. What Darnell didn't tell Leonard was that he was probably going to quit his job anyway. When Darnell found Melody's house and briefly checked out the neighborhood, he realized his only choice was to find a place to live in Marfa so he could make taking possession of the urinal his full-time work.

Leonard was furious when Darnell told him he was leaving his job at TOMT. He'd been underpaying Darnell for months and knew he wouldn't find anyone else to do all the work Darnell had been doing for the amount of money Leonard had been willing to pay him. Darnell was ambivalent about quitting his job for Leonard Bundy. If he wasn't able to find the urinal in Marfa, he might need to go back to work at TOMT. In the end he decided Leonard would take him back, if he ever wanted to work for the man again. Darnell packed up his belongings and added the few valuable items he'd been able to steal from Leonard Bundy to his duffle bag. He told Alger goodbye. Alger didn't understand why Darnell was leaving, and he cried as he watched Darnell's motorcycle pull out of the TOMT parking lot.

Darnell found a cheap place to stay outside Marfa—a room in a flop house with immigrant farm workers. Darnell hated his lodgings, but finding an inexpensive place to live was not an easy thing to do in trendy Marfa, Texas. It was all Darnell could afford. He watched Melody's house for a couple of days. He'd learned from Surry that she was a drunk, and he learned from his own surveillance that she had an erratic lifestyle. She slept at odd hours and worked on her sculpture at odd hours, mostly in the middle of the night. Once when Darnell figured Melody would be away from her house for a while, he'd gone inside on the off-chance he might find *Fountain* quickly. Melody's door was never locked, so he hadn't had to break into the house. He'd just walked in. He didn't find the urinal, but he found thousands of other things filling Melody's domain. It was a three-bedroom house completely stuffed with Melody's art supplies, and Darnell wondered if *Fountain* could be hidden underneath one of the endless piles of junk. Even though a urinal was not a small item, it was going to require more than a casual search to go through all of Melody's hoard. Darnell had always traveled light and had very few possessions. He was overwhelmed and discouraged by the prodigious number of things Melody had collected.

Her lifestyle was so unpredictable that Darnell was continually frustrated as he attempted, time after time, to gain entry to Melody's house to continue his search for *Fountain*. He knew it had to be there. He was sure Melody hadn't thrown anything away for years, so he was convinced the urinal was somewhere inside Melody's home, mixed in with her terrible mess of other stuff. Darnell's patience was running out. He was so close to his goal; he found he couldn't wait any longer. Melody was going to have to die. Eliminating Melody was the only way Darnell figured he would ever have enough uninterrupted time to do a thorough search of the artist's house.

Darnell's plan was to pretend to be Melody's nephew after she was found dead. He wanted to take possession of her house for a short time after she died so he could search it at his leisure. If Melody's death was not suspicious, he thought he could move in quickly and take over as her closest surviving relative. Darnell could be slick and charming when he needed to be. He felt he could convince the small-town law enforcement people into letting him take care of getting rid of Melody's stuff. Darnell thought the authorities would probably be relieved that somebody was willing to take on the job of sorting out her house full of crap.

Darnell knew that Melody went to the grocery store every few days. He had followed her into the store and pushed a cart behind her as he watched what she bought. She always purchased cat food, soy milk, and regular milk. She usually bought dry cereal and limes. Her other purchases were random, and she bought different fresh food every time she went to the store. He wanted to make her death appear to be from natural causes if possible, but that was always a very tricky thing to pull off successfully. If he couldn't make her death seem like an accident, he decided poison was a second-best choice. Everyone knew Melody drank. Maybe her death would be attributed to excessive alcohol consumption or food poisoning. He didn't really care as long as he was able to get possession of the house so he could search it.

Finding the poisons he wanted was not as easy as Darnell had thought it would be. He had to pay a lot of money to some very unscrupulous people to get everything he wanted. He was trying to be very careful and plan everything precisely. He was too close now to make a mistake. He prepared his deadly potions and followed Melody the next time she went to the grocery store. After she had loaded the regular milk and the soy milk into her cart, and when she was distracted and not paying attention, Darnell took her cart and pushed it into the next aisle. Working as fast as he could, he took the hypodermic needles out of his pockets. They were already loaded with poison. He quickly shot lethal doses into all six plastic bottles of the soy milk and into the quart of fresh regular milk. He put the needle in at the tops of the containers so the tiny pin prick of a hole wouldn't be discovered and, more importantly, wouldn't leak.

He left Melody's grocery cart in the wrong aisle. She was almost always three sheets to the wind, but Darnell knew she would eventually find her missing cart. He figured she wouldn't waste too much time worrying about how she'd become separated from her groceries. She would just be glad when she'd found them again.

He watched as Melody paid for her purchases at the check-out counter. He watched as she loaded the food and supplies into her truck. He smiled and congratulated himself that he was almost in control of Melody's house and the long-lost *Fountain*. He was already planning what he was going to do with the riches he was convinced were headed his way at long last. All he had to do now was to sit back and wait for Melody to drink the milk and die. He was almost a millionaire, maybe even a billionaire. He couldn't imagine what could possibly go wrong now. But everything did go wrong.

Darnell knew he had to continue to stay out of sight. A strange man wandering around in this neighborhood in this small town would attract attention. But he was so eager to have Melody die, he could not help himself. He had figured out that one of Melody's neighbors was a very old man who never left his house. Darnell decided he could hide out in the ramshackle shed in the neighbor's back yard, and no one would ever find him there. He was in the perfect location to keep an eye on Melody.

What he did not expect to see was Melody leave three doctored bottles of soy milk beside the man's door. Why would she leave her milk for her neighbor? Darnell knew that whoever drank that milk would die a very painful death. The milk had been intended for Melody. She was supposed to drink it. Darnell debated with himself about whether or not he should try to get into the neighbor's house and retrieve the soy milk. But he debated too long. By the time he finally decided to take action and broke a window pane on the back door, it was too late.

When Darnell found Jinx face down in his cereal bowl, sprawled across the kitchen table, he became enraged. He knew that sooner or later, somebody would find the old man dead. It was an ugly death. If Melody died in exactly the same way, law enforcement would become suspicious. If two neighbors who lived side-by-side both died from poisoning, the police would believe they had a serial murderer on their hands. Darnell saw his riches once again slipping through his fingers, and he completely lost it. His insanity consumed him. He ranted and raved around Jinx Carruthers' house; his fury had turned him into a madman.

Jinx had a very antiquated bathroom in his old house. When Darnell saw the old-fashioned fixtures, he mistakenly believed, in his delusional state, that Melody Granger had given *Fountain* to her neighbor, Jinx. Darnell's brain was on fire, and all he could think about was getting his hands on the prize. He knew there was a crowbar in the backyard shed where he had been hiding. He raced to the shed to get the crowbar and raced back to the house. In his hallucinatory frenzy, he pried the sink and the toilet away from the wall in Jinx's bathroom. He beat the bathtub and cracked the porcelain with the crowbar.

When his adrenalin began to fade, he realized what he had done, the stupid mistake he had made. He collapsed on the bathroom floor, screaming and crying about his terrible bad luck. Life had conspired against him. He was never going to find *Fountain*. Once again, Darnell had been taken over by the maniac inside himself. His fit of rage had completely sapped his energy. He fell asleep in Jinx Carruthers' bathroom, lying in the middle of the destruction he had created. When he woke up, it was morning. Darnell heard the sheriff breaking down the front door of the house. He had to get out of the place. He left through the back door and made it inside the shed just as the Presidio County sheriff discovered that Jinx was dead.

Darnell's plan had turned into a disaster. Melody didn't drink the milk. Her cat died instead. One of her neighbors almost died, and one of her neighbors did die. The police were involved, and everybody and their housekeeper were all over the place, in and out of Melody's house. The neighbors had even held a funeral for the cat on Melody's patio. Darnell's existence had become a catastrophe. He again became livid that nothing was working out for him. And now, Melody not only hadn't died; she had disappeared. Her pretend nephew no longer had any reason to come forward and take possession of her home. She was still alive, but nobody had any idea where to find her.

Because Melody's next-door neighbor had died, and everybody knew the soy milk that had killed Jinx Carruthers had come from Melody, her house had become a kind of secondary crime scene. Darnell wasn't going to be able to get the access to her house that he wanted. Darnell didn't have a plan B, but he knew he could come up with something. He had imagined himself living the high life within weeks of arriving in Marfa. Now he was going to have to stay in the squalid rooming house until Melody showed up again so he could have another crack at killing her.

As he continued to watch Melody's house, Darnell realized that law enforcement people were no longer paying any attention to it. The yellow crime scene tape was gone from Jinx Carruthers' house and from Melody's house. Melody's nosy neighbors and the nosy housekeeper were not paying any attention to the house either. Darnell decided he could get into the house and begin to search it, and no one would be the wiser. He decided he could even spend the night at the house, and no one would know he was there. He moved his things from the boarding house into Melody's.

He found everything else in the world at Melody's, but he couldn't find *Fountain*. She had collected plumbing fixtures of every kind, but there was not a single urinal in the house. Darnell had spent hours and hours going through every pile in every room. He'd left a terrible mess, but then, the place had been a terrible mess to begin with. He couldn't believe his bad luck. He'd been so sure this was the last stop on his journey. He was so sure he would be rich by now. He was beyond being furious with Melody. He could not imagine what she had done with *Fountain*. He had to decide if he wanted to give up his search or if he wanted to try to find Melody. She was the only person who knew what she had done with his fortune. Darnell was depressed. He had traveled a long and convoluted road, looking for the Marcel Duchamp treasure. Quite a few people had died because he had been so determined to find the priceless antique.

Even though he had stalked her for weeks, Darnell didn't know Melody. He didn't think she had any family. He had no idea where she would go to hide out. He had no idea where she had run to when she'd left her home in Marfa. She had left behind a house full of art supplies that Darnell assumed were valuable to her. She had left behind three towering unfinished sculptures on her patio. Would she ever come back to this place? Would she ever feel safe enough to return to her home? Would her work as a sculptor draw her back to Marfa? Would she feel compelled to complete her works of art? Would the hours and years of effort she had put into accumulating all of her "found objects" be enough to tempt her to return?

Darnell could not answer any of these questions. He was paralyzed with anger and disappointment and indecision about what to do. He wondered if he had been chasing windmills from the beginning of his quest. Maybe he should go back to TOMT and ask Leonard if he could have his old job and his old living quarters back. Where was Melody?

The Present...
Marfa

Chapter 32

llery wanted to join Augustus and me to open gifts on Christmas morning. Ellery said he hadn't celebrated Christmas for years and hadn't had a stocking or a gift to unwrap for a very long time. It made me sad to think he hadn't had anybody to enjoy the holidays with him in the past. Doug pushed Ellery's wheelchair into my living room. Augustus lit a fire in the fireplace, and the tree looked beautiful. Consuela had left two plates of her homemade cinnamon rolls with vanilla glaze icing. I carefully reheated the rolls in the microwave, and Augustus made coffee. We took turns opening presents, and Ellery even laughed a few times. Everyone loved their stockings and stocking stuffers, and I felt a burst of Christmas joy because I'd gone to some trouble to try to make Christmas fun for my small group of new friends. Doug was especially touched that I had given him a stocking and not just looked through him like he was the hired help.

Augustus had brought me another large box of the special dark chocolates that he knew I loved. He also gave me an exquisite silver bracelet that I knew was handmade and very expensive. I was thrilled and put the bracelet on my arm immediately. After an hour or so of Christmas fun, Ellery was ready to go back to the casita and rest. Augustus cleaned up the coffee cups, and I took a nap. Our reservation for Christmas dinner at the Saint George was at four o'clock. We would take the golf cart.

The Saint George was magnificently decorated. Fresh green garlands lavishly threaded with wide silver ribbons were draped everywhere, and the waiters and waitresses in the dining room were all wearing red velvet vests. The meal was expensive, but after all, it was Christmas. Augustus ordered a bottle of champagne, and we were seated at a table right beside the Christmas tree. It was decorated in tiny white lights, shiny blue and silver balls, handmade silver ornaments, and a touch of old-fashioned silver tinsel. It was lovely. We dined on gougères and olives, shrimp remoulade, lobster in a beurre blanc sauce, rare prime rib of beef with au jus, horseradish and sour cream sauce, Yorkshire pudding, dauphinoise potatoes, Brussels sprouts and asparagus, a spinach and pomegranate seed salad, and a parfait made with dark chocolate gelato and crushed peppermint candy canes. We were groaning from the wonderful meal. Augustus said it was the best Christmas dinner he'd ever eaten. I had to agree, especially since I'd not had to cook a thing.

Just as we were leaving, my favorite waiter, Hernando, brought two heavy shopping bags of food to the table. I gave him a questioning look, and he put his finger to his lips, the classic hush, don't tell, signal. He whispered in my ear, "Leftovers for you and dinner for Ellery and his nurse."

My face showed alarm, but Hernando again put his finger to his lips and shook his head. It was to be our secret. He and the kitchen staff at the Saint George were sending Christmas dinner to my house guests. I wondered once again how everyone always knew everything that was happening in this town. I gave Hernando a hug and kissed him on the cheek. I'd left him a Ben Franklin as a tip for the delicious dinner and meticulous service. He blushed, gave me a big grin, and hugged me back. Augustus drove the golf cart to Austin Street, put our leftovers in the refrigerator, and took the shopping bags for Ellery and Doug back to the casita. I was filled with the Christmas spirit. I might be living in the murder capital of the world right now, but Marfa, Texas was definitely home. I loved the people here. They had big hearts. It warmed my heart that I lived in a place like this. It had been a great Christmas.

I knew the reality of Ellery's slow recovery, the woman with the shoe, and the serial poisonings in the neighborhood would force me back into the real world the next day. But today I was able to put it all aside. I had a long, fun phone conversation with my daughter in San Diego. After hearing about my dinner at the Saint George, she was wishing she'd come to Marfa for Christmas. We made tentative plans for her to visit in February after her trial. I hoped things would have calmed down in Marfa by the time she arrived. It was tough to explain to one's child that neighbors on all sides and neighbors' cats had died or almost died. The last thing I wanted was for my daughter to become alarmed for my safety and decide I needed to go into a nice, safe independent living community. Ugh! Who wanted to do that? It sounded suffocating, boring, and quite dreadful to me. I'd rather live with murder and mayhem.

When I went to the kitchen the next morning, Consuela had gathered the beef bones from our Christmas meals, added some stew meat to the broth, and was making soup. She thanked me for the gifts I'd given to her and her children. She wanted to hear all about our dinner the day before. I thanked her for the delicious homemade cinnamon rolls we'd enjoyed for our Christmas brunch. She'd already been out to check on Ellery and said she thought he looked better. She wanted to know if I'd been in the pool yet. I told her tonight was the night. She'd taken one day off, and it seemed we had a great deal of catching up to do.

Augustus knocked on the back door. He said he'd just received word that he had to go back to L.A. for two days, but he needed to talk to me before he left. He wanted to tell me what he'd found out about the coins and the Euros that had been in the spy shoe. I'd been so focused on the microdot, I'd completely forgotten about the money.

"I haven't been able to pin down exactly how much the coins are worth. They are both very valuable, but I haven't yet found the right expert to confirm just how valuable. I've tried to be discreet about who I ask about the coins. I can't just go on the internet and post a picture of them. That would be asking for trouble. One of my coin experts will be back in the U.S. after the first of the year, and I have an appointment to meet with him. I'll know more then. I do know the coins are gold, and they were not mass produced. I think one is Peruvian and pre-Columbian. You can imagine how valuable that would be. The other coin is a Spanish doubloon of some kind, but very rare. Neither coin is in any of the coin collector's books. But the two Euros...they are the interesting part of this."

On his phone, Augustus brought up the pictures I'd sent him of the front of the two paper Euros. I had noted that some of the digits in the serial numbers were circled in blue ink on both of the two hundred Euro bills. Some of the digits also had lines drawn underneath them in red ink.

"I saw the circles and the underlining, but I didn't think that meant anything. From time to time, I've had U.S. currency that had things drawn on it. I got a bill one time that showed Alexander Hamilton with a moustache on his face. Another time I saw one that had a red stocking on top of Ben Franklin's head. Currency humor!"

"I don't think these markings were intended to be humorous. From the beginning, I've thought they were some kind of code. After doing some research, I think they are the numbers that lead to a Swiss bank account. I haven't cracked the code completely yet, but because of the total number of figures that are either circled or underlined, I'm pretty sure it's a numbered bank account. The five digits that are underlined in red identify a Swiss bank. I haven't figured out yet which Swiss bank. The account number has 12 digits—the blue circles. I'm still working on it with a cryptographer. This may have been our Taiwanese woman's insurance policy or her getaway stash. She never got to use it, but as far as I know, no one else has been able to access it either. You could be seriously rich, Margaret."

"I don't want to be any richer than I already am. I'm old, and I don't need any more money than I've already got." I looked at Consuela. "Of course, I could give it away, couldn't I?" I smiled at my housekeeper.

"Don't start giving it away just yet. You don't have the coins anymore, and somebody else might figure out before we do, why those numbers are circled and underlined." Augustus was such a smart and kind fellow. I'd grown used to the purple spikes in his hair. I didn't want him to go back to L.A., even for two days. I felt safer with him here in Marfa. He could see I didn't want him to leave, and I know he wanted to reassure me. "I have to go. Please keep a low profile while I'm gone. I'm bringing some muscle with me when I return from L.A. Can you stay safe until I get back? Promise me you won't leave the house."

"I will promise no such thing." Conseula looked at me with a frown. "But, I'll be careful. I'm going to be swimming for most of the next two days anyway." Augustus hugged Consuela and then he hugged me.

"Thanks for the best Christmas ever. Save some of that soup for me, will you?" He was gone. I'd been holding my breath and hadn't realized it. The news about the coins and the Euros and the numbered bank account, on top of the story about the shoe had left me gasping. Consuela looked equally dumbfounded.

I was concerned about Consuela. "Do you want to take some time off? I can understand why you might not want to come to work until all of this intrigue has been resolved. Sometimes, I wish I could run away for a while." I didn't want Consuela to be afraid to come to work for me.

Consuela turned the tables on me. "You could, you know, get out of town just for a few days. It might do you good. I'm not frightened to come to work. I feel perfectly safe here. I love my job, Ms. Margaret. I think you know that. You are a kind and generous boss. Maybe what you need is to try out your pool? I know you have been looking forward to it. It will relax you, and you will sleep better at night."

I decided I could swim twice today, if the first swim didn't tire me out too much. I'm allergic to elastic and latex, and because of the allergies, I can't wear a regular bathing suit in the pool. Even though my pool is treated with salt and not with chlorine, I have to wear an all-cotton swim outfit. It consists of ladies underwear with legs. I don't know what they're called exactly, but I bought a big enough size that they are just right for swimming. I put on my all-cotton men's undershirt as the top to my "swimming suit." I put a terrycloth robe over my all-cotton outfit and ventured out poolside. It was a cold morning, and I remembered why I usually waited until later in the day to swim. I had designed the pool so it would be easy for me to get in and out of, with plenty of railings and places to hold on to. There were sturdy railings on both sides of the steps that went down into the pool. The steps weren't steep, and I could walk gradually into the water. I felt confident I wouldn't fall getting in and out of my pool.

The water was heavenly. I sank into its warmth and luxu-riated in place for a few minutes. My plan was to swim laps, but I rested for a while and took some time to be thankful I'd decided to put in a heated pool at my new house. The natural gas to heat the pool would cost me a fortune, even in Texas, but it was worth it. I started my laps with the side stroke and then switched to the underwater breast stroke. I was out of shape with my swimming and didn't want to overdo it. I turned a few somersaults in the water and ended my workout with several laps of the elementary back stroke. I'd been in the water for about forty-five minutes. It felt wonderful. My worries about Melody and her cat and Jinx Carruthers and shoes and Euros and coins and all the other neighbor-hood drama faded away while I was enjoying the warm, welcoming, all-embracing water. I was going to urge Ellery and Doug to go in. It would be great therapy for Ellery.

When I'd renovated the house on Austin Street, I had added an exterior door to my new master bathroom. The door was just a few feet from my pool steps. I could walk almost directly from the pool into my bathroom to take a shower. What could be better than that? I wasn't going anywhere today, and I wasn't expecting any visitors. After my shower, I dressed in a navy-blue cotton fleece robe with a hood and warm matching slippers.

Consuela had my lunch ready. I ate the leftover Christmas dinner roast beef in a sandwich with horseradish mayonnaise and some potato salad from the Saint George. Bless Hernando and the cook there. They'd sent lots of extra rare roast beef home with us, and Hernando knew how much I loved their potato salad. I'd planned to write that afternoon, but after my swim and the excellent lunch, I fell asleep.

When I woke up from my nap, Consuela had left and there was a note on the table. My dinner was in the oven. She told me that Ellery and Doug had gone into the pool. They'd only stayed for fifteen minutes, but I was thrilled they'd been in there for that long. I knew it had to have felt good for Ellery to be in the warm water, even if he wasn't normally a swimmer. I hoped he'd want to go in again soon.

Chapter 33

ugustus Gemini arrived back in Marfa on the afternoon of New Year's Eve. He had brought fancy groceries from Los Angeles and announced that he was making dinner. Consuela was leaving early that day, and Augustus had brought her an organic ham as a gift. Consuela was skeptical, but the ham looked delicious. I could tell she was reluctant to leave and wanted to stay and watch what Augustus was going to create in her kitchen. He told her he would tell her all about it the next time she was here. She was taking the next few days off to spend with her family. She cherished her family time, but Augustus was such a compelling personality, I knew she hated to miss a minute of the fun and excitement he infused into any place he happened to be.

Augustus insisted that we eat on my patio that night. It was a mild evening for end-of-December weather. He arranged and turned on all my patio heaters. He set the outside table with my dishes and china and the beautiful hothouse flowers he'd brought on the plane from his favorite florist in L.A. He told Doug he expected him and Ellery to attend the special dinner he was preparing. It was Ellery's favorite—lamb chops on the grill. I was excited. I didn't think Augustus knew that lamb chops were also my favorite. He'd brought food in multiple coolers. The food was already prepared, including the vegetables and the salad and even the twice baked potatoes. Augustus said the potatoes were his weakness, and he loved them so much, he'd brought a dozen. He said we'd have leftovers. He worked so fast I could barely take in everything he was doing. He smiled and laughed, and I could see that even though he was working hard, he was loving every minute he spent producing this moveable feast from California. I knew I was going to love every bite of it, too. He wouldn't let me do anything to help.

I changed into a black silk caftan over a silver grey turtleneck. I added a silver pashmina. It was going to be a party, and I wanted to look like a party girl. Of course I put on the wonderful silver bracelet Augustus had given me for Christmas. It matched my outfit.

Doug pushed Ellery's wheelchair out onto the patio, and we gathered around the table to attack the seafood display, an elaborate cold seafood platter with several sauces that Augustus had lifted, already arranged, from one of his coolers. It was so beautifully presented, I could only think of it as a display. The arrangement of cold lobster, shrimp, scallops, crabmeat, and oysters were all sinfully delicious, as I knew they would be. Augustus brought out two bottles of champagne, and I happened to know that they were very, very expensive bottles. "What has happened in the five days since you were here, Augustus? Did you strike gold or land a really good script? You are so energized. We are delighted to see that, and we need it. But what is going on?" I was curious and couldn't keep from asking.

Augustus laughed, "All of the above. How did you know? I have struck gold, and I have landed a great new script. So eat up. We are not going to talk business tonight. It's New Year's Eve, and we are eating lamb chops and drinking champagne. I'm making brunch tomorrow and will tell you everything that is going on. It is all good news, and I am very excited to tell you about it. Tonight we celebrate our good luck – that Ellery is alive and recovering his strength." He lifted his glass in Ellery's direction. Ellery smiled and drank some champagne. Tears welled in my eyes. "I also want to drink to my good fortune in meeting and getting to know this lovely lady, Margaret Lennox. It has been such a pleasure." He made a small bow in my direction and lifted his champagne glass. Ellery smiled again, lifted his glass in my direction, and drank some more champagne. Augustus was in rare form tonight, and Ellery was smiling. We were celebrating. It was a wonderful time. We finished all of the lamb chops and all of the champagne. I'd imbibed a little too much and finally had to admit that this party girl was tired. Augustus said he would clean up, that there wasn't much to do. I gave everyone a kiss and went to bed.

The next thing I knew it was morning. I smelled bacon cooking. Thankfully, I didn't have a headache. Really good champagne is not supposed to leave you with a headache, no matter how much of it you drink—within reason. I guess my indulgence had been within reason.

The brunch Augustus was preparing was another culinary work of art. Ellery and Doug were in my dining room, which was open to the kitchen where the chef was working. Augustus talked and joked and kept up his running humorous commentary as he sliced onions and mushrooms and grated cheese. He made each of us an omelet to order. There was bacon, sausage, fried potatoes, and fried polenta with maple syrup. Augustus had squeezed what seemed like gallons of fresh orange juice, and the chocolate croissants tasted as if he'd just baked them, which he said he had. Where did the man get his energy to do all of this, and why wasn't he fat?

We laughed and made ridiculous New Year's resolutions. Ellery was even able to make a few jokes. He vowed to give up drinking soy milk. He promised himself he would stay out of Terlingua. The serious note was when he wistfully stated that he was going to walk on his own soon and get rid of the wheelchair. We all cheered him on with that resolution.

I resolved that I would not look for stray shoes or stray bodies behind my house. I resolved that I would swim every day. I also resolved that, if Melody ever returned, I would try to be more understanding of her drinking problem. Augustus choked and spit orange juice across the room when I made that vow. He said silly things like he was going to star in one of his own movies and give away millions of dollars to charity during the coming year. He said he hoped to buy a weekend house in Marfa. He winked at me when he said that.

When Ellery grew tired, he and Doug went back to the casita. Each time Ellery socialized with us, I thought he was growing stronger. Was that wishful thinking on my part? His recovery seemed like such an excruciatingly slow process. I knew Augustus was frustrated with the pace of Ellery's healing, and he was doing everything in his power to encourage Ellery and speed up his return to normalcy.

"I have some exciting things to tell you." Augustus had waited until Ellery and Doug were gone. He was cleaning up the dishes and putting food away. "You are a very rich woman, Margaret." My eyes got large and I started shaking my head in denial. "Before you start to argue with me and tell me that I went against your wishes, just listen to what I've done and my reasons for doing all of it."

"I told you I didn't want to be any richer than I already am."

"Hear me out. It's complicated. I think you will be happy with what I have to tell you." Augustus looked at me, and I tried not to look too disapproving. "I figured out what the circled and underlined numbers on the Euros were, and they led me to a bank in Zurich and a numbered account in that bank. Because I had the number, I was able to access the money in the account. There are all kinds of numbered Swiss bank accounts, and you became the owner of the account whose number was coded on the Euros you found in the dead woman's shoe."

Augustus looked like the cat who'd caught the canary when he announced that there had been ten million dollars in the account. "Of course, to a Zurich bank, that's not really very much. It was not a problem for me to transfer the money to twenty separate accounts in banks around the world." My eyes grew big again, and he put his finger to his lips. "I set up limited partnership corporations and trusts. It takes about five minutes to set up one of those over the internet, with tax ID numbers and all the rest of it. Everything I have done is completely legal. My tax people helped me with everything. Of course, you will have to pay income taxes on any interest your investments earn...except on the educational and other tax exempt trusts I've set up. These trusts are included in the twenty bank accounts. I consulted the experts — the very best tax and trust lawyers to do all of this. I knew you would never participate in anything unless it was completely kosher." He smiled at me and wanted me to smile back. I wasn't ready to smile at him yet.

"We will have to discuss at length what is to be done with all the money, but I wanted you to know that one of the trusts I set up is in Consuela's name. It's an educational trust that will allow all of her children to go to college." That brought a smile to my face. "I knew you would approve of that decision. I am very fond of Consuela, and I know you are, too. She's such a good person, and she has smart children. Her family would struggle to pay for the kids to go to college. Even with scholarships, they would still have room and board and books and other expenses. The educational trust will pay for everything. All three of her children will be able to attend college and go on to graduate school, if they choose to do that. It will all be paid for. Consuela and her husband will not have to finance anything out of their own limited personal resources. We have to talk about the best way to tell Consuela about this trust. She is proud and might not be willing to accept such a large gift from you. She will protest and refuse. So, I am thinking we should gift it to her anonymously. Your name will never be connected in any way with the trust, and she will not be able to trace it back to you or to me. She will strongly suspect, and she will know in her heart of hearts that the money somehow came from you. But it will be her money, and she will not have to be grateful or beholden to anybody to use it for her kids."

I put my arms around Augustus and hugged him hard and a long time. I could not imagine a better use for any money than the plan he had organized for Consuela. It was a

Christmas gift and a New Year's prize beyond belief. "I agree with everything you have done for Consuela. I think anonymity is best. You have scored beyond an A plus in my book."

"The reason I went ahead and claimed the numbered bank account for you was because I was afraid time was running out. I didn't want someone else to figure out what the numbers on the Euros meant, and I didn't want to give anyone else the opportunity to get the money from Zurich. The woman who was in control of this account is dead. She will never be able to access it. We can speculate all day long about how she happened to have so much money in a Swiss bank, but we will never know the truth. I decided I didn't want the Chinese to get the money, and I didn't want the U.S. government to get it either. I felt you and I could make better decisions about how to use this money. If our government got hold of the money, it would just go down the rat hole with all the rest of the money that goes down the rat hole every day. To a government, ten million dollars is peanuts. But to someone like Consuela and her family, the money is a miracle and a future with a promise. I knew tax laws were going to change in the New Year, so I went ahead and got it all together and transferred the money. I have a great tax accountant and a great tax lawyer. If it is okay with you, they will handle everything going forward. It's complicated to administer some kinds of trusts and limited partnerships. My people are the best, and they are happy to do this for us. Actually, my tax lawyer is a woman, and she is brilliant. Of course, they will be well paid out of proceeds from the various partnerships and trusts. You and I will make all the important decisions about where the money is to go. They will do all the paperwork and file all the necessary documents to keep us out of jail." Augustus smiled to let me know this was a joke.

Hearing all of this, the unexpected revelations about the bank account and the unexpected riches that had come my way, had worn me out. I was thankful for what Augustus had done for me. I wasn't going to argue with him or object to any of it. But I was having a hard time taking it all in. Augustus, always perceptive and considerate, could see I was overwhelmed by everything I'd just heard. He continued. "It will take a while to get used to all of this news. We will take baby steps. I will answer all of your questions, and you have full access to my accountant and my tax attorney. This will be fun. I think you will eventually agree with me that it will be fun to make people's lives better. You look tired. Go take a nap. I have to go back to Ellery's house and do some paperwork. I think you and I should go the Saint George for dinner tonight, if they're open. I'll give them a call."

The kitchen sparkled. Augustus was a genius at cooking and a genius at cleaning up. Consuela would approve. I didn't know if I would have enough energy to go to the hotel for dinner tonight. The year had certainly started out with a bang. I was feeling my age. It was only noon on the first day of the year, but it felt good to retreat to my room and climb back into bed.

Chapter 34

elody Granger marketed and sold her sculp-
ture under a name that was different from her own.
She thought her real name was uninteresting and
boring and not at all worthy of her talent. She'd adopted the
name Isadora Daphne as her nom d'artiste. No one believed
for a minute that Isadora Daphne was her real name, but it
was dramatic and cheesy enough to attract attention.

Not everyone appreciated Daphne's works of art, the
huge sculptures that made a statement and were created
out of "found objects" or junk. But there were more people
than one might expect who had a taste for the outrageous.
For whatever reason, Daphne's work had connected with
them. She had a following, and her following continued to
grow. Those who wanted art work that was very far out and
bizarre were attracted to her pieces. A number of movie stars
and television personalities had purchased her work, and
Isadora Daphne was something of a well-known, if minor,

celebrity among some of those in the Los Angeles and Las Vegas crowds.

Some of Melody's works of art were ideas she came up with on her own and created from her supplies of random second-hand objects that others had discarded. But Melody's most lucrative works were the commissions she accepted. As her reputation had spread, more and more of her time was spent on producing art that clients had hired her to create. Melody was not one to be constrained in her artistic expression by the opinions of others, so there was a trade-off when she agreed to create a sculpture to order. But the money from her commissions was so good, she couldn't very often bring herself to turn down a request for a custom piece. She was able to charge the rich people in the entertainment industry almost anything she wanted to charge, and she did.

The down side was that it took a very long time for Melody to complete a piece of sculpture. Those who commissioned Melody's art work knew this about her. The word was out that she was a drunk, and that was one reason it took her forever to complete anything. But lots of artists and writers and actors and entertainers are drunks and drug addicts. Melody's drinking was not the stigma it might have been had she been working as a kindergarten teacher or for a church organization. Those who wanted her work were willing to wait for it and were willing to put up with her procrastination, her erratic behavior, and her drinking habits. Her clients received their completed works of art whenever Melody got around to finishing them.

Melody had been working on a particularly large piece for almost two years. It had been commissioned by a very famous actress and comedienne who lived in L.A. but spent most of her time working clubs in Vegas. Melody was delighted to have this woman order a piece of her sculpture, and she'd worked hard on it. She wanted it to be just right, and she'd redone parts of it several times. The client was an ardent feminist and had hired Melody to create a large sculpture that the entertainer could display on her enormous terrace behind her palatial home in Beverly Hills. Because it was a piece for the outdoors, the sculpture had to be waterproof and substantial. It had to be able to withstand the wind, rain, and other elements of the weather that challenged any work of art placed in an open-air location.

Melody had gone to great lengths to make certain that all parts of her creation would stand up to any and all outside conditions in Los Angeles. It had required a great deal of extra time and effort to make it all secure and weatherproof. At the last minute, Melody had decided the piece needed a more secure base, and she had taken the entire thing apart and put it all back together again. Finally, she had been satisfied with her work, and she'd called the client to tell her the piece was complete. Arrangements had been made to ship the huge work to L.A. It had to be separated into three parts. Each piece had been crated separately and shipped to Beverly Hills. It would all be reassembled at the exterior site. It arrived at the client's home in California the day before Thanksgiving, and the client had been wildly delighted with the final product. In spite of her love of vodka and homemade wine, Melody had scored a success and received a check that would pay her bills for the next year and beyond. She had worked hard to earn the compensation, and she gloried in her triumph.

The sculpture had been fun to do. The client had given her a rough outline of what she wanted Melody to produce. For more than twenty years, this particular client had been building a collection of feminist artwork. All pieces in the collection had to be produced by female artists, and all had to articulate an obvious and even strident feminist message. Melody had certainly delivered on this particular project, and she was delighted that the client loved the piece.

Then Girdle had died, and then Jinx Carruthers had died. Before she'd had a chance to really enjoy the success of her latest sale, Melody's world had fallen apart. Everyone had told her that the poisoning deaths had been a mistake. Everyone had told her that she had been the intended victim, that someone wanted to kill her. She could not imagine who in the world that would be. None of her clients knew her real name or had any idea where she lived and worked. She didn't have any family, and she didn't really have any friends. She only had a cat, a cat that was now dead. Melody had finally come to believe that she'd been the intended victim, and it scared her.

When Jinx Carruthers was found dead after drinking the soy milk Melody had left for him, she decided to disappear. She'd had to leave several unfinished sculptures on her patio, and she had to leave behind all of the precious art supplies she'd spent years collecting. She'd decided she had to get out of town until law enforcement or somebody found whoever was trying to kill her. When that person was locked up in jail, Melody would think about returning to Marfa. Melody had just received a very sizeable check from a client, and she could use the money to pay for her escape. It wasn't cheap to leave your home and go into hiding, but Melody felt she had to do it to save her life.

But Melody, being Melody, couldn't stay away for very long. She'd gone to Santa Fe, a place where artists of all kinds liked to live and work, but she'd quickly concluded that the artists in Santa Fe were stuck on themselves. They weren't very friendly to a newcomer. And Santa Fe was terribly expensive. Marfa was pricey, but Melody had bought her house in Marfa before the town had been discovered and real estate prices escalated. She was staying at a hotel in Santa Fe until she could find a place to rent. After looking at several properties, she realized she couldn't find a place in Santa Fe that wasn't outrageously beyond her price range. If she was going to stay and continue her work in Santa Fe, she would have to find a place that was large enough to handle the giant sculptures she created. It was very discouraging, and after a few weeks at the hotel, she decided Santa Fe and its snobby artists weren't her style. She decided to return to Marfa and take her chances with whoever it was who was trying to kill her.

She traveled all day and all night to get back to Marfa and drove into her garage in the middle of the night. She immediately knew, because of the way her garage looked, that someone had been living in her house and had turned it upside down. When Jinx Carruthers died after drinking Melody's gift of soy milk, she had expected law enforcement to come to her house and search it. She knew they wouldn't purposely vandalize her property. When she went inside the house, she almost collapsed when she saw the mess someone had made. She knew she had a lot of stuff, but she'd known where everything was—or known where almost everything was. She had placed her found objects in categories, in different parts of the living room, in different bedrooms. Now everything was a complete wreck. She would never be able to find anything.

Who in the world had come into her house and done this? Had someone been trying to rob her? Had they been looking for something? They had left alone her works in progress on the patio. Melody decided she would probably never know what had happened or who had invaded her refuge. Maybe Margaret or Ellery had seen something? She was tired after the long drive from Santa Fe, but she would go to her neighbors' houses in the morning and question them about what they knew.

Chapter 35

I was so sound asleep, I tried to ignore the pounding at my door. I rolled over in bed and put a pillow on top of my head. Whoever wanted to get into my house was not giving up. I groaned and put on my wool robe. Whoever was at the door was going to have to take me as I was. I wished people would call before they came.

When I got to the door, I was shocked to see it was my neighbor Melody Granger who had disappeared into thin air several weeks earlier. "Melody, where in the world have you been? Are you all right?"

Melody brushed past me, in her usual rather rude way, without waiting for an invitation to come inside. She didn't answer any of my questions but jumped immediately into what was uppermost in her own mind, "Who has been in my house and torn it up? Somebody broke in and vandalized my place. Everything is a horrible mess. I'll never be able to sort it all out. Who would do such a thing? Did you see anybody poking around or anybody trying to get into my house?"

Consuela and I had gone into Melody's house on the day we'd buried Girdle. I'd gone in one other time to look for soy milk, and Consuela had searched for Melody's phone. But we hadn't disturbed the hoard of "found objects" that filled every corner of the place. Why would we have wanted to do that? We didn't want to touch any of it. It had been the usual terrible mess when we'd been inside. Someone must have gone into her house after the last time we'd been there. "Come inside and sit down, Melody. We have several things to talk about."

"I don't want to talk to you about anything except who has been inside my house." Melody seemed sober, but she was definitely in a bad mood.

"Consuela and I buried Girdle in the garden in your back patio." I thought that might get her to pay attention.

Melody's face crumpled and she began to cry. "They didn't cut her up, did they?"

"No. They didn't cut her up, but they did find out that she'd been poisoned...just like you thought she'd been. We buried her and had a short service and marked her grave. I can show you where she's been laid to rest."

"Later, you can show me later. Right now I have to find out who has been in my house."

"I haven't seen anything or heard anything. If someone has been in there, they were very quiet and careful and didn't cause any commotion."

"Where in the world is Ellery? I was over at his house today and banged and banged on the door. I know some-body's there, but he won't answer. I tried to get him to dig a grave for Girdle when she died, but he wouldn't come to the door then either. Is he mad at me? Is that why he won't come to the door?"

Allowing Melody to have access to Ellery right now was the last thing in the world he needed. She was a big dose to take when one was prepared and ready to take her on, but with Ellery in his currently weakened state, I was afraid she would crush him. And I especially didn't want her to know Ellery was staying in my casita. If she knew he was living there, she would be bugging him constantly. I had to tell some white lies to protect Ellery. Things were getting complicated.

"Ellery is still sick. He isn't at home. He's not mad at you. He just isn't able to do anything right now. I know he hasn't seen anything or anybody around your house. Is there anything missing? Do you think someone intended to rob you?" I was trying to change the subject back to the mess in her house and away from Ellery's whereabouts.

"What's wrong with Ellery? Is he still sick because of the soy milk, and where is he? I need to talk to him."

"That's not a good idea. He's being taken care of by a full-time nurse, and he's not seeing anybody right now. He's in a wheelchair and isn't able to resume his normal activities. He's going to be all right, but he's going to require a lengthy convalescence."

"He would want to see me. Do you know where he is?"

I groaned inwardly, imagining how much I was sure Ellery did not want to see Melody. "Let's go over to your house and take a look. If it seems like anything has been stolen, we need to call the sheriff or the state police. Give me a couple of minutes to put on some clothes. We can take the golf cart." I knew Melody loved to ride in the golf cart. I hoped I could convince her to refocus her attention onto her own house. I slipped into my bedroom quickly before she could ask more questions about Ellery. I closed my bedroom door, wondering if she would follow me in and continue talking to me while I changed my clothes. When she didn't come to the bedroom, I figured she was looking to see what I had in my refrigerator. She would be very curious about all the leftover twice-baked potatoes.

I ushered Melody out to my garage before she could start talking about Ellery or asking me about the potatoes. "So, when did you get back to town? We were all very worried about you but figured you'd been frightened by Jinx's death. Where did you go?"

"I evacuated to Santa Fe. I'd heard it was a place where lots of artists live. Of course you know, I am an artist. Santa Fe was a big disappointment to me. Nobody was at all friendly there. They all acted as if they'd never heard of me. Nobody was nice to me. The real estate was terribly overpriced, and I was very depressed by the place. I hated it and decided to come home. So I am home now, even if somebody is trying to kill me. Are you sure you didn't see or hear anybody breaking into my house?"

"You always leave your house unlocked, Melody. No one ever has to actually break in. All anyone has to do is open the door and walk inside." I didn't tell her that I actually had locked her door the last time I'd been there. Someone had broken in.

Sure enough, the house was an even worse mess than the last time I'd seen it. I could not have imagined that her house would look worse than it had before, but it did. Someone had been there, and it looked to me as if someone had been searching for something. Stuff was tossed in every direction. I wondered what in the world anyone could possibly have hoped they would find in Melody's hoard of junk. Melody was the only person who valued any of it.

It was hopeless to try to do any kind of inventory. Melody couldn't tell if anything was missing. She didn't want to call law enforcement until she'd determined if something of value had been stolen. I knew she would never be able to identify anything specific that had been taken. She would never call law enforcement. I had to think of something that might occupy her time and attention. I didn't want her coming over to my house and nosing around, and I didn't want her looking for Ellery, or even thinking about him.

"Nobody but you knows what was here and what might be missing. Maybe you need to do a written inventory of all these things, as you are cleaning up and reorganizing it all."

Melody looked at me as if I had completely lost my mind. "That's ridiculous. Why would I ever want to write down a list of all this?"

"I just thought it would be helpful to know what you had, so you would be able to determine what was missing. It's just a suggestion."

I could see that Melody was eyeing the cupboard where I knew she kept the vodka. I didn't know if there was anything in there, but I was sure it wouldn't be long until she headed in that direction to find out. If I'd been in Melody's shoes and had a houseful of chaotic junk staring me in the face, I think I might have wanted to find the vodka, too. I could understand a little bit better why she drank. It was time for me to leave. "I have to go home now. Let me know if you find that something has been taken. I'll go to the sheriff with you, if you want." Melody had stopped listening to me and was heading for the vodka cupboard. I slipped out the door and drove the golf cart home. I didn't expect to hear from her again today.

When I got home, I decided to go for a swim. I tried to swim every day, and I usually was able to meet that goal. The water felt wonderful. I took it easy today and purposely didn't tire myself out. I hoped to have the energy to go to dinner with Augustus. It had just started to snow when I was climbing out of the pool. I put on a terrycloth robe and went inside to my bathroom to take a shower. As I was getting dressed, I heard someone moving around in the house and wondered who it could be.

When I went to the kitchen, I found Consuela with three large tin boxes of Christmas cookies. She'd told me she was going to bring cookies as Christmas gifts, but she hadn't been supposed to come to work today. One of the boxes was for me, and she also had a box for Ellery and one for Augustus. During the Christmas holidays, she and her children had cut out and baked dozens of sugar cookies. They had carefully and artistically iced and decorated each one. There were traditional Christmas shapes and some southwestern ones as well. I especially liked the sombrero and piñata cookies. The kids had made liberal use of the red hots on those. I tried a cookie in the shape of a wreath, and it was so delicious. The colorful icing had a slight almond flavor, and every one of the cookies was a work of art. I was touched that Consuela's children had gone to so much trouble. Many kid hours had gone into decorating the dozens of cookies. I helped myself to a second cookie, and Consuela was pleased that I was happy with her gift. She made us each a cup of tea, and we sat at the table to drink it. I told her Melody was back home and recounted the story about her house being vandalized. It was peaceful as we looked out the back windows and watched the snowflakes fall softly on the patio and on the pool.

Augustus knocked on the door and came into the kitchen to join us. He was amazed at the artwork displayed by the richly decorated cookies with their vibrant icing colors and generous toppings of red hots, silver balls, and other colorful sprinkles. He took quite a few pictures of the cookies with his phone. Consuela made him a cup of tea, and he settled down to eat some of the inviting and sugary treats. It was a quiet afternoon, the second day of the year. All was right with the world, and then all hell broke loose.

Chapter 36

arnell had been watching or living in Melody's house off and on for weeks. He'd suspected she would come back sooner or later. He knew he couldn't watch her house all the time, and he knew he couldn't stay in Marfa forever, waiting for her. He'd decided that he would spend one more week in Marfa after the first of the year. If she hadn't turned up by then, he would return to TOMT and ask Leonard for his old job back. Living on the second floor of the warehouse with Alger wasn't a terrible existence. Darnell had earned a paycheck, and he hadn't had to do much to earn it. He knew he'd move on from Dallas eventually, but for now his dream of finding Duchamp's *Fountain* had almost come to an end. He wasn't going to find Melody, and he wasn't going to find his fortune.

Then his luck changed again. He was driving by her house on his motorcycle when he saw her riding up to her front door on her next door neighbor's golf cart. Both women went inside for a while, and then the neighbor left and drove the golf cart home. Finally! This was Darnell's chance. It was his last chance. He knew Melody's house well by now, and he went in through the back door. Melody was in her kitchen, sitting at her kitchen table drinking vodka out of a jelly glass.

Darnell always had his plastic handcuff ties and his duct tape with him. He thought he could quickly overpower Melody. But Melody was stronger than she looked, and she resisted. The lifting that had been required to build her large sculptures called for a good deal of upper body strength, and Melody was no pushover. She put up a good fight. Darnell was shocked that Granny Haircape could give him such a battle. They struggled, and Melody shouted and yelled as loud as she could. But nobody could hear her. Darnell grabbed a vase in his hand and struck her over the head with it. Melody briefly went limp from the blow. Darnell was able to press his advantage and immobilize her arms.

He secured her arms and legs with plastic ties and put duct tape over her mouth. He explained to her why it was important that she should not scream. Melody's eyes were wide with fear. She had no idea who this man was or why he had barged into her kitchen and attacked her.

"Where's the urinal, Melody? What did you do with it? I have looked everywhere in your house, and it isn't here. Tell me what you've done with it, and I won't have to kill you. All I want is the urinal."

Melody was completely confused and had no idea what this crazy person was talking about. She hadn't had a chance to drink much vodka, so her brain was still working pretty well. She stared at the man, and he knew she didn't have a clue.

"You dragged the urinal out of a dumpster in Dallas. Do you remember? It was three or four months ago. I want *Fountain*. Tell me what you've done with it, and I'll leave you alone."

Melody searched her memory to try to remember the urinal. She often traveled to Dallas and often went dumpster diving for her art supplies. She didn't remember the urinal.

"It had J. Mutt and 1917 painted on the side of it with black paint. You have to remember that. Where is it? What have you done with it?"

When the man mentioned the black paint on the side, Melody remembered it. The urinal had been a very old-fashioned style, and she had worried that it might not work in the place she needed to use it. She'd been thrilled to find it in the dumpster, but it had been almost impossible for her to get it out of there and into her truck. Once she got it back to Marfa and took a good look at it, she'd worried that it wasn't the right shape or height. It had to work with the others. In the end she'd made it work, but it was long gone now. How could she tell that to this man who was clearly insane? She could not possibly tell him the truth about what she had done with the urinal. He was going to kill her if she didn't give it to him. She knew he intended to kill her, even if he did get the urinal. Melody no longer had it, and she couldn't get it back.

Darnell's rage was building. He was losing patience with Melody. He had given up on finding *Fountain*. Now that he finally had Melody in his clutches, his expectations had soared. He was ready to kill again to make his fortune. He took his knife out of his pocket and held it to Melody's throat. She made noises as if she wanted to talk. Darnell continued to hold the knife to her throat. He ripped the duct tape from her mouth.

Melody knew she had to say something to this person before he completely lost control and killed her. "I have the urinal stored in my garage. It's in a secret closet in there. You'll have to untie me so I can show you how to get to it."

"You can tell me how to get to it. I'm not going to untie you. Forget that. Tell me where it is. Then I'll let you go, and only then." Darnell had no intentions of letting her go or letting her live. Melody was going to die tonight, urinal or no urinal.

"It's hidden in a secret space in the garage. There's no way you can get into it on your own. I have to show you. Just undo the restraints on my legs so I can walk. You can leave my arms in the handcuffs. I'll walk with you to the garage and show you how to get into the hidden cabinet. It won't take a minute."

Darnell didn't think it was a good idea to allow Melody to walk to the garage, but he decided it was the only way she was going to show him where the secret hiding place was. He released her legs and continued to hold the knife to her throat. She stumbled a bit and limped into the garage. She headed for the back wall where she kept many of the tools she used to build her sculptures. She knew there was a tire iron someplace on the work bench. She moved closer to the wall and turned around to face her enemy. She felt behind her, along the work bench with her still-handcuffed hands, and picked up the tire iron. She finally had it in her grasp and brought the tire iron up behind her back as close as she could. She gathered all of her strength and swung her whole body around. She put the full force of her strength into the swing and tried to direct the her weapon downward towards Darnell's legs.

But Darnell had seen her reach for the tire iron. He leapt for her neck and would have sliced Melody's carotid artery if she hadn't turned away at the last minute. As it was, her artery was nicked, and blood began to spurt out. She knew the chips were down, and her adrenalin kicked in. She swung the tire iron again, and this time she was lucky and hit Darnell solidly in the knees. She heard a loud crunch and knew she had destroyed something important. The next thing she had to do was to get away.

Bleeding profusely and growing weaker, Melody ran out of her garage and headed for Margaret Lennox's back yard. Melody still had the plastic restraints around her wrists, but she was determined she was going to get away from this madman. Margaret would help her. Margaret would beat him with her cane.

She ran screaming towards Margaret's back door. She collapsed as she pushed through the door into the kitchen.

The three of us, who were gathered at the kitchen table drinking tea and eating Christmas cookies, were stunned when Melody fell through the door. She was covered with blood and her hands were tied behind her back. Augustus knelt down beside her to assess her wounds. He reached for a tea towel and pressed it firmly against her neck.

"Call 911. She's bleeding to death. Someone has cut her throat. Tell them to hurry. She'd already lost a lot of blood, and I don't know that keeping pressure on the wound can save her."

Consuela knew the dispatcher and most of the EMTs in town. She spoke in rapid Spanish over her cell phone. She stayed on the line until she was sure the dispatcher understood how urgent it was. They would come as quickly as possible. I hobbled to a drawer to get fresh towels for Augustus. The one he'd been holding against Melody's neck was already completely soaked with blood. We were losing her.

Before any help arrived to save Melody, there was a huge commotion on my back patio. I looked out and saw a scruffy looking man stumbling past my pool. He was shouting and waving a gun in his hand. He headed for my back door. I couldn't let him come inside my house with a gun. We would all die. Consuela grabbed her purse and ran towards the back door. I didn't know what she was going to do, but I wasn't going to let her confront the madman alone. I followed her outside, limping on my cane.

The man was still waving his gun around and weaving back and forth around the patio. He saw Consuela and me and aimed his gun at us. Consuela reached into her purse and brought out small pearl-handled revolver. She raised her arm and aimed it at the unknown assailant. She fired at the same moment he fired. Her shot hit him somewhere in the middle of his body, but he didn't stop. He kept on coming towards us. He fired two more shots. Consuela fired two shots at the advancing mad man. I felt a sharp pain in my arm and knew I'd been hit by one of his bullets. I was incredibly angry that he'd shot me. I moved towards him and pushed him backwards into the pool. I don't know what I thought that was going to accomplish, but he ended up in the water. He thrashed around and thrashed around. He didn't look like he knew how to swim. He looked like he was going under. I was not about to jump into the pool to save him.

Consuela kept her small gun aimed at the man as he fought to keep his head above the water. He still had his gun in his hand, and as long as we could see the gun, no one was going to go in after him. He didn't seem to be able to aim his gun at anything, but Consuela kept her gun aimed at him until he went under for the last time. I'd collapsed beside the pool, blood dripping down my side. Consuela was on her phone again, calling 911 for a second time. The last thing I remember was looking at my pool and seeing a dead man in the water and the beautiful blue water turning red.

I learned later that the EMTs had tended first to Melody, and then they'd tended to me. They airlifted Melody to Alpine. My gunshot wound was less serious than Melody's knife wound, but they airlifted me to Alpine, too. Augustus insisted on traveling in the helicopter with me. Consuela was left behind to explain it all to the sheriff, who was her cousin's father-in-law. Who would have ever dreamed that Consuela carried a revolver in her purse? But thank God for it! At first, no one knew who the dead man in my pool was or why he had attacked Melody. If she recovered from her injuries, Melody might be able to shed some light on that.

Chapter 37

*B**y the third week of January, my doctor told me* I could begin swimming again. The gunshot wound in my arm had healed sufficiently. There was no longer a dead man in my pool. The pool had been emptied, scrubbed within an inch of its life, and refilled with clean water. The salt water was heated, and the pool was again ready for me. I refused to let the fact that a scumbag murderer had bled to death in my pool keep me from enjoying it in the future. I was going to swim, and I was going to forget all about the fact that I'd been shot, that I'd pushed Darnell Anthony Jackson into the water, and that he'd died there. It was one of life's unfortunate happenings, and it had ended with as good a result as anyone could have hoped for.

Consuela had undoubtedly saved my life, and Augustus had managed to keep Melody alive until help arrived. The authorities all knew Consuela, and she was a hero. She was related to everyone in Marfa, it seemed, either by blood or by marriage. Her little pearl-handled revolver was totally legal, and she had a license to carry a concealed weapon. Who could have ever dreamed that up? Thank goodness for her courage and her foresight.

Melody's recovery was ongoing. Her heart had stopped twice in the helicopter on the way to Alpine, but the EMTs had brought her back both times. She'd had three surgeries on her neck, and she was going to be fine. One piece of bad news for her was that they'd had to cut her hair when she'd had the surgery. Granny Haircape was no more…or at least until her hair grew back. She'd been transferred to a hospital in Dallas for plastic surgery, and in a few weeks, she would be back home in Marfa. Law enforcement had questioned her numerous times about why Darnell Jackson had stalked her and tried to kill her. She wasn't able to remember much from the attack. Ellery told her that more about what had happened might come back as time passed.

Melody had already started on the vodka when Darnell had attacked her in her house. She vaguely remembered that he'd been desperately looking for something she'd used in one of her sculptures, but she couldn't remember what that something was. She did remember she no longer had whatever it was he'd wanted. She had tried to knock him out with a tire iron rather than give him the bad news that she'd gotten rid of the thing he was so determined to find.

Darnell Jackson turned out to have died from drowning rather than from the gunshot wound to his stomach. No doubt being shot and the resulting profuse bleeding had all contributed to his demise, but it turned out he couldn't swim. His official cause of death was drowning. No one felt any sense of guilt or loss about his death. He was a murderer and had almost killed Melody and me. He had waved his loaded gun around and could have killed Consuela or me if she hadn't been as savvy and brave as she'd been.

The FBI became involved in the investigation, and they confiscated the gun Darnell had used to shoot me. They had found a second identical gun in a locked compartment of his motorcycle. It turned out that these two guns had been used to commit several murders in the Dallas area. Darnell had killed at least four people. No one had any idea why he'd killed two people in Plano, Texas or why he'd shot a man in Arlington, Texas and a woman in Ft. Worth. The authorities could only conclude that Darnell Jackson was some kind of crazed serial killer.

Leonard Bundy and Alger Duncan at TOMT were both interviewed about Darnell. The only potentially useful piece of information the authorities could gather from these two was that Darnell had been looking for a person named Chuck. Chuck had something Darnell desperately wanted to find. One of the people Darnell had killed was named Charles Grimaldi. Investigators speculated that the Charles he'd murdered might have been the "Chuck" that Darnell had been searching for. If indeed Chuck and Charles were one and the same, what did Chuck have that was so valuable that Darnell was willing to kill him to get it? No one was ever able to satisfactorily answer that question. The bottom line was that Darnell Jackson was a very bad dude, and Texas was glad they hadn't had to waste any prison space or any chemicals or electricity to put him to death. Consuela and I had taken care of Darnell for Texas.

Augustus Gemini bought a small house, two doors down from Ellery's house and right across the street from mine. He had great plans for fixing up his weekend retreat. He'd always loved Marfa, and he'd always wanted a place to get away from the harum scarum world of the L.A. movie business. I suspected he also wanted to be sure Ellery continued his recovery on track. Augustus was determined to return Ellery to the point where he was able to write his wonderful musical scores again. I know Augustus liked me, too. We had trusts, foundations, and limited partnerships to administer together. How fun was that going to be! With everything else that had happened, we hadn't found an anonymous way to let Consuela know yet about the educational trust that had been set up for her children. That would happen in time and in the right way.

Augustus had been so enthralled with the beautiful Christmas cookies Consuela's children had decorated, he'd decided to do a short documentary featuring her children and their cookies. He had interviewed the kids and planned to have the film ready for release before next Christmas. He talked about this production constantly. He was going to fly his best cinematographer to Marfa to film the cookie-decorating project. I had decorated cut-out sugar cookies as a child and had decorated thousands of cookies with my own children. I wondered if Augustus had ever had a childhood of any kind. I knew he hadn't ever decorated Christmas cookies as a part of that childhood.

Augustus was flying in on Friday night and bringing dinner from his favorite Greek restaurant in L.A. We were going to eat on my back patio now that it was back in commission and no longer a crime scene. That evening we were going to make a real effort to build new memories around the pool. It was an attempt to dispel some of the tragedy that had happened there. Ellery and Doug were going to join us for dinner.

Ellery seemed to be making slow progress. He had even shown a little bit of interest in his musical instruments. He had asked Doug to bring his guitar and his flute to the casita. When I told Augustus this news, he'd been ecstatic. I warned him not to raise his expectations too much, but he couldn't help himself. We held our breath and prayed that Ellery would soon begin to make music again.

Even Ellery laughed a little bit during dinner. After we'd eaten and Augustus had cleaned up the dishes, Ellery walked, tentatively, but on his own, into the casita and brought out his flute. He played the slow, sad tune he had written. It was a haunting melody that touched us all. Augustus was very familiar with Ellery's music and his style. I could tell that Augustus had been caught by surprise when he heard this new original composition. Even I could tell that Ellery's music was different somehow, different than it had been before he'd almost died. It was more contemplative and had more depth. When Ellery played his flute, all of us who listened had tears in our eyes.

Somewhere in Time...
Los Angeles

Epilogue

It was to be her biggest party ever, her wildest extravaganza.
The actress and comedienne was home from Vegas for a
month between shows. She invited everyone she knew and
hired the best caterer in L.A. Anybody who was anybody
would be there. She was pulling out all the stops. She had
added three pieces to her outdoor art collection, and this
party was a kind of unveiling or "coming out party" for the
new sculptures. One sculpture in particular was enormous
and incredibly dramatic. The famous personality loved
it and had given it the most prominent position in her
outdoor gallery.

   Over fifteen feet tall, from a distance it appeared to be
a black and white striped monolith. Wide at the bottom,
it tapered slightly towards the top, similar to a light house
painted with black and white horizontal stripes. The touch
of yellow at the top was intriguing, almost like the light at
the top of a lighthouse. The name evoked both its feminist
roots and its appearance. The sculptor, Isadora Daphne had
named the piece, *NOT A LIGHTHOUSE: THE BATTLE
OF THE SEXES.* Was the sculpture a tribute in part to
Virginia Woolf's book, *To The Lighthouse?* No one was

quite sure about that. The name of the sculpture was as enigmatic and thought-provoking as the sculpture itself. It was as complex and mysterious as the woman who had created it.

On closer examination, one could see that the piece was made of layers piled on top of each other. Alternating layers were painted black and white. The layers were made up of objects that were distinctly associated with either males or females. Every other layer was male, and every other layer was female. All objects in the male layers were painted glossy black, and all objects in the female layers were painted bright, glossy white. Every individual part of the composition was a found object, something the artist had rescued from a dumpster or a landfill or from someone's trash can.

Because the piece was displayed outside, the artist had covered anything that was not inherently waterproof with black or white stucco. The work weighed more than a thousand pounds. No wonder it had taken so long to create. No wonder it had to be taken apart into three sections to be shipped to California. No wonder it had been so absurdly costly to transport. It was a masterpiece in the eyes of the owner, so all the time and money and difficulties involved with bringing the work of art to her California home had been more than worth it.

The huge piece by Isadora Daphne drew the most attention at the party. Everyone was jostling for a front row position to be sure they saw everything in the complicated and multi-layered work. A great deal of analysis was underway. Symbolism, which had probably never occurred to the artist, was being read into the various parts of the sculpture and into the work as a whole. It was definitely a conversation piece.

The bottom layer, the foundation of the piece, was a male layer, and it was painted black. The next layer was a female layer, and it was painted white. The structure of the sculpture built upon itself, layer after layer, black and white, male and female. The base was made up of six urinals bolted together. All of the urinals were painted with coats of glossy black paint. The choice of the plumbing fixtures as the foundation of the art work brought a chuckle to all who viewed it.

The next layer was made up of masses of alternating toaster ovens, toasters, sewing machines, hair dryers, and vacuum cleaners, strung together and coated with bright white glossy stucco. The next layer was sports equipment, representing sports played mostly by men—footballs, ice hockey pucks and sticks, baseball bats, golf clubs, and jock straps, all artfully arranged and reinforced with glossy black stucco. The next white layer represented the traditional women's roles in various professions from the past – nurse's caps and shoes, stenographer's tablets, a teacher's blackboard painted white, and typewriters. The artist had even fashioned a mobile made of chalk and black erasers. It dangled from the side of the sculpture. Near the top of the piece were layers of men's and women's clothing, all coated in black or white stucco. Men's pants, neckties, button-down collar shirts, suspenders, blazers, and boxer shorts were displayed in hardened black. Women's bras, girdles, slips, garter belts, and pantyhose were artistically arranged and coated in white stucco. Hats of all kinds, black and white seemed to float at the top of the work of art. Men's hats were coated in black. Women's hats were all in white. At the very top of the tower was a doll's baby carriage, coated in yellow stucco. It was a fascinating work, and the celebrity's party was a huge success, in large part because of her new and undeniably fabulous piece, *NOT A LIGHTHOUSE*.

The bottom layer of the sculpture was closest to the crowd, of course, and this was the easiest part of the artwork to see. Party guests were intrigued by how the artist had bolted the six urinals together to make the base. The urinals were all different. They were different sizes and shapes and styles. It had not been easy to get them all to work together as a secure and sturdy foundation for this imposing and immensely bulky piece. A few of the guests who had an interest in engineering even lay down and looked at the urinals from underneath, to see exactly how they'd been fastened together. The base of this enormously heavy work of art had to be incredibly strong and well-balanced. One man noticed that one of the urinals that composed the base was quite old. It was a very antiquated style, and he thought he saw the year 1917 outlined under the glossy black paint. He was lying on his back, trying to read what else was written on the old-fashioned porcelain fixture. But the writing was so faint, he couldn't get a good view of it and decided it was probably just a trick of the light.

Someone remarked that this bizarre sculpture, touted as having been made entirely out of found objects, didn't have any one thing in it that was worth much, but that, when it was all put together, the whole must be worth a fortune. The work of art was truly priceless.

Acknowledgments

Heartfelt thanks to my readers and editors. I couldn't have done this without you. Thank you to Jamie at Open Heart Designs who developed the beautiful cover and who does everything else to turn my manuscript into a book. Thank you to my photographer Andrea Burns who always makes me look good. Thank you to all the friends and fans who have encouraged me to continue writing.

About the Author

CAROLINA DANFORD WRIGHT
*is a grandmother. She uses a blue
and white cane. She has lived in
many places and traveled far and
wide. Carolina has had several
fulfilling careers and began writing
mysteries when she was seventy.
She believes that behavior has
consequences and that it is critical
to fight for truth and justice. The
women of the Granny Avengers
series echo Carolina's crusade to
help right the wrongs of the world.*